I0684905

Beltway Bub

Tripping on Truth in the 1960s & 70s

by

Warwick J. Knox

Copyright © 2012 Warwick J. Knox

All rights reserved.

ISBN: 10:061561471X
ISBN: 13:978-0615614717
LCCN: 2013912381

To Joyce.

PREFACE

I wrote the first draft of this book back in 1995, and then I shelved it. My initial inspiration was the result of some bad medical news, and whenever that happens most of us have a tendency to worry. As I thought to preoccupy my mind, I figured that writing might help. Then I recalled someone saying, "If you're going to write about something, write about something you know a lot about." That finally led me to think about myself and the hand I was dealt at birth—an unusual name, a strange accent, being small and left-handed, wearing glasses, attending Catholic schools—you get the picture. Now it's eighteen years later, and certain circumstances led me to return to the book. This is a work of fiction. Names, characters, places and incidents either are products of my imagination or are used fictitiously. Any resemblance to actual events or locales or persons, living or dead, is entirely coincidental.

Beltway Bub is the story of a kid named Riddick "Bub" Kellow, whose identity problems and strong passions cause him to rebel against the status quo as his family relocates inside the Washington, DC, Capital Beltway. As he enjoys the psychedelic era of the 1960s and '70s, he identifies with other kids whose families reside in the rich town of McLean, Virginia. Since he's a perfect fit for the hippie counterculture and spiritual revolution, he experiences tremendous highs and lows while using drugs and alcohol. When the party is over, though, he realizes he's created a world that leaves him to wonder, *What the fuck just happened, man!*

CONTENTS

ACKNOWLEDGMENTS

As I wrote this book, it dawned on me that everyone I've ever met has played a part in my inspiration to write *Beltway Bub*.
Thank you.

Cover illustration by Shannon Knox.

1. PROLOGUE

By the time Riddick "Bub" Kellow had moved from Downingtown, Pennsylvania, to Vienna, Virginia, in 1966, he was frustrated by his unwanted social complexities. He was just thirteen years old, and already his family had moved five times. Every time they'd moved, he was pestered by bullies, because he was small, had odd names, wore glasses, and he sounded strange. Of course, all those traits were due to heredity, so it seemed that he was destined to deal with them as best he could.

His Australian mother was a well-educated socialite who'd met and married his father in Sydney after World War II. Then they moved to a tiny town in Northern Minnesota, where they started to raise a family. When her turn came to name their second son in 1953, she picked the unusual Irish name of Riddick (*Rihd-ayk*), which means "smooth field." Then Riddick acquired the nickname of Bub from his fun-loving brother, Robbie, and sisters, Darla and Jessie, who found humor in his mother's use of the Australian slang term for a baby boy. Little did they know that there was an American definition of *bub*, which was "a disrespectful way of addressing a boy or a man."

Soon after Bub was born, he'd experienced long and deeply traumatic nightmares, which puzzled both his parents and the doctors. As he learned to walk, those nightmares would cause him to run around the house, and his family would give chase. Fortunately for all, those episodes became less frequent as he grew older. Nevertheless, they made Bub sensitive and insecure, which caused him to constantly wonder who he was and why he was alive.

In addition to those characteristics, Bub had other differences that made him more or less distinguishable. He'd been born cross-eyed, so he had an eye operation that resulted in his having to wear glasses. As he learned to walk, he acquired the diction of his Aussie mother combined with the dialect of his fellow Minnesotans, so he sounded strange by anyone's standards. Since he was raised as a Catholic, he also attended Catholic schools, where his religious education stood in contrast to the natural sense of logic he was developing. That caused him to become confused, and his constant questions tested the patience of his teachers. Of course, having a weird, non-Christian name and being left-handed didn't help either, since it became an obvious concern to some of the more traditional nuns.

As a result of his characteristics, Bub was bullied by some of his classmates. He always found himself at a disadvantage, because he was small for his age. He would try to explain why he was the way he was, but reasoning didn't seem to help. Therefore, he learned the meaning of adaptation. Every time his family moved, he'd try to fit in by applying all that he'd learned from his past harsh experiences. As he quit wearing glasses and did his best to act cool, he noticed it was fairly easy to fool people. That made him skeptical, as he was developing a certain amount of spite toward the status quo.

Bub was also sensitive, because he was the youngest of four children. He'd been teased a lot, because his mother was always doting upon him while affectionately calling him Tweedy. Of course, that name was funny, and it caused his siblings to come up with the name of Tweedits. That bothered young Bub, so he started to make blubbery fart noises or jokes about his "doo-doo" to change the subject. While that ploy seemed to work, it became one of the facets of his character that would attract the type of friends that he'd come to make.

Bub's childhood wasn't all bad, though. Despite the threat of nuclear war and the occasional sound of sonic booms, he enjoyed all the fun that comes with the change of seasons. Starting with the Space Race and Kennedy's election, the trends of the sixties were fascinating to everyone. Electronic products were getting better and cheaper, and rock 'n' roll was there to stay. There was a strong resistance to a rebirth of free thinking, but it was clear to most that the times were changing.

As Bub moved from place to place, he tried to stay abreast of the "cool" kids. He wanted to be treated like an adult, so he cussed and experimented with cigarettes and alcohol. Of course, that meant getting caught once in a while, but, he wasn't too concerned. His behavior seemed normal to him, since many kids were doing the same things, and besides that—he figured that all he had to do to be forgiven by God was to confess his sins to a priest.

2. ADAPTATION

In 1966, Bub was thirteen years old when his family relocated for the fifth time. They had moved just outside of the Capital Beltway of Washington, DC, and rented a house on the west side of Vienna, Virginia. His new school would be a public intermediate school in the Fairfax County School District, and he was happy about that. He'd attended Catholic schools all his life, and now he wondered what a "normal" school would be like.

He knew his problem would still persist with the embarrassment of his new teachers trying to pronounce his name. His names seemed to be an unavoidable problem wherever he went, but they were his, and that was that. Since he had one good eye, he quit wearing his glasses, which had also been the source of ridicule, and now he was hoping to fit in with the "cool" kids who'd bullied him the most.

Bub was healthy, since, while living in the beautiful Pennsylvania countryside, he'd broken the nasty habit of smoking cigarettes. He still wore whatever clothes his mother bought him, except for his pointy black shoes. They'd been given a rest all summer long in lieu of his more comfortable sneakers. He still liked to experiment in front of the mirror with his hair. He'd usually comb it back before pushing it forward, to get a wave effect. Then he'd snap his head backward, just to get the final Elvis thing going. Once in a while he'd check his pelvic region, only to be disappointed by his lack of pubic hair. Yes, Bub was definitely a late bloomer, standing four feet nine inches tall and weighing in at ninety-eight pounds. He dreaded the thought that there was going to be plenty of mature classmates who were going to make him look like a runt and probably make fun of him to boot!

Aside from his impending social dilemma, Bub thought that his neighborhood location was nice. The school was about a quarter-mile walk, with no major crossroads. There was a community pool three blocks down the street, surrounded by a large wooded area behind it that extended to the boundaries of his school. Then he discovered the local railroad tracks about five blocks from his house.

The railroad tracks were fascinating to Bub, since he always wondered where they went. He'd spent a lot of time on them in Minnesota and Wisconsin, and just touching the rails made him feel as if he and his old friends were still connected. He admired the heavy drone of the massive locomotives as they approached and the rumble of the ground shaking as they passed. Aside from that thrill, there were always some interesting things to do around railroad tracks, and Bub loved to feel free and explore.

On the first day of school, Bub was filled with anxiety as he sat in his homeroom. His grades from the previous year weren't good, and now he realized he was going to have to work extra hard in order to finish the eighth grade. The morning announcements came over a loudspeaker and that was something new to him. Although he wanted to listen, his mind was preoccupied with the impending roll call. Then his fear manifested when the homeroom teacher tried to call out his name.

"Rid … Rid-*dick*?"

Bub squirmed in his seat and shook his head in obvious frustration, and then he corrected her with a crooked smile.

"*Rid*-dick."

Then the teacher smiled as she said, "By the way, students. We have a new classmate this year! Where on earth did you get that unusual name, Riddick?"

Bub had been through this drill before, and it bothered him. Still, he told everyone how his father had met his mom in Australia during World War II, and that it was his artistic mother who'd named him. Then the teacher asked him if he went by "Riddick" and he said, "No. My friends and family call me Bub." That made everyone laugh, and Bub found it hard not to do the same. He laughed for different reasons, though. He was amazed at how predictable people were, while he was thinking how pathetic his dilemma seemed. As the laughter died down and roll call resumed, many eyes were upon Bub. Since he was mainly introverted, he just folded his arms and felt humiliated, until he was saved by the bell.

Switching classrooms every hour was something new to Bub, and he hoped that it would relieve the monotony and boredom that he'd experienced at his previous schools. What he didn't figure on was having to explain his weird names as he went from one class to the next. He'd soon realize that there were many students who would have to hear his explanations more than once!

His first day of school wasn't all bad, though. During the embarrassing moments, Bub would merely avoid direct eye contact with his fellow students. Then, after the subject had been changed, he'd glance around the room to check out the girls. Bub's type of girl had to be appealing in some unusual way, since typical beauty alone didn't do it for him. His mom had big eyes and full lips, and since she was gentle and loving, he correlated her attributes to the apple of his eye.

Bub's biggest surprise came during his fifth-hour gym class. That's when he and his new next-door neighbor, Duncan Callahan, discovered that they were in the same grade together. Duncan had seen Bub when the Kellows moved in, and mistook him for a much younger kid. Conversely, Bub had seen the red-haired Duncan, with his five-foot-ten, 165-pound frame, and mistook him for a high-school student. Therefore, they were both blown away, and an instant bond seemed to take place. At the end of the gym period, while they were getting dressed, Duncan asked Bub if he wanted to walk home together and meet some of his friends.

"Sure," Bub replied, and now he was excited!

Little did Bub know that he was befriending a member of the biggest clique in the school. He would think this was an answer to his prayers, since he'd been the target of a clique called the Preppies, while he was living in Milwaukee, Wisconsin. The Preppies consisted of kids who'd come from very well-to-do families and lived along Lake Michigan. Bub had painfully learned the meaning of economic class division from them, and after being relegated to hang with other "social rejects," he'd become spiteful. Their prejudice had made him dissatisfied to be who he truly was, and he was longing to be a part of the "in" crowd. Well, that was then, but now that his chance was approaching, he would sell his soul to take it.

After school Duncan led Bub toward a path that went to the community pool. As they made their way across the football field, Duncan kept glancing at Bub, sizing him up.

"Shiiiit," he finally said, then laughed. "Where did you get those shoes!"

Bub smiled proudly and said, "They're my shit-kickers!" Duncan laughed louder, and then he coughed and spat to the ground. After reaching into his London Fog jacket, he pulled out a pack of cigarettes and offered one to Bub.

"Smoke?" he asked.

"Why not?" Bub shrugged, wanting to gain favor by revealing his wild and reckless side.

As they got on the path and entered the woods, Duncan stopped to snap open his fancy flip-top lighter. After using it to light his cigarette, he held it out for Bub.

"If you're going to hang with me and my friends, you're going to have to restyle your hair and get some decent clothes."

Bub looked up at Duncan while taking his first drag a little too deeply. Duncan raised his eyebrows and let out another big laugh before pausing to blow some perfect smoke rings. Then he poked his finger through the last smoke ring and smiled at Bub.

"Come on, let's go," he said.

As they continued on, Duncan explained some relevant facts to Bub. He told him that his friends dressed in a style they called "collegiate," and he then he explained to Bub what that implied.

"When we're not wearing Chucks, we wear loafers or wing-tips, and we only buy shoes that are brown, burgundy, or oxblood, okay? Black is a no-no. We wear ribbed single-colored socks that match our shirts, and we don't wear any of that plaid crap. We wear earth-tone pants that are made with natural fibers, such as corduroy or hopsack. Just be sure to avoid that polyester shit. Look for solid or pinstriped shirts that have Oxford button-down collars. Basically, they should be excellent name-brand stuff. Are you getting all of this?"

Duncan glanced behind him to see Bub's nod.

"Is this too much for you?" he said with a smile while turning to walk backward.

"I guess so," Bub said in an unconvincing tone. Then he quickly added, "Maybe you should go shopping with me and explain it all again. Anyway, I'm going to have to hit my old lady up for some cash. She's the one I usually ask, since my dad is pretty tight—he's this practical type of guy who won't spend money, unless he absolutely has to."

They walked on in silence long enough for Bub to feel guilty about bad-mouthing his parents. Then Duncan broke the silence as he flicked his cigarette to the ground.

"I'll explain some things to your parents, if you want—they'll come around."

"Gee! That might actually work!" Bub said.

Then Duncan laughed and added, "I'll lend you a few of my *Playboy* magazines, and they should tune you into the latest fashions. Just don't jizz on them, okay!"

After letting out a loud belly laugh, Duncan stopped abruptly and bent over to pick up an empty clear-glass beer bottle.

"Hmm—what have we got here? This dead soldier's still warm—the label's not faded."

Duncan unzipped his pants and proceeded to pee in the bottle while giving Bub a little more insight.

"These woods are a favorite drinking place for intermediate and high-school kids, and sometimes they stash their beer in secret hiding places. Saturday and Sundays mornings are a good time to hunt for it— when I've got nothing better to do."

When he was through peeing, he held the bottle up to the sunlight and said, "It looks just like beer, doesn't it? Wouldn't that be nice!"

Duncan looked back toward the school.

"Here comes that dopey kid."

Bub looked to see a boy with blond, Beatle-styled hair in the distance.

"Who's he?"

"You'll find out," Duncan said. "Let's keep going."

After walking about fifty yards, they came upon a meandering creek. Beyond that stood a tall chain-link fence that surrounded the community pool.

"I know where I am now," Bub said.

The path ended where the creek made a ninety-degree turn. There was a large, cement storm culvert located on the opposite bank, and it had caused some erosion. Bub figured that this was a hot spot for the local kids, since there were thick vines dangling from the trees. They looked as if they'd been cut, and now they were perfect for playing Tarzan. As Duncan started to tell Bub a story about this place, the boy they'd spotted finally caught up to them.

"What have we got here?" the boy asked as he approached with a big smile.

"Just some—*beer!*" Duncan exclaimed while still holding the beer bottle.

"Oh, Duncan—can I have some, please—*please!*" The blonde boy begged.

"Na, you wouldn't like it," Duncan responded while staring at the bottle and tilting his head. "It's kind of warm, so it tastes like piss."

In his excitement, the boy failed to grasp Duncan's allusion, so he persisted.

"Well damn, boy! If you insist," Duncan said as he calmly extended his arm.

With that the boy quickly grabbed the bottle. He put it to his lips but stopped short of drinking, as he remarked, "Ew, it *is* warm!"

"I told you so!" Duncan exclaimed. "Didn't you hear me? We just found the damn bottle in the woods and... oh, forget it! Here—give it back."

After shooting a brief deer-in-the-headlights stare at Duncan and then Bub, the boy suddenly put the bottle back to his lips and started drinking. Immediately, Duncan slapped his knee, and Bub exclaimed, "Oh God!" With that, the boy jerked the bottle away from his mouth while spraying Duncan's urine into the air.

"Ew—that *does* taste like piss! It's salty," the boy exclaimed while frowning and touching his lower lip. As he looked at Bub and Duncan's facial expressions, he knew that he'd been duped, so he quickly turned away as he began to cough, hack, and spit.

Then Duncan made a wisecrack, as if to put icing on the cake. "That's funny—that's just what I was telling Bub here a little while ago!"

"By the way, Bub," Duncan blurted out between fits of laughter, "that there—is Bill O'Reilly!"

Finally regaining his composure, Duncan motioned to Bub to follow him. Together they crossed the creek beside Bill, who was still tending to his oral hygiene. As Bub carefully followed behind

Duncan, they made their way up onto the concrete culvert and followed it to the mouth of a large storm pipe. Once there, Duncan stopped and put his hand to his ear before calling out into the pipe.

"*Who goes there!*" Duncan shouted.

"Who in the fuck wants to know?" came a male voice, from deep from within the pipe.

Bub and Duncan could hear girls giggling.

"Come on, Bub," Duncan said, as he leaned forward and disappeared into the darkness of the pipe. Bub stood there for a moment because he remembered his babysitter locking him under a dark staircase when he was just a little kid. As a result, he was experiencing a mild case of claustrophobia.

"Well? Come on, man!"

Reluctantly Bub crouched forward and followed Duncan while seeing a dim light from a distant drain inlet. Upon reaching the wider inlet area, Duncan took a seat on a ledge beside a boy who was sitting across from two girls on the opposite ledge. Apparently, they'd just been sitting in there, talking and smoking cigarettes. One of the girls was named Sheila, and, as it turned out, she lived a few houses down from Bub and Duncan. Bub thought she was beautiful, and he watched her body language as she joked with the other boys.

After Bub's brief and unremarkable introduction (except for his having to explain his names), their chatting continued. It was the normal girl-guy stuff, each trying to say something clever or sexy. At one point, after Duncan made some sexual comment to Sheila, she put her shoeless foot up between his legs. Duncan returned her gesture with a devilish look, while curling his tongue through his teeth. Bub was not used to such displays of sexual promiscuity, and in his embarrassment he looked away. When the conversation ended, everyone filed out of the sewer pipe while squinting against the sunlight.

As the group of kids prepared to go their separate ways, Bub finally got a good look at Tommy. He was a good-looking kid of Spanish descent, and he was just one inch taller than Bub. As Tommy and his girlfriend went in another direction, Duncan, Sheila, and Bub walked to their homes. As they did, Sheila and Duncan continued their flirting, so Bub felt more at ease walking a few steps behind them.

Later during supper, Bub saw Sheila walking to Duncan's house. He watched her until she entered, and it wasn't more than twenty minutes afterward that he saw her leave. When he later saw Duncan outside on his driveway, Bub decided to go and ask him if Sheila was his girlfriend. Duncan suddenly grinned. "No—but I did just fuck her!"

Bub was dazed by Duncan's tersely crude but honest response. He never imagined that people would have sex without having deep, emotional feelings. Up until now, he had only kissed a girl, because he was naive and shy. For him that had been thrilling enough, since he was mainly attracted to their beauty and gentle nature. Now he realized that he was of the age where some girls might expect him to go all the way, or "get lost!"

Since Bub had been befriended by Duncan, he figured that he was locked into a new groove, and, although he had some reservations, he was okay with that. Although his intention had been to hunker down and focus on his academics, his social life suddenly seemed more interesting and important to him. He told his parents about his new collegiate friends and their dress code. They saw no harm in Duncan's style, so they gave Bub the money he needed to buy the clothes that he thought would establish himself with the coolest kids in his school.

When Bub and his new friends would get together, they'd drink alcohol, smoke cigarettes, and try to conduct clever conversations. All the while they were aspiring to be the promiscuous young adults that the American college life exuded. In that realm Bub was now feeling secure, since he felt that he was on the right track while being under the protection of his new, hard-hitting pals.

Bub would use the powers of his new clique to avoid harassment. Such was the case when he was walking home from school one day, and a big boy had snuck up from behind and snatched away his cigarettes.

"You're a dope for smoking! Do you think you're cool or something? I'm going to crush these, and then maybe I'll kick your ass!"

Not to be intimidated, Bub calmly replied, "Those belong to Duncan Callahan, and if you don't hand them back to me, he'll probably kick *your* ass." That frightened the big boy, who knew of

Duncan's reputation as a scrapper, so he immediately handed the cigarettes to Bub and apologized. Although Duncan later praised Bub for his quick wit, while gloating upon his own reputation, Bub felt slightly ashamed. He knew that the bully was right. Still, he figured he'd had his reasons for the way he acted, and he wasn't about to explain them to anyone.

* * *

Duncan's older brother, Shane, was a dishwasher at a fancy restaurant in Vienna. Sometimes he'd put stolen beer into a large trash can before hauling it out and emptying it into the Dumpster. He'd arranged a deal with Duncan to take a percentage of the beer if he'd retrieve it from the Dumpster and stash Shane's portion in a local wooded area.

It was on one such occasion that Duncan recruited Bub and Tommy to help him get the beer before visiting with two girls named Becky and Alice. Bub was excited because he'd been having some encounters with some of the girls in his clique. All he would do was kiss, though, and maybe feel their breasts. He was scared to go beyond that, because the female anatomy was a mystery to him, and besides, he still hadn't reached full puberty. The girlie magazines that Duncan had lent him contained jokes about small penises, and he wasn't sure how his measured up.

After getting the beer, each one of the boys wrapped their jackets around a six-pack before walking to Becky's house, whose parents were out for the evening. When they got there, the two girls raced for the door and opened it while giggling and smiling. Then they all sat around drinking, smoking, and laughing, and finally, when their silly conversations had run dry, Duncan suggested games.

"Do you have any cards?" Duncan asked, and Becky nodded. "Well, let's play strip poker!" Silence followed, with wandering eyes checking facial expressions in order to weigh in on the final decision. When Bub looked at Duncan, he had a devilish grin. When Bub looked at Tommy, he was smiling and slowly nodding. Then he looked at the girl's expressions, and they looked mortified!

Bub felt the same way the girls did, even though he appeared to be calm. So, as the other boys' gentle persuasion shifted toward coercion, he decided to chime in.

"Hey guys—let me tell you about *my* first game of strip poker. It happened about two years ago when I was growing in up in the small town of Forest Lake, Minnesota. I was hanging out with my best friend, Jackie, when we decided to pay a visit to Grazer's barn. Old man Grazer hadn't been seen for some time, and there was speculation that he might have died. Anyway—his huge barn sat high atop the highest hill around, and it'd become a popular place to goof off."

"Once we got inside the barn, we climbed up to the high loft to smoke cigarettes, and that's when we came across two boys and a girl. The boys were named Dickey and Jeff, and they were old friends of mine who'd since joined a greaser gang. If not for some of older boys in the gang, I might have joined, too—but that's another story. The girl was named Gigi, and she was a nice-looking French girl who liked to cuss a lot."

"They had a deck of cards, and they invited us to play strip poker. Since the barn was equipped with a track-wheel and rope, they said that the loser would have to swing to the other end of the barn and then swing back. I was scared that I'd lose, but just the thought of seeing Gigi naked changed my mind!"

"As the game progressed, I was being dealt good hands and after a while, Dickey lost all of his clothes. I thought, damn! The game is over, and I didn't get to see Gigi naked? What a drag!"

"We all laughed while Dickey took his underpants off and grabbed the rope, but he was impressive as he swooped from one beam to the next with the grace of a chimpanzee! After he got back to the hay loft, we all cheered, and then we went to get dressed. That's when we were surprised by two older greasers who had slipped into the barn, and apparently they'd been watching us. One of them just happened to be Gigi's brother, Kurt!"

"'*Next!*' Kurt shouted as he came over the top of the ladder, and I almost shit my drawers!"

"'Where did you guys come from, and what do you mean, "next?"' I asked."

"'Well,' Kurt explained, 'There's only going to be *one* winner, and that's the way *I* say it *works*!'"

"I was stunned, so I just stood there with my mouth open. Then I looked at everyone else, and they were shrugging and nodding. Well, I didn't want to get my ass kicked, so I sat back down on a hay bale, and we resumed the game."

"I started to get lousy hands, and I had to take more clothes off. After losing one hand, I argued about having to pull two socks off at once, since the other kids hadn't done that. Well, Kurt shouted at me to take them both off, or else! Then Gigi laughed because, while I was pulling them off, I lost my balance and fell backward and bumped my head."

"Then my luck changed, and I was laughing, because Gigi's luck had finally run out. She'd already lost her top, but her brother Kurt had said that it was all right if she left it on, until she lost her undies. Now, at last, she'd have to strip naked, and that was the moment I'd been waiting for!"

"When she got undressed, I was stunned, since it was my first good look at a real-live naked girl! Then I saw that she had some pubic hair and I thought, *How can that be? Gigi has pubes, and I don't?* As Gigi swung from one beam to the next, I started to imagine myself having to do the same thing, and that made me feel pretty sick, since I was standing there in just my Fruit of the Looms!"

"Sure enough! As the game resumed, it wasn't long before I was the next victim. Everyone could see my face turn red as I rose to meet the challenge, and my mind raced as I tried to think of a plan. I walked to the rope and got it into position while turning my back to everyone. Then I dropped my drawers, grabbed the rope, and started running sideways! I had to run fast to make it to the beam, but I tripped, and my feet dragged, just as I was going off the edge of the damned loft! As I hung there swinging and twisting, I was embarrassed by the laughter and jeers. Shit! Even my best friend, Jackie, was having a field day!"

"*What am I going to do now?* I asked myself. Then someone yelled, 'Hey, check it out!' and that was all I needed to hear! I loosened my grip, and, as my hands slipped down the rope, they began to burn, so I let go! I must have dropped at least twelve feet, and after I landed, I rolled onto my back. By now, I was so embarrassed that I jumped up like a ninja! Then I saw a burlap gunny sack that was hanging on a rusty hook, so I ran to get it so I could cover myself. It was dirty and crusted with pigeon dung, but that didn't matter to me."

"As everyone continued to bellow with laughter, I wondered, *What next?* That's when I realized that I'd have to climb up the ladder to get my clothes! I needed both hands, so I tossed the burlap over my shoulder and climbed the ladder. When I got to the top, though, I discovered that Kurt was holding my clothes under one of his arms!"

"'Okay, numb-nuts,' Kurt said. 'Do it again and this time, do it *right!*'"

"Everyone else laughed, but I was really frustrated. To make matters worse, I had to wait while my friend, Jackie, retrieved the damned rope! By the time he brought it to me, I was determined to do it right, so I threw down the burlap and said, 'To hell with it!' Then I ran as fast as I could, and, after swinging from one beam to the next, I finally pulled it off."

"When I returned to the loft, I discovered that Kurt had thrown my clothes down to the floor of the barn. That only added to my humiliation, and now I was more perturbed than embarrassed. So I climbed down the ladder, got dressed, and waved good-bye without looking back."

"That was my first experience playing strip poker and after that, I never wanted to see another deck of cards!"

Since Bub's story had obviously finished with the shaking of his head, everyone began laughing and relating to his embarrassment.

Finally, one of the girls said, "That's my problem, too! I would be embarrassed as hell, since it's that time of the month, if you know what I mean."

"I know exactly what you mean," the other girl quickly added, while nodding in agreement.

That pretty much put a halt to the idea of strip poker, and Bub was relieved that his ploy had worked. Meanwhile, his male friends were pouting, since their eyes had lit up every time he'd talked about Gigi. Finally they decided to play spin the bottle, and, whenever Bub got his turn, he got a thankful smooch from one of the girls.

Many nights were spent that way. The boys would find some alcohol and then meet up with some girls. Alcohol was liquid courage when it came to being bold and shedding inhibitions, and it didn't matter if they fooled around in the woods or at someone's house while the parents were away. In consideration of that, it was a new and exciting life for Bub, and he was having a blast—as long as he got to keep his underwear on!

* * *

Mark Hipbath had a thick and high flat-topped haircut, which matched his bushy eyebrows and dark, heavy-rimmed glasses. He was a natural joker with a big smile full of gangly, white teeth. His parents worked long hours, so they were rarely home, and, with their fully stocked bar in the basement, Mark let everyone know that they were welcome.

Upon receiving that gracious invitation, Bub and his friends began spending a lot of after-school hours at his house. Mark would play bartender, while the guys and gals would drink and flirt. After a while, some of them would disappear into the bedrooms, but Mark was cool with that. Bub like to joke that Mark lived up to his name, since he'd carefully apply a pencil "mark" to his parent's booze bottles for the purpose of adding tap water after the party was over. In response to that, Mark would point out that hard liquor was not Bub's drink, since he had a tendency to be a "guzzler"!

On Easter Sunday of 1967, Bub and his buddies skipped church while hiding out around the railroad tracks. After getting bored, they started hurling stones at the glass covers used to stabilize the high-voltage wires that followed the tracks. A couple of direct hits proved that the glass was too thick to be affected by mere stones, so they began to hurl rocks. As Bub reached down to pick one up, a rock thrown by Tommy ricocheted off a utility pole and struck Bub on the left side of his head. It sounded like hatchet hitting a coconut, and everyone freaked out as Bub staggered back and involuntarily slumped to the ground. As he struggled to maintain consciousness, blood began flowing freely down his face and the left side of his head. His white Sunday shirt began to get soaked with blood, so Tommy quickly took off his own shirt and pressed it to the wound.

"Ouch! Damn, it stings!" Bub said, as Tommy pressed down.

"Hold that there, Bub. We're going to get you out of here, okay? I am so, so sorry!"

As Bub left the railroad tracks and walked down the street, everyone who saw him gasped in horror. Meanwhile, his friends would quickly explain what had happened, and although the horrified people would offer their services, Bub was focused on walking straight home. All the while, he wondered, *What will my parents say, and how are they going to react?*

Naturally his parents freaked out.

"Where were you! You were supposed to be at church," his dad scolded while rushing to get his car keys.

Then off to the emergency room they went, and Bub's dad continued to press him.

"Look, son—I realize that I travel a lot, and that your mother is practically raising you by herself. For that reason, maybe I don't understand the way you think! When I was raised, people called me square, because I always did what was right. Nowadays, the word *square* is used by those who don't place any value on what it means to be good, and that concerns me. How do you feel—would you rather be square or hip?"

Bub drew a deep breath and said, "I think being square is okay, since you put it that way—but can't I be both?"

"Well, that depends, and it's a tough path to follow," his father said. "It all depends on your temperament and your ability to reason—maybe we just don't talk enough."

Bub received five cat-gut stitches deep under his scalp and nine on the surface. He also received a tetanus shot to prevent infection. The deep stitches stung, as did the burning shot, so he left the doctor's office with a sore and throbbing head.

Soon after Bub got home, he was over at Duncan's house, showing him his bald spot and bandage.

"Let's go over to Mark's and drink to your speedy recovery," Duncan said with a soft smile. So off they went.

Bub's head pounded with every step he took, and he could feel his pulse in his head wound. Duncan praised him for being a trooper, so he wasn't about to turn back.

Since Mark's parents held their business open on Sundays, his house was hopping! Bub had never seen Mark's parents so now was starting to doubt if they even existed.

"What will the injured soldier require?" Mark asked, with a big, shit-eating grin.

"Whiskey, and make it a double," Bub retorted, while shaking his head and forcing a smile. He said that because that's what he'd always heard on TV whenever some hero got hurt and asked for a drink. Meanwhile his young teenage friends were drunk and laughing loudly, as they ran up and down the stairs and though the hallways. Doors were slamming, and no one had to guess what was going on in the bedrooms! Still, Bub was content to sit at the bar while hoping for his condition to improve.

It wasn't too long before Bub's headache worsened, so he went to find Mark.

"I've got to lie down—do you have any aspirin, Mark?"

Mark led Bub to his parent's bedroom, which was the only bedroom that was empty. Then he fetched him some aspirin. As time passed, the throbbing headache became more intense, and Bub began to get the chills.

Out of the bedroom now, Bub announced, "I'm outta here," but he noticed that the smashed partygoers didn't even notice him. Not caring one way or the other, he left abruptly and walked the long hike back home.

Finally, Bub lay in his parents' bed. "I … I'm having trouble breathing!" he cried. "What's happening to me!"

His mother didn't know that Bub had been drinking, and therefore she made an educated guess. "You must be having a reaction to the tetanus shot. Just try to relax and take shallow, quick breaths."

Bub was beginning to panic, and he wondered, *Am I going to die?* He felt as though his chest muscles were cramping, because he couldn't get his lungs to work.

His mother went to the medicine chest and returned while ordering him to lie still. Bub did his best to cooperate, while she smeared eucalyptus oil on the inside of his nostrils, and soon the worst was over. Then his mom gave him a spoonful of honey with some crushed aspirin in it.

"Here, Riddick. Suck on this, slowly," she told him.

"Thanks, Mom," Bub whispered. Then he licked the spoon clean before curling up on his side and entering a fitful but much-needed sleep.

* * *

As time passed in Vienna, Bub continued to feel his way along. He was a normal kid, for the most part, doing whatever he could to entertain himself. He would play touch football, mow the lawn, wash the family car, and that sort of stuff. However, when night came he would usually head out with Duncan to smoke and drink, and do whatever.

Bub was missing tobogganing, which he'd enjoyed while living in Minnesota. Therefore, he decided to make an eight-foot flatbed wagon and constructed it with old wagon wheels, plywood, and two-by-fours. Well, build it he did, but, after testing it with some brave neighborhood volunteers, Bub got a good road rash and a broken big toe. As he explained it, "The contraption worked great while going down the hill, but when I tried to turn the damn thing, all hell broke loose!"

A week later Bub was still on crutches when he decided to skip church again. This time he and his friends went to the area of a creek bed where they'd stashed some malt liquor. Bub got so inebriated that when he tried to walk home alone, he didn't make it more than twenty yards before one of his crutches slipped on the muddy path, and into the water he went. That was good for a laugh from his friends, but Bub wasn't having any fun as he crawled back up onto the path!

A Good Samaritan saw Bub hobbling down the sidewalk and gave him a ride home in the back of his station wagon. This surprised Bub's sister, Darla, who'd stayed home and was washing her car. After getting him out of the station wagon, she helped him to get undressed before putting him to bed. Then she stashed his dirty clothes and later explained to his parents that he came home suffering from a terrible headache.

Bub's brother and sisters varied in their temperaments, but they all looked out for one another. In that regard, there was a big generation gap in the 1960s, and since their attitudes were becoming more liberal, they were pretty much in tune with one another. In fact, the times were changing so rapidly, they were all experiencing new thrills while riding the wave of what was to come. Darla was the oldest of the four Kellow children. She was six years older than Bub, and with long, dark-brown brown hair, she was very attractive. She was an avid reader and her intelligence was apparent due to her gentle and curious nature. Robbie was five years older than Bub and he was his only brother. He had a gift for making people laugh and he loved to take things apart just to see how they worked. With his slender six-foot frame and neatly styled blonde hair, he'd made a worthy impression as a singer in a rock 'n roll band. Jessica was three years older than Bub and she was the most spirited child in the family. With long blonde hair and piercing blue eyes, she had the ability to tell when someone was lying, and, if she thought they were, she would unleash her fury! She was crazy about animals and she loved to ride horses.

*   *   *

As the school year was drawing to a close, Duncan introduced Bub to a new way of getting high—glue! Although Bub thought that Duncan was off of his rocker, he conceded that he'd been a decent mentor. After all, Duncan had been a shining star within the ranks of the biggest clique, so how bad could it be? Besides, Bub was ready to experience a different type of high, so he was curious to see what it was like.

Duncan bought some model airplane glue, and into the woods they went. As Bub took low and deep breaths from the paper bag, he began to sense a vibration in his entire head. The initial effect was as if he were surrounded by a swarm of cicadas, as a strong vibration loomed in his head. Then he entered a lucid dreamlike state, whereupon his mind wandered and observed stark and strange images. When he finally lowered the bag from his face, he regained normal consciousness and was amazed by the experience. Then he tried it again, but, after getting a headache, he quit.

Upon later learning that glue burned brain cells and fearing that it could produce bad side effects, Bub vowed never to sniff it again. Still, he'd been mystified by the experience, and now he was curious as to how other drugs might affect him. At the same time, Bub figured that if Duncan Callahan was into sniffing glue, other drugs couldn't be all that bad!

Just as it looked like Bub was going to attend high school in Vienna, his parents announced that they were buying a nice brick home in the upscale town of McLean. That meant that the Kellow family would be moving for the sixth time, and as far as good-byes went—well, they were used to that by now.

3. PSYCHEDELIA

Bub's family moved to McLean during the early summer of 1967. Since his dad had worked his way up in the federal government, and his parents had actually purchased this particular house, Bub figured that they'd finally reached their permanent destination. Their new house had two split levels, and Bub's room was located on the ground level, alongside his brother's room. Both of their bedrooms were just off the recreation room, and there was a three-quarter bath located at the end of a hallway that led to a back door. Bub liked his room because it had large windows that would come in handy whenever he wanted to smoke, or sneak in and out of the house.

Bub was quick to explore the immediate neighborhood, and then he walked to the business district to give it a good, long look. Once outside of his subdivision, he enjoyed the hilly, uncurbed roads that gave the McLean area a nice town-and-country effect, but when he reached the center of town, he became a little disappointed. *Not too much here*, he figured, as he surveyed the town. The only thing that appealed to him was the liquor store, a couple of restaurants, and the bowling alley. It was a small town, when compared to Vienna, and now he was missing his friends.

After hitchhiking from town, Bub was walking up a side street toward his home when he saw Joey. Joey was a small boy, like Bub, and he appeared to be the same age. Bub nodded as he approach Joey and Joey nodded back, so Bub said, "What's up?"

"Are you from around here?" Joey asked.

"I am now," Bub replied.

After exchanging names and some background information, Bub learned that Joey was an only child whose dad worked for an intelligence agency and whose mother drank a lot. After hearing that, Bub thought Joey might need a friend. Joey claimed to be part Native American, and since he had brown eyes, olive skin, and straight, blue-black hair, Bub believed him.

"What do you do for kicks around here," Bub asked, whereupon Joey slowly smiled.

"Come on in, and we'll shoot some pool," Joey responded, and in that instant they became friends.

As they racked the balls, Bub told Joey about his collegiate friends, from Vienna.

"I used to be a collegiate, too," Joey said dryly.

With that comment, Bub examined Joey's style. He was looking a lot like the hippies whom he'd heard of, with his long hair parted down the middle, a collarless shirt, bell-bottomed jeans, and pointy boots.

The British Invasion, Bub thought.

The clothes fit him like a glove, and as Bub nodded in quiet approval; he liked Joey's style.

Joey told Bub that he had a best friend by the name of Thad, who was an only child, like himself. Thad's father was a colonel in the US Army, and like Bub's dad he'd moved several times. Most recently Thad had returned from Germany, and since his dad was now stationed at the Pentagon, he'd bought his family a magnificent new home in McLean.

When Bub and Thad were finally introduced, they clicked and became immediate friends. He was a very good-looking boy, with perfectly styled blonde hair, a big smile, and a huge propensity for having lots of fun. Although he spoke fluent German and was German by descent, Thad was an all-American kid with no hint of a foreign accent.

That summer the three of them had loads of fun together. Joey and Thad had minibikes, and they let Bub ride them. It was his first experience at riding a motorized bike, and he loved the sound and feel of the stout little engines. By law, they weren't allowed to ride them on the street, but that just made it seem all the more exciting. They also explored all the woods in the area and spent a lot of time in town, where Joey introduced Thad and Bub to other kids he knew.

There was a high pile of peat-moss bags that were stacked next the town's drugstore. They'd become "the place" for restless kids to sit while looking for action. It was a convenient spot, because there were three phone booths located next to the bags, and there was a soda fountain in the drugstore.

During that summer, Bub developed a relationship with a girl who was a friend of Joey's girlfriend. She was a nice girl, and Bub was happy and excited every time they got together. Her mother was divorced and worked a lot, so people hung out at her house during the day. Since the house was located by a small park, they met more kids there as well.

It was at that park, one evening, when Bub first smoked marijuana. At first, it didn't seem to have any effect on him, but within the span of a minute, he started to experience complete euphoria. At the same time, the volume of his thoughts increased, as he began to sense different parts of his body while analyzing every function that was taking place. Then, as if on autopilot, Bub pulled out a cigarette and put it to his mouth, much to his dismay.

My lungs, he thought, as euphoria was suddenly replaced with panic. *My God! What am I doing to my lungs!* Then his girlfriend hopped on his back, nearly knocking him to the ground.

"This is great—why isn't pot legal!" Bub exclaimed.

Joey and Thad were very much like Bub in that they shared some important feelings. They were tired of the rigors of conformity, because they equated conformity with a stunted experience of the unknown. They also shared a contempt for social inequality and prejudice, which they'd all experienced while growing up. For those reasons, they felt justified to hang with people who got stoned to rebel against the status quo. They knew they were heading into new and exciting times, and now they were eager to share them together.

Freshman Year: 1967–1968

As Bub roamed the halls of his new high school, he was groggy due to lack of sleep. The anticipation of his first day at school, plus the fact that the family television set was now parked just outside his bedroom door, had taken its toll. His parents enjoyed watching *The Tonight Show Starring Johnny Carson*, and Bub liked his monologue too.

He finally found his homeroom, packed with all the kids whose last names started with a *K*. *It's funny how last names that start with a K always sound so goofy*, he thought.

After exchanging hidden glances with the other kids, the teacher started with the roll call. Expecting his name at any second, the teacher fell silent before blurting his name as if it were one word: "Riddickkellow."

Bub winced, because he'd been taunted as "ridiculous" by some mean kids. Therefore, he quickly and carefully enunciated his name for his teacher and the students.

Not understanding the necessity for his correction, the teacher looked confused and somewhat annoyed. Then she made a half-hearted second attempt. "Just call me Bub," Bub sighed. Of course, he expected the laughter that followed, and, as he shook his head and sank low in his seat, the teacher smiled while shrugging her shoulders.

Bub figured that with his small frame, long hair, and new style of clothes, he'd become easy prey for the collegiate crowd. He knew that he could've dressed the part and talked bullshit in order to fall right in with them, but now he'd had it with that scene! He equated the collegiate lifestyle to an old-fashioned social groove that paved the way to a pretentious, materialistic, and narrow-minded society. As a result, his men's magazines had been replaced with underground newspapers.

He'd learned that the Beat generation had laid the foundation for the hippy counterculture, which had expounded on the importance of free thought and new social concepts. Meanwhile The Man was pushing back as if to say, "Stand down and be silent." Bub figured that intolerance had only fed the flames of protest, while the need for ethical reform had become self-evident. That civil unrest was not just a simple matter of being drawn into a controversial war to stop the spread of communism. It started with the witch hunt of McCarthyism and arguments centered on the notions of true individual liberty. At the same time, the Afro-American Civil Rights Movement, the Women's Liberation Movement, and the Environmental Movement were in full swing, and together they were ushering in a period of civil unrest that was greatly feared by traditionalists. Therefore, a consensus had been formed amid the rising chaos, as defiant politicians took to the media to state their constituents' concerns.

Bub was hardly a traditionalist, so he believed that there was a need for change. Now he was willing to help with whatever it would take to make that happen. He'd listened to Buffalo Springfield's "For What It's Worth," and that song had become his mantra. It made him more aware of the propaganda campaigns that were being aimed toward the oppressed, and that made the notion of demonstrating against "the powers that be" a very noble and interesting cause. At the same time, he realized that he and his friends were merely the children of a greater intellectual force that was opposed to the moral aversions to individual equality, and the unjustified contempt of elected leaders who seemed determined to maintain the status quo. Since Bub was now attuned to those revelations, he was content to merely demonstrate his opposition by growing his hair long and smoking pot while getting into the mental groove of "the movement." While that lifestyle was exciting to him and his new friends, they were getting paranoid while developing a mutual resentment of "the pigs."

Bub didn't drop out of school, but he didn't do much homework or pay much attention in class, either. To him, high-school classes were pretty damned boring, with few exceptions. He claimed that was due, in part, to the dullness of his teachers' ability to stimulate or challenge him, but he was quick to add that he'd really rather be "where it's at." So, before the first bell of the day would ring, one could usually find him on the edge of the school grounds, smoking pot with his friends and making future plans.

As Bub's excitement grew with the stimulating news and music of his subculture, so did his energy level. Each morning he'd rise out of bed and perform the calisthenics that he was taught to do during the Kennedy administration. He would snap off sixty pushups, sixty sit-ups, twenty windmills, and twenty jumping jacks before standing on his head against a wall. Then he'd admire his bulging veins and muscles before jumping into the shower. All the while he would think about the mysteries of spiritual revolution while wondering where his life would take him.

Musicians were producing powerful music that connected with Bub's soul, so he wanted to learn more about the human spirit. He borrowed an Eastern philosophy book from his older sister Darla, who seemed to have a deep sense of wisdom. It was an introductory book related to the notions of preexistence and reincarnation, and it was written in an accessible way that would clarify his understanding.

As he absorbed the occult material, he equated the Christian definition of Providence to the author's observation that universal laws govern circumstance—the force of which is guided by virtue. That made him think, *That's heavy—if the universe is governed by laws—that means God doesn't have to watch everybody all the time!* Then he read that the human race was composed of souls who are at various stages of development. That made him think, *That explains why some people are more advanced than others! Hmm—I wonder how advanced I am?* After that he put the book down, because he was overwhelmed while realizing that he had to give those notions some serious thought.

When Bub told Joey and Thad about what he read, Joey scoffed. "You don't believe that bullshit, do you?"

With that remark, Bub never brought the subject up again, since he didn't want to appear weird to his friends. Nevertheless, he was eager to talk about what he'd read, so he consulted with his sister Darla. She enjoyed his enthusiasm, and they played ESP games while burning incense and listening to soft music.

It wasn't long before Bub began to try a new group of drugs called psychedelics. Joey wanted to try some acid, but not alone. He rationalized, "Everybody's doing it! The US Army even gave it to their own soldiers, so they could see what it's all about!" He didn't have to coax Bub, though. "Incense and Peppermints" by Strawberry Alarm Clock had been a big hit, and now "Journey to the Center of the Mind," by The Amboy Dukes, was topping the charts. So Bub, Joey, and Thad made a plan to score their acid at a new hamburger restaurant in McLean. It was a popular place for kids to hang after high school, and during that time it was touted as "Drug Central."

Upon their arrival, Joey moved about the place, making subtle inquiries, until he was finally told to sit tight with his two friends and wait. They didn't have to wait long before they scored some purple double-domes from a rough-and-tumble, long-haired fellow who sat down slowly while giving them a wide-eyed stare. He was an ominous figure of a man who appeared to be of Scandinavian or German descent, due to his massive forehead and thick, blond hair. He was pockmarked, scarred, tattooed, and lean, with a muscular build. His braided leather vest, spiked belt, rumble bracelets, torn-up jeans, and engineer boots led Bub to believe that this drug dealer might be from Falls Church and perhaps a member of a motorcycle gang. The dealer just sat there and calmly folded his hands while staring back at Joey, who was looking very nervous. Then the dealer slowly raised his folded hands to his chin while keeping his elbows on the table and voilà, the little purple pills appeared. Joey quickly followed suit, mimicking the actions of the stranger, and Bub was impressed. The drugs disappeared, replaced with money, and with that, the tall, evil-looking man performed his disappearing act without ever having said a word.

As they left the restaurant, Bub's hunch panned out. They were just in time to see their connection roar off toward Falls Church on an obnoxiously noisy and outrageously raked knucklehead chopper with a side-shifter.

"That's the first time I've ever seen anybody like him in McLean!" Bub said.

It was late in the afternoon by now, and Thad, Joey, and Bub dropped their acid while walking home.

"This is crazy," Bub suddenly realized. "I'm going to have to go home to eat supper!"

They stopped by Joey's house and sat around, waiting to get off. Since it was a Friday night, they discussed a couple of parties that they'd heard about.

After a while, Bub said, "I've got to split, man—I've got to go eat and check in with the parents. I'll meet you dudes back here in about an hour, okay? By the way, I don't feel shit, man. I think we got ripped off!"

Joey just shrugged, and Thad shook his head as Bub disappeared out the door.

As Bub took the short walk home, he began to feel a slight swelling in his throat. It wasn't painful. It was just a feeling. So he rubbed his neck with his hand, but it felt normal. Then he felt a floating sensation, but his head was clear. In fact, it was clearer than it had ever been. Then he grinned, as he was overcome by sudden rush to his head, which caused him to feel light on his feet. It was as if he were floating now, and his body motions were effortless.

"Man—I feel like a wild beast!" he said out loud, just to experience the sound of his own voice.

Suddenly, a rush of energy flowed down from the top of Bub's head to his feet. *So this is tripping—Wow!* As he rounded the corner to his house, he began to notice that everything looked extremely vivid to him. The colors of everything he saw grew in intensity. The cicadas and the birds grew louder in his head, causing him to look about. At the same time, the smell of the thick honeysuckle filled his sense of smell. *And what is this?* he wondered, as the different shades of gray in the street began to ooze up and down while slowly transmogrifying. That made Bub grin from ear to ear, and, while he knew that he was wide awake, he felt as if he was having a lucid dream. *Who am I?*

Bub bounded up the three steps to the front door of his house, and, as he extended his hand to the doorknob, he marveled. *It's as if I'm the Wizard of Oz and working a damned robot!*

"Wash up, dinner's ready!" His mother greeted him with a smile.

Bub was already smiling, and he waved as he dashed down the steps to his bathroom. As he started to wash his hands, he looked into the bathroom mirror while focusing on his eyes. *What are you doing in there?* he wondered, as he slowly moved his head from one side to the other. His pupils were so dilated that his hazel irises had all but disappeared. He felt very warm, and his face was slightly flushed. His pores seemed to be wide-open and tingling. In fact, everything about him seemed to be on heightened alert.

He washed his hands and face, and then he combed his hair.

"You look great," he said, as if he were talking to someone else. Then he clenched his fists as he thought, *I feel great, too!* He was wearing a gold, V-neck body shirt, and it had some sparkling polyester fabric in it.

"Captain Kirk, I presume," he said while grinning and then left the bathroom.

His family was already seated at the dinner table as he took his place, and all the while he was grinning. Apparently, it was infectious, because everyone who looked at him smiled.

"What are you so damned happy about?" his brother, Robbie, asked.

"Nothing much—I just feel *good*," Bub replied.

Then, as if out of nowhere, his mom plopped a big plate of steaming spaghetti with garlic toast in front of him.

"Whoa!" Bub said, almost involuntarily. "I don't think I can eat that!"

"What? You can and you *will*," his mother scolded.

Bub very carefully broke down what his mother had just said to him, and it was "you will" that intrigued him the most. *You will,* he repeatedly thought to himself, and as he did he twirled his spaghetti with his fork.

At this point, he realized he didn't want to draw any more attention to himself, so he merely glimpsed at everyone as they ate. His family loved his Mom's spaghetti, so now they were eating it with gusto. *We are animals,* Bub thought. *How beast-like they appear—I have got to get out of here!*

It wasn't too long before everyone had finished their supper and put their dishes into the sink. *Thank God for garbage disposals,* Bub thought, and, when the coast was clear, he scraped most of his serving down the drain.

"I'm going to hang at Joey's," he called to his parents, who had already settled down in front of their television. "I'll see you later," he added, as he left the house.

It was nearly dark outside on that perfect, early October evening, and the sky was clear and bright with a huge, gold, harvest moon hanging on the horizon. As Bub walked to the back of Joey's house and passed a basement window, he could see Thad through the picture window, gesturing to Joey with his hands. Thad's face was flushed while bearing a telltale grin.

As Bub let himself in, his two partners in crime grinned while searching his face for what they already knew was happening.

"This is some fairly awesome shit, no?" Bub said while moving his hand slowly across his face in order to watch the trails.

"*Fairly,* my ass!" Thad responded in a high but restrained voice. "It's *fucking out-of-this-world* awesome! Come on—let's play a game of pool!"

As Joey finished rolling a joint, Bub racked the balls and Thad chalked every cue stick he could find. Then they passed the joint as they played pool. As they marveled at the trails the balls made with each passing shot, Bub was amused while thinking, *Even though Joey's dad works for an intelligence agency, Joey always stinks up the whole house with pot!* The three boys spent a lot of their time in Joey's basement, they were becoming sharpshooters. Therefore the game was nearly over before it had started.

"Let's go up to McLean," Joey said, and with that, they were out the door, breathing in the crisp, cool, evening air.

The full moon created an electric-blue light on all that they saw, and as they passed through the darkness of Pimmit Run, the moonlight made the woods seem mysterious. Then their shadows passed them under the streetlights as they continued to share thoughts on the drug's strange and interesting effects. Once again, Bub felt as if he were dreaming.

When they finally arrived at the drug store, they found Frankie sitting alone on the peat moss bags. Frankie was a small French kid, with long, dark curly hair; and he was always sporting a big smile beneath his thick goatee. He was waiting to meet another friend and told the three grinning trippers that everyone had gone to Kent Gardens Park, to "party down" in the woods.

"Shit! That's right behind my house!" Thad exclaimed. So the three of them stocked up on cigarettes and sodas and headed back toward the park.

Upon reaching the edge of heavily wooded park, they took a trail that would lead them to a bridge that crossed over Pimmit Run. There was a clearing there, and it was a popular hangout for teenagers. As they made their way down the moonlit path, a young man came running from the opposite direction and stopped, with his chest heaving.

"Don't go down there, man! The cops are there, and they're busting everyone!"

Then, as quickly as he'd stopped, he was off running like his butt was on fire. Bub laughed. "Shit! They've got nothing on us! Besides—we're sober, and we live around here."

So the three continued on, anxious to see what was happening.

When they arrived at the bridge, all was quiet, except for the sound of the bubbling brook. Then a glowing flashlight suddenly appeared about twenty yards in front of them. As it grew nearer, the three just stood there, observing the patent leather shoes that shined beneath the light.

"What are you kids doing here?" came a deep voice, filled with authority.

It was a county policeman, and he was accompanied by two plainclothes police officers.

"What *kids* are you talking about, man!" Bub retorted.

Then Thad quickly and humbly interjected in an effort to smooth down the tone. "I live right over there, sir. We were just passing through to get to my house."

Then the officer's tone continued. "We have complaints of loud mischievous activity in this area. Are you kids aware of the posted park hours?"

"No," Bub responded. "We were only aware of avoiding the dangers of crossing a creek while walking a the poorly lit, uncurbed street—and everything seemed peaceful to us, up until now!"

The policeman looked at Bub and then frowned. "You seem to have an attitude problem, boy!"

As Bub squinted to see past the flashlight, he knew the officer was merely looking for unconditional respect. Nevertheless, Bub had experienced abuse by people who had authority, and he was tired of overblown attitudes. Besides, he and his friends would have run if they'd done something wrong, so now he wasn't going to yield, despite the consequences.

"It might seem that way to you, *sir*, but I think that attitudes, in general, reflect the attitudes that we perceive—don't you?"

That was *not* the response that the officer wanted to hear, and, with his colleagues mumbling and growing impatient beside him, he lost his patience. "All right, let's go! You kids are coming with us!"

As they were led to a police car, Joey and Thad shook their heads and laughed as Bub continued to agitate the cops. "Don't you guys have something better to do? You'll be hearing from our attorneys—our parents are taxpayers, you know."

Once at the police substation, the boy's parents were called, and each arrived only minutes apart to claim their own. When Bub's dad arrived, he looked confused and annoyed. "What's the problem here, officer?" he demanded.

The officer explained about the neighborhood complaint and said that the boys had obviously been drinking. With that remark, Joey's dad and Bub's dad approached their boys to smell for alcohol. Then they looked at one another and shrugged.

"Don't you police officers have any sense of reason in these matters?" Joey's father asked.

Without an answer, the boys were released to their fathers' custody. As Bub left the substation, he grinned at the officers while scratching his head with his middle finger.

The next day, Bub felt as if all the vitality in his system had been depleted. The drug had kept him awake until about four in the morning, and now he realized that he had to mow the lawn. Other than that, he felt okay, and he figured his experience with acid had been a good one, except for his brush with the law.

Come Monday, he and Joey told their story to some acquaintances at school and one of them, who claimed to know the long-term effects of the drug, admonished them. "Don't you know that there are consequences to dropping acid? Once you take it, you're incapable of making critical decisions, and there's a pretty good chance that your children will be deformed!"

While Bub figured that the boy was full of crap, his words were none the less planted deeply within his mind.

Soon thereafter, Bub experienced an incredibly strong déjà vu. It happened when he was climbing into the backseat of Joey's dad's car. Joey's dad was reaching between the bucket seats to grab an umbrella, and that's when it hit Bub. He had experienced déjà vu before, but this time he was positive that he had dreamt of that same instance just the night before. It was in the initial flash of his new experience that he had first recalled his dream. That caused him to excitedly relate his strong perception, but Joey and his dad just smiled as they looked at each other. Of course, Bub understood their skepticism, but that profound experience reinforced his notion that there was definitely something strange going on behind "the big curtain."

* * *

Up until now, Bub had been expected to attend church and catechism at least once per week, until finally, he complained to his mother.

"Pops never goes to church, and you miss Mass every now and then—and catechism! They don't even want to discuss the validity of their interpretations. They tell me that logic and reason are a ploy used by the devil! Anyway, I've already absorbed what Jesus said, and as for the rest of it—blind faith just isn't my bag."

As he stomped about the kitchen while making his breakfast and continuing his harangue, his mother had finally had enough! "Oh, well—God knows I've tried, Riddick!"

Although Bub had explained his interpretations of life to his mother, she figured that his notions weren't doing him much good. She'd heard him rant about the hypocrisy and ignorance of the government, and she tried to make him understand that all would be better if he concentrated on his own defects of moral character. She realized that his mind had become shaped to his bad experiences, so she warned him that an ill fate might be his teacher. That was okay with Bub, though, and he thanked her for trying to teach him her religious beliefs. The next time he went to church, it was to relieve the offertory box of five bucks, so he could score a gram of hash. That action not only surprised his friends but himself as well. It was not only an outlandish display of his contempt for his former church but also an indication of just how far he would go to satisfy his growing lust. As Bub had put it, "I shall take from the rich, so as to give to the needy!"

During this period, Bub also developed new relationships with a couple of his brother's friends, Barry and Jeff. Barry was a charismatic young man with good looks and a great sense of humor. He was also an avid, self-professed cocksman, and he liked outrageous-looking muscle cars. Jeff, or "Bouncer," as his friends called him, acquired his nickname because he was tough. His parents lived in a large mansion off Georgetown Pike, which was very close to Barry's home. The mansion had large, castle-like turrets on it, as did the detached four-car garage that Bouncer lived above. What was originally a chauffeur's quarters made a nice, private abode, and he and his friends could come and go as they pleased, without disturbing his parents. The multi-acre property was situated high on the south bank of the Potomac River, and it provided magnificent views.

There was a trail near Barry and Bouncer's homes that led all the way down to the river's edge. It winded through thick woods and finally followed the west side of a tributary that flowed into the river. Across from that confluence was a long and narrow island and then the state of Maryland. The closer the tributary flowed toward the river, the higher the stone cliffs grew on the eastern side of it. On the west side of the tributary stood an old wooden house that was about 150 yards from the river. Just down the hill from that stood a stone bungalow surrounded by the greenery of the flat river plain. The inside of the bungalow was raw and rustic, with a stone floor and big, square timbers that ran across to support the pitched roof. It was fairly small, but it had a large, stone fireplace, and the window that faced the fast-flowing Potomac River made it inviting.

There was a sad story concerning an artist and his spouse who'd lived in the house while raising a family. The river flooded after a huge downpour and claimed the life of one of their little children. They mourned the loss but persevered only to have that same calamity befall them again. Then they moved on. Bub figured that the bungalow had been constructed by the artist for painting pictures, since the view of the Potomac wasn't obstructed by the dense treetops.

This area proved to be a favorite hangout for Barry, Bouncer, and the local kids from another high school, and party they did! There were huge, drunken fests that had taken place there, and finally, the big wooden house was burned to the ground. That was shame for them, but it was a blessing from Bub's point of view. The stone bungalow remained intact, and since the rowdy people had quit partying there, he claimed this area as one of his favorite haunts. He loved to sit on a huge, oblong rock that jutted out toward the confluence of the swiftly moving river and the tributary. There, the energy and sound of the shallow, hard-flowing river filled his senses—the same feelings that he'd experienced as a child while growing up in the raw beauty of Northern Minnesota. It was then that Bub was a toddler, and sometimes go with his dad as he drove deep into the woods to inspect the operation and condition of various lookout towers. Together, they would hike past Smokey the Bear signs and climb the long and scary stairways that ascended to the high towers. When his father was through with his inspections, they would go the maple trees where he had bored a hole and inserted a spout to catch syrup in buckets. After heating and pouring the syrup into cans, they would also hike around the shores of lakes to pick choke cherries so the girls could make jam. Therefore, Bub felt happy and at home in the woods, since they reminded him of a time when life seemed simple, wondrous and care free.

The high cliffs on the other side of the tributary, together with the steeply sloping grades on all opposing sides, formed a large, seemingly private area of magical beauty. The trees made a cool canopy for the more delicate ferns and shrubs that grew on the low ground, and the fast-flowing river provided a steady, thunderous rumble as it flowed over smooth and slimy rocks. To add to the natural beauty, the moon and sun, whenever unobstructed, made the river shimmer and shine.

Bub excitedly told Thad and Joey about the place, so they told their parents they were spending the night at a friend's house. Then they gathered all the necessities, such as sleeping bags, food, beer, and cigarettes, and hitchhiked down Old Dominion Drive, toward the river. After the long hike down the path, they inspected the bungalow, whereupon Bub claimed the old, rusty cot. Then they placed their beer in the cold water of the tributary before collecting firewood.

Within a short time, Thad and Joey were busy eradicating the bungalow of huge wolf spiders, while Bub began to build a fire. As each of the three boys settled in with a beer, and the flames grew larger, Thad suddenly shrieked! There were dozens of bats, hanging upside down from the support timbers, and since it was darker outside, the bats were getting aroused. Thad immediately grabbed a flat board that Bub had used to adjust the wood in the fireplace, and with it, he began to wail on the bats. That caused a flurry, as bats began flying through the air, so Bub and Joey ran outside. Then they watched in amazement until they heard one final splat, and all seemed quiet.

"*All clear!*" Thad shouted.

Joey and Bub cautiously made their way back into the cabin. There they found Thad proudly smiling while holding one of the dead critters between his fingertips.

"I nailed at least four of these little suckers—hungry?" he asked, and grinned.

As they sat around, smoking pot and drinking beer, Thad took up a charred stick and inscribed *BAT SPLAT* on the board. Then he made four notches on it before putting it up on a rafter. It was pitch black outside by now, except for a few shards of electric-blue moonlight and the glow of the river.

After they went outside to take a leak, the river's twinkling reflections and powerful rushing sound drew them closer. It was a fine night indeed, and, after exploring the area in the dark, they became thirsty once again. The thick and musky air was getting cooler by the minute, and the firelight, glowing dimly through the bungalow window, provided a welcome beacon as they hiked up the gentle slope from the river's edge.

As they settled down, with Thad and Joey struggling to get comfortable on the uneven block-stone floor, Thad kept complaining that one of the stones was sticking up too high.

"Go get some brush and put it under your sleeping bag, man," Bub murmured while mesmerized by the fire.

Frustrated and annoyed, Thad kicked his covers off and stood up. Just as he was walking for the door, Bouncer kicked it open, and at the same time, Barry appeared at the window with a bloodcurdling scream! That made Thad pee his pants, and, as he doubled over while trying to stop the warm flow, he said, "You *assholes*—what the fuck!" His face had turned raspberry red, and, since Joey and Bub hadn't freaked out nearly as badly, everyone's laughter was aimed at poor Thad.

Barry, and Bouncer came through the door, holding big sacks of cold beer and potato chips. Jokes and laughter followed into the early hours of the morning while everyone enjoyed singing Ninety-nine Bottles of Beer on the Wall and playing Cardinal Puff. Finally, Barry, and Bouncer got bored and decided to hike up to Bouncer's place to crash, but not before Bub asked them not to tells his brother or parents he was there. He was relieved because he and his groggy friends wanted to get some sleep, and he desperately needed to smoke a cigarette.

Many camping trips to the river's edge would follow, and all were memorable to Bub. Some of his brother's friends became river rats, so they became Bub's friends too. Together they'd get so drunk that they'd do outrageously silly things. Oftentimes they would stumble through the dark, slip and fall into water, or trip and fall into the campfire. One night, after they waded to the island, one of the guys shot himself through the calf of his leg. Not to be deterred, he poured whiskey on the wound, tied it off, drank the rest, and passed out. In Bub's estimation, he was a true partier extraordinaire.

*   *   *

All during his freshman year, Bub had done a good job of concealing his increasingly bad habits. He was building a tolerance for alcohol, so he wasn't getting sick afterwards, and, since his parents smoked cigarettes, they couldn't tell if he did, too. All the while he seemed like a normal kid, since he liked to watch baseball and football, and he was good at playing chess. Unfortunately, he was also good at the art of deception, so no one in his family was hip to the full extent of his latest antics. Then Bub's family took a trip to Ocean City, Maryland during the summer of 1968, The two-week vacation was good for Bub despite getting a bad case of sunburn. He would sneak out to smoke every now and then, but the serenity of the beach environment slowed him down. He didn't drink any alcohol while he was there, and he enjoyed a lot of fun activities with his family. By the time he returned to see his friends, the sun had turned his hair blond, and his skin was darkly tanned. Therefore, it seemed as though Bub was a chameleon to his social environments. When he was with his friends, he drank because he felt he needed a crutch, but when he was with his family, everything seemed more joyous, simple and secure, and, in that relaxed state of mind, his health glowed.

Sophomore Year: 1968–1969

By September 1968, the United States was experiencing hard times wrought by a tremendous clash of moral perspectives and political power. The view of the Vietnam War had shifted, since the My Lai Massacre had been brought to national attention, and the Martin Luther King Jr. and Robert F. Kennedy assassinations resulted in unprecedented civil unrest and disobedience. The 1968 Democratic National Convention showcased the violence that politicians aimed toward demonstrators, with no regard for their safety or even that of bystanders and journalists. Meanwhile, the environment was a major concern to those who realized the detriments of polluting the earth without regarding natural consequences. There were factories belching carcinogens into the atmosphere and waterways, and there were heavy and unrestricted vehicles that ran the roads on high-octane, high-emission, leaded fuels. As for the social contract with state governments, public safety and awareness continued to be an issue. Despite many people's complaints, cigarette smoking was still allowed in most buildings, and office parties continued to be outrageous. That brought a focus on "Corporate America," whose profit-at-any-cost attitude often seemed indifferent to the welfare of the common man. For those reasons, the chaos of the sixties was steadily increasing, and if you asked Bub if he gave a damn, his attitude would range from caring to cynical. He liked Jim Morrison's point of view: "The end is always near, so roll, baby, roll!"

Bub dreaded being back in school because, even though he was starting with a fresh slate, he knew his grades would eventually suck. Still, he was relieved as he thought, *At least I'm not a freshman!* New faces passed him in the hallways, and some of them were the young kids he'd met at the peat-moss bags. He was small during his freshman year, but now he was continuing to grow. His spiritual thoughts were on hold in lieu of his growing social status, and he was anxious to experience the "high" times that his friends eagerly wanted to share.

Since Bub was no longer embarrassed by his lack of "manhood," he was looking for a girlfriend. His most-recent girlfriend was nice enough, but she'd dumped him because he wasn't aggressive enough. Since then, a few girls had made advances toward him, but he didn't like assertive girls. He dreamed of a girl who was cute, cuddly, intellectually stimulating, and just somewhat uninhibited, but, due to his increasingly reckless behavior, that was becoming a tall order to fill.

One day, Bub and his friends ducked into the woods and smoked a joint before going into town. After arriving at the drugstore, Bub took a seat at the soda fountain and ordered a drink. The auburn-haired girl who served him studied his bloodshot eyes and then served his drink while laughing. He loved her charm, and she seemed to be just the kind of girl he'd been looking for. Alas, his heart skipped a beat, and he was in *love*—or so he thought. Sadly enough, as Bub got to know her better, his love for her grew stronger, but he was always too high or shy to let her know.

The time came when Bub was old enough to get a driver's permit, and his sister Darla taught him how to drive. She had a

1965 Impala SS convertible, and it was sweet! It was gold with a white top and interior, and it had sparkly, wire-wheeled hubcaps. She was a good teacher, but was Bub an appreciative student?

Occasionally, when everyone was asleep in his house, he would sneak Darla's keys and go for a midnight joy ride. Finally he got bold one night, while returning home, and decided to floor the gas pedal for one last thrill. He got going so fast that he didn't see a sharp turn up ahead, and when he suddenly came upon it, he went into a state of panic. He slammed on the brakes and skidded about twenty yards, but when he turned the steering wheel, the car continued to slide forward. In that same instant, he pushed the brake harder, and his foot slipped off of the pedal! Of course Bub freaked out, but, since the wheels were spinning freely now, the car ripped through the corner like it was glued to the pavement.

Bub was amazed at his luck! At the same time, his head was spinning, and his body was shaking from an adrenaline rush. He took great care as he drove his sister's car straight home, and, with tender loving care, he finally parked the car. Then he defaulted to his old habit of making the sign of the cross before creeping back into the house. After that experience, he vowed never to sneak Darla's car again!

When the day came for Bub to get his permanent driver's license, he was a nervous wreck. His mom had driven him up to the testing station in their new, baby-blue, 1969 Ford Galaxie 500, and the car seemed huge to Bub. Nevertheless, he had to take the driving test in it, and, when the state trooper told him that he had passed, he was highly elated.

"Park the vee-hicle and come inside," the stone-faced trooper dryly said as he got out of the car.

As Bub attempted to follow his orders, he managed to put a good-sized dent in the passenger door while parking. That happened because he hadn't squared his turn in the crowded parking lot, and he'd hit someone else's bumper. When he told his mother, who was waiting for him inside the testing station, she winced.

"Strewth, Riddick! You've dented your father's brand-new car! He won't be happy with you, mister!"

Bub was ashamed, but all he could do was shrug and apologize. "I'll pay for it—I'm really, really sorry!"

After his mother allowed him to drive home, Bub pulled up to a busy intersection that had no traffic light. His vision was obscured by a railroad trestle, and by now he was making his mother as nervous as he was.

"Be careful and look both ways, now!" she warned.

Bub did as she instructed, but, as he started to make his move, his mother exclaimed, "Riddick, there's a car coming!"

An experienced driver would have just stepped on the gas and got the hell moving, but Bub panicked and stopped flat in the middle of the intersection! That caused the oncoming driver to skid to a halt as Bub nervously shifted into reverse. Then he floored the car backward without looking behind him and smashed into a Pontiac Grand Prix, which had already moved up to the stop sign. With the sudden impact, the trunk of the Ford had buckled and popped open, and his mother screamed, "Riddick!"

By now every driver had stopped, so Bub sheepishly pulled forward into a gas station across the street while the guy driving the Grand Prix followed. As the two parties inspected the damages, it became apparent to the owner of the Pontiac that there was no damage to his car at all. His big, pointy bumper, however, had speared the back-end of the new Ford and bended it into a V shape. The extent of the damage was an embarrassment to Bub and his dear mom, because the trunk lid wouldn't shut and stay closed. This in turn prompted Bub to try to ease his mother's distress by interjecting some levity.

"Hey, the dent that I put in the door at the testing station doesn't look so bad now!"

His mother was not amused, though, and neither was his dad, who later inspected the damage, and said, "God almighty, Riddick!"

As Bub took the heat from his dad, his siblings found the situation to be quite humorous. Dejected but undeterred, Bub begged to drive the car, but his dad refused, saying that he would let him use it only while in the company of an experienced family member. Bub understood his dad's decision, but he still felt dejected. Now he dreamed of one day owning a car, whereupon he would enjoy an unencumbered feeling of freedom.

* * *

Bub knew of a sweet girl by the name of Eleanor whose daddy was a longtime county judge. The judge had bought a big Ford Galaxie convertible with a 390 four-barrel, and Eleanor was always driving it. Bub had never met the judge, and he was happy about that. Nevertheless, now that he had his driver's license, he was ready to take Eleanor up on her generous offer of letting him drive her daddy's car. As it turned out, she seemed to have a crush on Bub, so she let him drive wherever they went, as long as she got to sit next to him. Often, there were other girls with her who like Bub, too, so now he was feeling great!

Since Bub was driving Eleanor's car nearly every day, he started to get more reckless and daring. He liked to flip the air cleaner lid upside down, for added performance. Then he'd power-brake the car and pull hole-shots and power-slides while rat-racing other friends all over town. Meanwhile, his antics were starting to scare the crap out of the girls, and Eleanor was becoming leery of his intentions, so finally she refused to let him drive.

Shortly thereafter, Bub and a male friend named Tony were riding in the backseat of Eleanor's convertible, while Eleanor was driving and her sister was riding shotgun. It was a fine day, and they had just smoked a big, fat doobie. They were heading east on Georgetown Pike when they drove over the crest of a hill, and Eleanor had to slam on the brakes for a slowpoke who was driving a Camaro. After some patience, she realized that she could not pass, and since the driver refused to speed up, she began to honk her horn. As a result, the Camaro driver slowed down even more, and since Tony was on the driver's side of the backseat, he decided to hop out and run up alongside the slowpoke.

"Either speed up or get the fuck out of the way, man!"

The Camaro driver, who was apparently startled, suddenly floored his car, and off it went, like a shot! With a shrug and a look of amazement, Tony hopped back into the convertible, and they proceeded to laugh about the whole affair. Then, as they went over the next hill, they saw the Camaro stopped on the road, blocking their way, again! This time, it was the Camaro driver who jumped from his car, and he was brandishing a long and heavy-looking revolver. As he stomped toward Eleanor's car, he raised it with both hands while cocking the hammer back with a click.

"DRIVE!" Tony yelled, but Eleanor's instincts told her to stay put.

The man had a shaved head and wore a tight white T-shirt, and he appeared to be flushed red with anger. Bub figured him to be in his mid-twenties, and he noticed that there was a girl in his car who was watching him do his thing. *The guy is embarrassed after getting frightened, so now he's pissed*, Bub thought. Then the man carefully aimed his big-bore revolver at Bub's face who, while staring down the barrel, started to do some fast talking!

"Hey, what's the problem, man? Be cool! We're just trying to get down the road!"

While everyone else joined in the protest, it became quite apparent that this guy never saw exactly who had scared him. Still fuming and yelling, the angry man was suddenly surprised by other approaching motorists. So, pointing his pistol slightly upward, he slowly released the hammer while stepping backward. Then, after spitting on Eleanor's father's car, he quickly turned and ran back to his car.

Bub, who had been stiff with apprehension, slowly sank back down into his seat and took a deep breath.

"Jesus H. Christ! Find me a bathroom, please! What the fuck just happened, man!"

Eleanor and her sister were savvy and quickly noted the guy's license-plate number. Then, after some cars had driven around them, they carefully continued on their way. Within a mile, they came upon a fund-raising festival at the Great Falls Volunteer Fire Station. At Bub's beckoning, Eleanor abruptly swung the car in and parked near some policemen. As they quickly got out of the car and approached one of the officers, they were being carefully observed, and Bub knew from experience that most cops did not like longhairs.

As Bub frantically began to explain what had just happened, the policeman checked him. "Calm the hell down, boy!"

Bub took a deep breath, and, as calmly as he could, he started from the beginning.

"He's getting away," Eleanor interjected in protest.

Bub looked at her, and then he looked at the cop, who adjusted his stance with his hands on his hips. Bub resumed his account, but before he could finish, the cop interrupted him.

"It sounds to me as if you all might have had it coming!"

With that, Bub glared at the policeman's badge. "Okay, man, I've got your number! Thanks for nothing!"

Realizing what Bub was up to, the cop clutched his badge with one hand while pointing with the other. "Go—get the hell out of here, *now!*"

When Bub later explained the entire incident to his parents, they immediately called the police. Subsequently, two plainclothes detectives came over to their house to interview Bub. He was uneasy, because he didn't like cops, but he knew that the weirdo who'd wielded a hand cannon had to be stopped.

A week after the interview, the detectives called his father. They told him that the agitated man was a security cop, and that he, and the officer whose badge number Bub had given to them, would be formally reprimanded.

Upon hearing that news, Bub bitterly complained. "Big, hairy, fucking deal! I nearly get my head blown off, and those assholes merely get reprimanded? What a crock of *shit!*"

Although his father was angered by Bub's use of bad language, he also understood his son's uncontrollable bout of frustration. He explained to Bub that intelligent people express their anger with constraint, and that getting overly angry in such circumstances would only bring him more despair. That caused Bub to calm down and ponder his father's wisdom, before apologizing for his sudden outburst. Upon hearing that, his father reiterated his concern for Bub's safety, and told him he was going to become more lenient with Bub's use of the family car.

Soon thereafter, Bub took advantage of his father's understanding and generosity when he borrowed the family car to drive into town to buy some cigarettes. It was a beautiful Saturday morning, and he was anticipating the fun times he might have with his friends. While heading back home, he nailed the gas pedal to the floor, and the big sedan dropped into second gear. As he sped along Old Dominion Drive, the car approached eighty miles per hour before it finally shifted into third gear, and now Bub's knuckles were white on the wheel. As he observed a blind curve coming up fast, he began to back down, and, as the car went into the curve, he suddenly spotted trouble ahead. There were two cars stopped in his lane, and there was a long line of approaching traffic. Bub instantly slammed on the brakes as he gripped the steering wheel even harder, but it seemed as though the car was barely slowing down. As he gritted his teeth, the rear of the car in front of him came up fast and with a loud crash his car smashed into it, causing it to lurch forward and smash into the car in front of *it*! Luckily for all, none of the cars involved were forced out into the oncoming traffic, or who knows what might have happened.

No one was injured, but the resulting damage was not good, to say the least. The hood of the big Galaxie had popped open and folded back, causing the windshield to shatter. The front fenders had flared out from the impact, and they overlapped the doors, making it necessary for the nervous and rattled Bub to exit through a rear door. Meanwhile, steam was coming from the busted radiator, and passing cars were running over miscellaneous debris that was scattered all across the roadway.

Surprisingly, the car wasn't totaled, which annoyed the hell out of Bub's father. After all, he'd just purchased the car a short while ago, and already the front, rear, and side had been smashed. To add to his misery, the last repair had been a lousy one, and now he feared the next one wouldn't be much better. Aside from that, he was just relieved that no one had been hurt.

The policeman who investigated the accident had merely given Bub a ticket for "Failing to Maintain Proper Time and Attention." The officer claimed that he was being very fair, all things considered. It appeared that only two wheels had skidded for a distance of about forty yards, and therefore he told Bub that the car might have faulty brakes. Bub laughed about that later, while drinking beer with his friends. He figured that the brakes were fine, and the rear wheels were probably too light to leave a skid mark due to the high speed and forward thrust of the car.

As his sophomore year in high school progressed, Bub continued to party. On the weekends, he would tell his parents that he was staying at a friend's house but then crash at the river or just party all night long while roaming the streets. If he decided go home, it was usually very late, and his brother and sisters would almost always be up partying with their friends. It was often the case that their exasperated parents were awakened, and Pops, as Bub fondly called his dad, would yell, *"Pipe down!"* That was a term that he had acquired in the navy, during WWII.

As the "Age of Aquarius" was still filling the airwaves, the summer of 1969 gave way to more mind exploration through "experimentation." On one such occasion Bub, Joey, and Thad had scored some "robin eggs." Robin eggs was an appropriate name given to clear capsules of a light blue synthetic mescaline, interspersed with dark-blue specks. The high was said to be the best ever, so the three boys were eager to give them a try.

The hype proved to be correct when the trio found themselves sitting in a tree, laughing in joyous disbelief over the profound effects of the drug. There were no ill side effects, whereas some hallucinogens had been laced with strychnine, and it was just shy of being mentally overpowering. As a result, Bub entered a calmness whereupon he was certain that he'd finally connected with some divine stream of knowledge. That is to say, life's complexities suddenly seemed crystal-clear to him, and the only thing that disturbed him was the thought of losing his wonderful insight. Needless to say, he eventually would, but for the time being, he felt that he had crossed the line that day and found further proof of another plane of existence.

In August of 1969, Bub tried to find someone who would take him to Woodstock, but apparently it wasn't meant to be. He had considered hitchhiking with a friend, but they reckoned it was too far away. Besides that, he had no money, so he finally gave up. It was a bummer for him, though, because he wanted to experience the sensation of the hippie revolution by listening to awesome music while drinking and sampling assorted drugs.

Bub's first two years in high school were very entertaining, if not productive. He had made a lot of friends, and he looked forward to having fun whenever he could. Whether he was headed to the hamburger joint or the peat-moss bags by the drugstore, there was always somebody he could hook up with. Once he would find some willing partiers, they would usually brainstorm where they might find something, and somewhere, to get high on. If they were fortunate enough to have some means of conveyance, they'd go to some beautiful place, such as The Maze, Scott's Run, The Barn, Sugarland, or some other place that was not normally patrolled by the oinkers. If neither Bub nor his friends had wheels, they'd just settle for a local haunt, like The Planet, where they could get high in relative peace.

The Planet was a secluded area located in a patch of woods not too far from the peat-moss bags. It was a magical place, or so Bub and his friends imagined. It gave them the illusion of being in the wilderness, because the focal point of the party spot was high in the air, and it was surrounded by thick trees and heavy undergrowth. The fact that it was so remote-feeling caused some people to jokingly claim that they saw a hobbit every now and then. At the far end of a clearing was a twenty-foot-high cliff, which overlooked the bushy green valley below. At the edge of this cliff stood tall, shady cedar trees whose twisted roots made for natural stirrups to sit in. The view was excellent from that location, and it was an ideal vantage point for ditching the cops, should they decide to pay a visit.

The Maze was another name for the Potomac School property. In those days, the church and school were modest, but grounds were expansive and beautiful. The Peat-Moss Gang gave it its name because of the way the rolling grounds rambled on with isolated areas of beautifully manicured grass, bordered by thick forestation. Some partiers would bring their Frisbees and whoop and holler in the utopian atmosphere, while others just got stoned and laid back, experiencing the quiet and reflective aura of nature. Then there were the lovers, who sought the seclusion to deepen their relationships. Other nice features of the grounds included a natural grass amphitheater and a tree-swing, which was located on the highest hill in the area. While the amphitheater was great for sledding, the long swing provided an opportunity for people to meditate on a splendid view as they pumped with delight.

The Barn was old, and it was located in Langley, just off Dolly Madison Boulevard. Although it was located within a hundred feet of the busy road, it was secluded behind shrubbery in a beautiful country-style atmosphere. At first, the old German farmer who lived in the distant house would come out and yell "Hooligans, hooligans!" whenever Bub and his friends would go there. Then the man was introduced to Bub by his brother and his river pals, and he gave Bub permission to bring his friends to the barn.

Scott's Run was a tributary that dropped in a magnificent waterfall just shy of the Potomac River. It was located on a gorgeous tract of land, and, since it wasn't a park, it was an excellent place to party. People could often be found swimming or skinny-dipping in the deep pool made by the falls, and the high rocks that surrounded them offered great views of the river while Bub and his friends were getting high.

All those were terrific party hangouts, and Bub loved them all. There were other, more distant places to romp and party, such as rivers, quarries, and historic places, but none were more interesting and educational than what was happening with the war demonstrations in Washington, DC. Since January of 1968, the Tet Offensive had raged in Vietnam, and with nearly 525,000 American troops fighting on the ground, sea, and in the air, their casualties were high. Bub was concerned for his brother, who'd been attending college and was now eligible for the draft, so every now and then he'd skip school or use his summer days to attend war demonstrations. Even though he knew the war-hawk politicians wouldn't exit the war without a victory, he still enjoyed partying among "his kind of people." All the while, he'd chant and march, and if things heated up—he'd run!

Junior Year: 1969–1970

By the early fall of 1969, the Vietnam War had cooled only slightly. At the same time, incredibly talented rock musicians were filling the airwaves with powerful sounds and relevant lyrics. In Washington, DC, music and love were served up in the morning and early afternoon hours, followed by peaceful street demonstrations that turned ugly into the night. That was not only an occasional occurrence, either. There were a large number of antiwar protesters camped out all over DC at any given time, and because of that the police presence had swelled.

It made Bub sad to think that many of his classmates did not see eye-to-eye with him about the war, and he failed to grasp their ignorance. He wondered, *Is it because they relate the antiwar movement to the yippies and hippies, who they view as a group of "social rejects?" Maybe it's because they've adopted the political views of their parents, or some kind of mentor—such as a high-school teacher or a preacher? It could be from the spin surrounding the spread of communism—who knows!* While all of those thoughts raced through his mind, he knew that religion, prejudice, and politically backed propaganda were instrumental in shaping people's attitudes.

*   *   *

Regardless of how much dope anybody had, Bub liked to have at least a quart bottle or a six-pack of beer. Alcohol had become his drug of choice, since he had a tendency to be introverted and it helped him to feel at ease. Of course getting drunk would become monotonous, so if anyone had some drugs for sale, he was usually willing to give them a try. Like his friends, he wasn't a prolific pill-popper or dope-shooter, but he liked to experience different type of drugs just to see what they were like.

Bub had grown to five feet-four inches tall by now, and his hair was getting longer. He'd become more involved with the growing number of people that liked to congregate at the peat moss bags, so his exclusive encounters with Joey and Thad were diminishing. He still hung with Joey a lot, because he lived one block away, but since Thad lived one mile away and his parents didn't like him hanging around town, Bub saw him less frequently.

That's where Sam came in. He was a new roustabout in Bub and Joey's neighborhood, and, since moving from the Bronx to McLean, he had taken a shine to them. He had an accent that made Bub laugh, and Bub's Northern accent, mixed with his mother's Australian way of speaking, made Sam laugh too. Since Sam was older, he already had a driver's license and a car. So, having temporarily become a threesome, Sam, Joey and Bub would ride around and find other friends, before going to all the remote spots to party.

As time passed, Sam began to display a mean streak that turned Bub off. It became apparent when Sam was driving, and he would often yell at other drivers while flipping them the bird. At school, Sam took a fellow student to task just because of the way the boy looked at him. That bothered Bub, because Sam then reminded him of a bully who had recently hit Bub in the stomach during gym class. For that reason, Bub laughed and made a joke when the boy flipped Sam upside down on the hood of a Volkswagen Beetle, before making him say he was sorry. That angered Sam, so he began to prefer the sole company of Joey. Bub figured that Sam liked Joey, anyway, because they were both becoming fond of the effects of heroin, and the culture that went with it. Since they shared that affinity, they finally managed to get strung out on the drug.

Bub's grades weren't too bad at the beginning of his junior year, even though he skipped a lot of classes. He often attended his classes after getting stoned, but he still managed to remember things that interested him. As far as textbooks went, he found them too cumbersome to carry to the peat moss-bags, and besides, he knew he wouldn't read them anyway. His curriculum included English composition, analytic geometry, and earth science, and, although they required homework, he was managing to get by on test scores alone.

4. REALITY SUCKS!

By October of 1969, Bub's focus on his scholastic achievement was like a roller coaster. At this point, he was at his peak, but every time he began to make some headway, something would happen to bring him down. One day, near the end of his health class, a boy who was sitting behind him snuck the books out from the bottom of another boy's desk and quietly placed them into Bub's. When the bell rang, the victimized boy hollered foul, and, when Bub realized what had probably happened, he simply passed him his books. Bub explained that they had both been bamboozled, but the boy was mad at Bub and raised his voice. That angered the gym teacher, who ordered Bub to approach his desk. As Bub tried to explain what had happened, the teacher stopped him short and ordered him to go directly to the principal's office. As Bub rolled his eyes and did an about-face, the teacher rose from his chair and delivered a hard, stabbing kick to Bub's lower back. The force of the kick caused Bub to fly off the teacher's elevated platform so fast that one of his shoes came off his foot. As Bub gasped for air and turned to get his shoe, the teacher grabbed him by his shirt and cursed as he yanked Bub along to the principal's office.

Much to the disappointment of the gym teacher, it was lunchtime, and the principal wasn't there. Still, the small and stocky man angrily promised to exact vengeance before allowing Bub to go on to his next class. Bub was humiliated by that experience, and it made him loath authority even more. He knew that the gym teacher hated boys with long hair, because he'd seen him dish out his sudden and violent corporal punishment before. To him, the teachers and administrators at his high school always seemed to treat the vast majority of the students like naughty little kids instead of young adults, and that was turning him off. He thought, *I am who I am, and if others can't accept that, then they're the world's worst kind of assholes, as far as I'm concerned!*

Even though he knew he'd done nothing wrong, he chose not to tell his parents or the administrators. Instead, he made a plan to come to class the next day while pretending he had a stiff neck, and it worked. The gym teacher watched him as he took his usual seat, and all the while Bub would turn his head with his whole body to look this way and that. When he later approached the gym teacher's desk to hand in a pop quiz, the teacher sheepishly asked him how he was.

"I'm stiff, man," Bub replied.

He'd figured the gym teacher for a bully and a dumbass who could be fooled, and now he knew that he was right.

Later, Bub compared this episode with one that he had had in the sixth grade while attending a Catholic school in Milwaukee. The rich preppie boys had become a problem for him, and, when they weren't pushing him around in the schoolyard, they were pulling pranks on him in class. One day in the classroom, as the nun was demonstrating a math problem on the blackboard, Bub noticed one of the preppies staring at him with an evil grin. Then he noticed that the kid was bending a paperclip into an elongated position. After that, the kid proceeded to take a red pen and draw a large mark on the back of his hand. That was strange behavior, and by now he had Bub's undivided attention. Finally, the kid produced a rubber band, and, as he flipped it onto Bub's desk, he yelled, "That hurt!" That quickly got the nun's attention, who twirled around to see the boy holding up his red-colored hand while pointing straight at Bub. Bub laughed as he held up the rubber band to explain the hoax to the nun, but the old nun, who was half blind, wasn't in the mood to listen. She scoffed as she pulled Bub by his ear to the principal's office, and he could see his classmate laugh as she did.

Bub pleaded his case before the principal, but his teacher was held in higher esteem, so he was admonished and placed on detention. He was required to take a letter to his parents, and, while they believed his story, he begged them not to make a big deal out of it. Well, they did, and, just as Bub had figured, his social dilemma only became worse.

After that recollection, Bub wondered how teachers could be so closed-minded and harsh. Then he thought about the pranksters who'd caused him trouble. After this latest episode, the world looked hopeless to him, and justice did seem blind at times. For that reason, he'd taken matters into his own hands by putting on an act and lying to the gym teacher. Due to his success in resolving that matter, he vowed to use similar ploys when operating the doors he wanted open and shut. As far as his focus went—it was no longer attuned to his academic interests, and now he was heading for a new low.

*   *   *

As a result of Joey and Sam's heroin addiction, their pale and expressionless faces made them look very mature. That made Bub curious, so every now and then he'd tag along as they tried to score their shots. Since they'd only recently become addicted, they didn't know any major heroin dealers. That meant that they were at the mercy of small-time heroin users, who welcomed the money of new addicts in order to support their own vice.

Most of the junkies that Joey and Sam knew came from well-to-do families. After talking with them, Bub figured that physical effects weren't the only reason they injected the powerful and deadly drug. Some of them seemed to be very interesting and well-educated, while having deep and troubled intellects. Moreover, they seemed be to have a problem with the hypocrisies, intolerances, and prejudices that were pervading society, so, to them, life seemed like a joke.

As time went on, it became apparent that junkies would even rip off their best friends, if it meant getting their next shot. Therefore, treachery seemed commonplace, and honor among them was nowhere to be found. Such was the case one night when Joey had asked one of his good friends to score him and Bub some hash. The junkie told them to wait in the lobby of a hotel on DuPont Circle while he took the elevator up to score the dope. Then he came back to tell them that there was a price increase. Surprise! After getting more money, he then took the elevator to the garage, whereupon he escaped with the cash. That was the kind of deceit that Bub experienced as he got burned in elaborate rip-offs, and, he finally figured that was the cost of a street-wise education.

After studying the mindset of the more complicated junkies, Bub thought about their intellects while smoking a bowl of Columbian by his open bedroom window. They made him think about his own perceptions of society and how his refusal to accept many of the truths they readily accepted caused him to feel demoralized. Then he integrated those feelings with the bad experiences of being constantly bullied due to his unique and unavoidable identity traits. That caused him to wonder, *Is there a single word that describes that condition?* After taking another hit off his pipe, Bub shut his window and lay down on his bed. Then he thought about the true meaning of *social rejects.* To him, it seemed to be a term given to those who questioned the status quo, and as a result, had been rejected and labeled by their society. "Ah, yes," he suddenly laughed. "Beltway Bub! Spurned by the scorn of *rejectionism!* Ha—dealt a bad hand at birth and led astray while having to deal with the adversity of his own twisted mind! Oh boy, that's rich! No wonder some people go apeshit and start killing people!" Although Bub realized that there were simpler reasons why people got addicted to any drug, he thought that one was the saddest.

Eventually, Bub realized that his mere presence was loathed among the growing group of junkies. He didn't know if that was due to his unwillingness to commit to their type of addiction, or, they didn't trust him, because he was fairly new to the area. In reality, most of them saw Bub as an "uncool" beer drinker, whose interjections of foolish humor weren't well received. Besides that, Bub was usually broke, and they needed money. At that time Bub would never have guessed that some of them would change their minds, as they would eventually find ways in which he could be useful.

* * *

When Bub wasn't hanging with anyone special, he would occasionally befriend a dejected student who had suddenly found the pressures of being a high-school scholar or athlete too demanding. That was both sad and interesting for Bub, because he didn't want to see anyone fail, but at the same time he was curious as to why some of his classmates were. Sometimes their grief stemmed from a family dispute, and other times it came from academic or peer pressure. Whatever the reason, those people were turning to his group of friends, and he didn't think that was necessarily a good idea!

Then there were those who'd "crossed the line," because the Vietnam War was becoming unpopular with the moral majority. That made getting high on pot more popular and acceptable. As those occurrences were becoming frequent, more people started falling in with the Peat-Moss Gang. Whenever that happened, Bub would be amused as he watched "a newbie smoke a doobie" and try to deal with the combination of alcohol and pot. After all, it took only about three beers and a couple of tokes to get a person smashed, and it usually caught them off guard.

Even with all of his insight into the minds of others, Bub was becoming aware of his own problems. He was into a pattern of partying hard and hell-raising, and he knew that there was no stopping it. That was obvious to his friends, who seemed to have a better handle on their drinking. Since his original friends had now split into groups of varying degrees of drug and alcohol abuse, he was finding it more and more difficult to fit in. While he found more comfort hanging with those who knew where to draw the line, he also enjoyed the depravity of those who didn't. As much as he tried not to show it, he was losing control of his passions, and as he did, he was becoming troubled and confused.

*   *   *

It was the night before Halloween, and Bub's dad was going to take him, his mother, and his brother on a scenic ride down Skyline Drive. Bub had been dry all day, and now he was feeling like a caged animal. He pleaded with his dad to let him use the family sedan while trying to assure him that he'd learned a great deal from his accidents. Although his father was leery, he eventually threw him his keys.

Bub couldn't find his friends at the peat-moss bags, so he got Billy the Wino to buy him a six-pack. After guzzling about four beers, he got impatient, so he decided to drive to The Maze to see if anybody was there. As he drove along Dolly Madison Boulevard, he spotted a carload of his friends traveling in the opposite direction. He quickly hit his car horn and waved them down. After seeing an opening in the median, he turned the car sharply to the left, in order to negotiate a fast U-turn. He was going too fast, and he lost control of the car. With a loud bash, the car had slid sideways into the curbed median strip, and it bounced high while pushing Bub up into the ceiling.

"For crying out loud!" he fumed.

Not wanting to get hung up on the curb, he immediately mashed the gas pedal, which inadvertently caused passing cars to get showered with rubber, rocks, and dirt. Then he cursed as the rear wheels dropped off of the curb with a slam and a squeal, leaving blue sparks and a cloud of smoke in its wake. His friends, who had pulled over and witnessed the event, were stunned.

"Wow, man, you really fucked your old man's car *up!*"

After Bub sheepishly retrieved two hubcaps, which had popped off and rolled down the street, he and his friends quickly skedaddled. Then Bub stopped at a mini-mart to inspect the damages before heading to The Maze to share some cold beer with his bewildered friends. While there, each of them claimed to have seen Bub act crazy at one time or another, but after this most-recent incident, they all laughed as they agreed it was never an act. Later that night Bub waited until his family was most likely to be asleep, whereupon he quietly crept into bed.

The next thing Bub heard was, "Wake up, Riddick—wake up NOW!"

Bub's head was throbbing as he lifted his face from his pillow, and he looked through bloodshot eyes to see his dad staring down at him with disgust.

"Robbie tells me that you've wrecked the damned car again!"

Bub rolled off the bed and rose slowly to his feet.

"What do you mean?" he mumbled innocently.

"Don't give me that crap, Riddick! Just get your clothes on, and let's get moving!"

His dad was very nice, considering the fact that Bub needed his ass kicked.

As Bub stumbled out of the house for some much-needed fresh air, he observed Robbie examining the damaged car.

"What seems to be the problem, man?" Bub asked, with a wiry grin on his face.

Robbie stuck his head out from under the car and looked up at the still-inebriated youth.

"I'll tell you want the problem is—the frame is bent, you idiot! Man, look at your hair!"

"Jeez! No shit!" Bub exclaimed half-heartedly. Then his throbbing brain tried to comprehend the significance. "What exactly does that mean?"

Robbie got up and dusted himself off.

"It means that this car is going to do some serious dog-walking, and the tires will wear down unevenly and prematurely."

"Jeez—*that's* a bummer," Bub said, and with that he went back into the house to chug some milk out of the carton.

When they got moving, his dad noticed that the steering wheel was crooked, so Robbie filled him in. That made his father so mad that he lectured "Riddick" for about twenty minutes. As he did, Bub thought about guzzling the contents of an airline whiskey bottle that he'd swiped from his father's liquor cabinet—just to take the edge off.

*   *   *

The Kellows always followed Christian traditions, and Bub looked forward to family gatherings. His mom was an excellent cook, and she served exotic dishes, which were popular in Australia. When Christmas arrived in 1969, Bub was prepared. He bought his sisters wine, so he could drink it after giving it to them. Of course, they were hip, but they didn't care. After all, they knew the boys would always get drunk, and since Bub was usually broke, they knew the wine was cheap.

In January of 1970, Robbie had just finished with college, when the US Army drafted him. It was devastating news for all the Kellows, even though they knew it was coming. Robbie thought that the war was wrong, but he had a sense of duty. Unlike Bub, he expressed his opinion in different ways. Robbie's main staple for copping a buzz had always been beer, and even though he loved his little brother, he didn't tolerate illegal drugs *or* their users. On one occasion, he caught Bub with a pack of cigarettes and nearly whipped his ass! For those reasons, he'd been the apple of his father's eye, and Robbie's strict adherence to his own moral standards made his parents extremely proud of their tall, blond, and protective son. As for Bub, Robbie was like a second father to him. He was no dunce when it came to electronics and mechanics, and he'd taught Bub a great deal while enjoying a cold one or two. So now the Vietnam War was greatly affecting all the Kellows, and, when they wished Robbie farewell, they were extremely sad.

In the aftermath of Robbie's departure, Bub thought about the differences between him and his brother. Robbie was his parent's first son, and therefore he'd inherited his father's name. In addition to that, Robbie was five years older than Bub, so he'd always been the son who got the cool toys. In contrast, Bub figured that he'd more or less become his mother's son, and since his dad was frugal, Bub had been left to play with his brother's older toys. While he understood how that all seemed natural, he wondered how that might have affected him. That, in turn, made him think about his father's role in the family. He was the breadwinner and the man of the house. Therefore, he'd always called the shots while enjoying his leisurely time reading the newspaper or watching TV. Meanwhile, as was the par norm for the sixties, his mother was left to clean the house while doing her best to keep the children in line. Of course, she'd often complained about that arrangement, but Bub knew that she was grateful while always doing her best. His dad was a good man, and he'd often shared his wisdom at the dinner table, but, as far as Bub could tell, it was not within his nature to delve into long and deep personal conversations, unless spurned to do so.

Bub had had a few love interests during his junior year, but they hadn't lasted too long. Interestingly enough, he'd developed those relationships outside his circle of friends. They were nice girls, for sure, but the relationships had culminated only to the point of mental and physical exploration before dissolving from conflicts of interest. That was mainly because Bub was still scared to take relationships too far while his drinking was causing him to develop an unpredictable and irritating Jekyll-and-Hyde personality.

Toward the end of his junior year, Bub started to get bad acne on his face. Oddly enough, it was soon after he had called a girl who suffered from the same affliction "pizza face." He had made that remark while he was drunk, in an ill attempt to amuse a friend.

Upon sobering up, he suffered greatly from the recollection of his cruelty. Bub figured his acne to be instant karma, while his mom told him it was probably due to hormonal changes. Whatever the cause, he was deeply embarrassed, since his youthful good looks had suddenly turned ugly.

Shortly thereafter, Bub contracted hepatitis A and became extremely weak while oozing yellow sweat. His urine became as dark as coffee, and his parents were dumbfounded as to how he might have contracted it. Their guesses ranged from bad food to hanging around the river. Then Bub learned of another possible cause when he went to the clinic. The doctor told him about the dangers of sharing syringes, and he went away thinking, *Did I miss that fact while skipping school? The only drug education I remember was related to alcohol, pot, and acid! One film showed an alcoholic's brain being sawn in half, and the other one showed some long-haired dude looking at his reflection on a doorknob! Damn!* His parents were not in the doctor's office when that had been explained to him, so while he agonized over his dark little secret, he decided to make them none the wiser.

Just as his health was improving, his family to Ocean City, again. He always had a fantastic time there, either swimming, lying in the sun, playing in the arcades, or just reading good books. Every now and then, one of his brother's or sisters' friends would tag along, and they would all play games. Toward the end of this enjoyable vacation, Bub inspected his face to find that the saltwater and sun had totally cleared his skin, at least for the time being.

That vacation during the summer of 1970 seemed to pass like a cool breeze for Bub, and it gave him time to reflect. His good memories had been the warm evenings when the world seemed to stop, and he could hear black birds singing in the dead of night. That coincided with his great appreciation of The Beatles, whose *White Album* was his among his favorites. His bad memories included his failed female relationships, drunken driving episodes, blackouts, and terrible hangovers. Although he considered that behavior to be normal for a daring young man of the sixties, it was everything but normal!

After returning home, Bub "borrowed" the family car one afternoon, before his father got home from work. Then he found his friends on the peat-moss bags, and one of them had some acid and hash. After getting Billy the Wino to score them some beer, they all piled into his dad's car to go for a spin, and as they did they listened to loud rock 'n' roll while smoking the hash and waiting for the acid to take effect. The ride was fun, and the kids were all squawking like birds. Meanwhile, Bub was feeling great and anticipating a wonderful night.

As he turned the car onto another street, The Amboy Dukes' "Journey to the Center of the Mind" came on the radio. Then someone yelled "Turn it up!" Bub turned the volume up loud and looked over his shoulder to take the burning hash pipe. Then someone yelled, "Watch out!" and Bub instantly hit the brakes, but he was too late. The big Ford Galaxie, filled with wide-eyed kids, had plowed into a parked car with the front-right bumper. The force of the impact pushed the car he'd hit into the car that was parked in front of it.

They all sat in stunned silence, except for the psychedelic song that was blaring through the speaker. That was followed by much cussing, fussing, and dismay, as Bub quickly threw the car into reverse and mashed the gas pedal. Once detached from the pile-up, he made his getaway. As the car revved through the gears, he wondered how something like that could happen on a road wide enough to land a good-sized jet!

The adrenaline rush from the accident triggered the LSD that Bub had swallowed, and now it was oozing like cool pancake batter from the top of his head. Then, as he tried to comprehend the stark reality of what had just happened, he involuntarily grinned.

"WHAT THE FUCK JUST HAPPENED, MAN!" he hollered while laughing and shaking his head. Meanwhile, "Journey to the Center of the Mind" was still blaring from the radio.

Bub returned to the drugstore parking lot and parked his dad's car. He opened his door, but his front-seat passengers couldn't open theirs. The right fender had been pushed back, once again, and it was a mess.

"Jeez," Bub exclaimed. "The Old Man is going to have a *cow*!"

Bub's dad was terribly alarmed with Bub's increasingly deviant behavior and understandably so. It was clear to him that his once-bright kid was drinking like a lush and simply couldn't be trusted, so he took his car privileges away and put him on a curfew. So Bub now hitchhiked, walked, or rode the bus, and it was pretty much in that order. As far as the curfew went, he knew that was *hogwash*!

Senior Year: 1970–1971

There comes a great relief when you finally become a senior, and Bub was thrilled at the prospect of putting his high-school years behind him. In his anticipation, he attended any party that he could find, but as he did he began to notice that the parties he attended were becoming increasingly violent. The Peat-Moss Gang that he had hung out with for the past three years had steadily grown, and it was attracting a cast of characters who had different aims. They were not attracted to the "peace and love" concept of the original crowd. Instead, they were simply attracted to the large number of people and the alcohol and drug abuse that'd become the trend. Therefore, they had no "cause" other than getting extremely drunk and doped up with the intention of kicking ass and raising holy hell.

Bub had witnessed the redneck ways of some of the newcomers, and he didn't quite know how to handle it. He'd experienced their type of intimidation while growing up, so humiliation wasn't his bag, and neither was fighting. He'd hoped to remain a mere observer of their crass behavior, and avoid confrontation. Nevertheless, anxiety swelled up in him every time one of those guys picked on someone they thought was weaker, and his lack of intervention bothered him.

That concern finally came to a head one evening when Bub and a group of his friends rode out to Great Falls after learning a party was in progress. Upon arriving, they found a group of people congregating at the entrance to an abandoned cabin. As Bub got out of the car, he walked past a group of the rowdy young men, whose oldest member was a guy named Jake.

"What's happening, Manny?" Jake said.

Not wanting to be compared with one of his friends, Bub put his hands on the top of Jake's shoulders and smiled. "Hey, man— the name is Bub," he said.

As Bub's attention was suddenly diverted by a friend, the long-haired Jake hit Bub upside the head! Then he instantly charged forward while knocking Bub to the ground. As they wrestled back and forth, they rolled across the dirt driveway and came to a rest in a clump of sticker bushes. Bub was blown away, and his mind was spinning. He had no idea that he'd pissed Jake off, but now that he was pinned on the ground with stickers in his back, he figured he had no choice but to fight. Just as he took a deep breath and was about to give it all he had, Jake smiled and spoke up. "Ready to call it quits, Bub?"

Although Bub was perturbed, he was also confused by Jake's smile. *Did I deserve to be knocked down, or is this Jake's idea of a good time?* he wondered. Realizing that now was not the time to deliberate, he said, "Sure, what the hell." Jake stood up and offered Bub a hand. Then, after they were both on their feet, they laughed as they shook hands.

Bub didn't realize the mistake he had made by being passive, but the simple fact that he didn't fight to the finish would surely come back to haunt him. Later, during the same party, he noticed Jake joyfully gloating among a group of buddies. Meanwhile, a couple of Bub's closer friends scoffed at him for not retaliating and kicking Jake's ass right then and there.

Later on that same night, Bub and his friends siphoned some gas so they could drive to Ocean City. After being further shamed by his friends, Bub had some time to think as they traveled along. Their criticism seemed very stupid to him, but it increased his anxiety and caused him to feel further humiliated. *This is the very condition that I've been trying to avoid,* he thought. It was then that he realized that if he'd stood up against that type of violence in the first place, he wouldn't be suffering from despair.

That experience changed Bub's outlook with regard to his carefree lifestyle. He didn't want to go to parties if hell-raisers were there, but that seemed improbable. Instead of living up to his old moniker of Obnoxious Bub, he was prepared to remain on the sidelines and engage in casual conversation—just like adults do while the children are at play. In that transformation of becoming an intellectual drunk, he would curtail the full flight of his rowdiness, since he preferred peace in lieu of becoming "one of them."

*   *   *

Bub smoked some pot one morning after taking a shower, and in his solitude he began to reflect upon his life. When he smoked pot by himself, it always brought about a certain amount of panic with regard to his physical self-abuse, and that caused him to run down a checklist of his current conditions. As it was often the case, he was dehydrated from drinking too much the night before. He recalled smoking two packs of cigarettes, and that was one more than he would have, had he remained sober. As a result, his mouth was unusually dry and smelly, and his chest was tight. That caused him to wonder if he'd reap some grizzly fate, such as cancer or emphysema. He knew he wasn't heading in the right direction, and he considered giving up alcohol altogether. He figured if he went straight, he might delve deep into some thread of philosophy or science, which was something he'd always wanted to do. Even so, the intense effect of the pot would fade away, and his deep-rooted desire to join his friends for fun, frolic, and alcoholic debauchery would grow strong once again.

It was after one of those strong desires that Bub got bored in school. It was a gorgeous day, so he forged himself a fine note to excuse himself from the rest of his classes. Since his parents were visiting relatives in Australia, he figured he'd walk home and use their car to take a joy ride. When he got there, he ate some food before using his secret key to start their car. Then he drove back to the school while hoping to pick up a couple of his buddies during their lunch break.

When he arrived he found Thad and Manny, who were just beginning their break, and he asked them if they wanted to take a little joy ride. Manny was a good friend of Bub's and he'd packed enough lunch to share it with Thad. So, after getting into the big Ford Galaxie, Thad ate while riding shotgun and Manny ate behind him while enjoying the entire backseat. As Bub drove away from the school, he asked them where they wanted to go on such a fine day, whereupon Manny eagerly made a suggestion.

"Hey, man! There's this really neat, super-hilly road that goes down toward the Potomac River! It's off Georgetown Pike, and it's a blast, man. The experience will knock your damned socks off, I guarantee it!"

"Okay. That's sounds like a plan, man!" Bub said, so off in that direction they went.

As they headed toward the "super-hilly road," Manny loaded a pipe with some very strong hash. Bub didn't want to smoke too much, because it normally caused him to experience great anxiety when he was doing something he knew he shouldn't. Then Manny kept passing the pipe, and after a couple of lung-buster tokes, Bub realized that he was overwhelmed.

After turning onto the road, it seemed as though it wasn't so hilly, after all.

"Don't worry," Manny said. "This is going to be fun—just go faster!"

Bub brought the car to sixty miles per hour as the first hill appeared, and it rose quickly and leveled off nicely. It gave them a weightless sensation, and they were thrilled.

"Here comes another one—FLOOR IT, NOW!" Manny screamed.

With that Bub mashed the gas pedal to the floor, and the car pushed them up the hill at eighty miles per hour. As they reached the crest, Bub saw an elderly gentleman fetching his mail from his mailbox up ahead. As he watched the startled man quickly duck down, he soon discovered why. The car kept rising up into the air, when it should have been going downward, and within a split second, it was well above the old man's head! Since the boys realized that the car had gone airborne, with the road nowhere in sight, they suddenly sounded like the Three Stooges. As it was evident to them now, the road did not even out at the top like the last hill. Instead, it went steeply downward, almost right away!

Bub's eyes were glued straight ahead, but all he saw were treetops and sky. Then the car slowly yawned to the right because there were two boys on that side of the car. Meanwhile, Thad and Manny were screaming for God's forgiveness, while Bub was hugging the steering wheel so tightly that his ass wasn't even touching the seat. As he gritted his teeth, Bub thought, *This could be all she wrote!*

To Bub it seemed like eternity before the right-rear of the car first made contact with the pavement. Then the front end slammed down with a thunderous crash, and the car suddenly decreased its speed like a roller coaster does when it returns to the loading platform. In that instant, the three stonies started babbling to themselves, as Bub brought the car under control before slamming on the brakes. "WHAT THE FUCK JUST HAPPENED, MAN!" Bub screamed!

As the car had skidded to a complete stop, it made some pretty weird noises. Before inspecting for damage, Bub figured that there was the business of kicking Manny's ass to attend to!

"What in the fuck were you thinking, Manny!" Bub angrily exclaimed as they emerged from the car.

Manny immediately started to apologize. "I'm really sorry, guys! I've never come down this road *that* fast before! Shit— please believe me, Bub—I'm so sorry, man!"

That quick and heartfelt apology caused Bub to rein in his anger while realizing that Manny wasn't entirely to blame. Then he quickly turned his attention back to his dad's car.

Upon giving the car a close inspection, he discovered just how lucky he was. The noise that he'd heard toward the rear of the car was the air-cleaner lid that he'd stored in the trunk after removing it to make the engine sound louder and seem faster. Then he raised the engine hood, only to find that the rest of the air cleaner had turned cock-eyed. Next, he peered under the front of the car, and everything checked out, except for some thick gravel and bare metal on the cross-frame.

"Hmm. What's up with that?" he wondered aloud, while rising to his feet.

"Holy shit—check it out, man," Manny exclaimed, as he pointed back up the road.

They all walked back to examine a section of the black-top road where, evidently, the cross-frame had created a fresh, deep divot that was about twelve feet long and a foot wide.

"Shit! That would explain why we stopped so fast!" Bub shook his head and smiled in disbelief.

"The angels were with us today," Thad said while still looking as white as a ghost.

After that episode Bub took his friends directly back to school and gingerly drove his parent's car home. As time passed the car didn't develop any problems, and for that he was grateful. Just for him and his friends to have experienced a ride like that and come away injury-free gave him the shudders whenever he thought about it.

*   *   *

As Bub bumbled his way through the first two semesters of his senior year, he continued to skip school, and his grades became worse. Finally, a school administrator called his parents to inform them that "Riddick" would have to repeat his senior year. When confronted by his distraught mom and dad, Bub told them it was probably for the better.

"Don't get too uptight, because it's probably a blessing in disguise. There's a private school in downtown DC where some of my friends go, and they say they treat you like a real human being!" Then he went on to explain how their curriculum would enable him to finish his senior year in just six months, but what he neglected to tell them was that his "friends" were troubled junkies.

Bub's parents visited the school, which was in a good location near DuPont Circle. After researching statistics and getting some good references, they gave Bub the green light. By that time Bub had told most of his friends about his plans, and, to his delight Joey, Thad, and Manny decided to join him.

"I'm Eighteen" by Alice Cooper was at the top of the charts, and it was a song that Bub could relate to. Although he'd formerly been dejected and confused, his new environment was helping his self-esteem. The school was surpassing his expectations, in regard to the mutual respect shown by the administrators, since they always greeted him with a smile. In the classrooms, students were treated as adults. They were allow to drink non-alcoholic beverages, smoke, and even cuss if they felt it was the best way to express themselves.

One of Bub favorite classes was "Vocabulary." He enjoyed learning lots of new and descriptive words while figuring they might come in handy when bullshitting his way into some type of future employment. As a means of remembering the words, he would use them whenever he could, and while his friends laughed and called him weird, he noticed he wasn't cussing as much.

The night classes that Bub attended were filled with troubled teenagers and adults who'd come from well-to-do families. For that reason, instructors would oftentimes leave the classrooms during quizzes and tests while knowing that their students would cheat. Since Bub had received a fairly good education prior to enrolling at the school, some of his classmates would rise up out of their seats to view his answers. Bub didn't object to that. In fact, he was flattered!

Since Bub and his friends took turns driving, his dad agreed to help him buy his first car. After all his son had done to his car, he was only too glad to do it! His dad was a pragmatist, so he wasn't going to waste much time shopping for a cheap car with Bub. After visiting a couple of used-car lots with no success, they finally came upon a sunbaked 1962 baby-blue Rambler American with a sale price of only $200.00. Bub was immediately turned off and called the car "butt-ugly," but his father insisted that it was that, or nothing!

Since Bub had no choice in the matter, he looked the car over. It had a cast-iron flat-head six-cylinder, with a three-speed manual shifter on the column. The paint was faded, and the plain interior was made of stiff, gray vinyl. Worst of all, it was a Rambler, and they were known to be slow. To Bub's way of thinking, that was a mortal sin! Nevertheless, it was soon to be his to call his own, and that made him appreciate the car, because it represented more freedom.

Bub and his friends attended school only at night, which meant that, with his new wheels, he could now get a day job. So, he found one at Tyson's Corner Shopping Mall, sweeping up cigarette butts and emptying trash cans. It was a great job, because the mall was dead-quiet during the morning, but eventually it always filled up with nice-looking girls. It had great ambience, with high ceilings, beautiful fountains, giant bird cages, skylights, and various exciting aromas. Ah, life was better for young Bub—at least for now!

Bub loved the Washington, DC, location of his new school. He made a habit of attending the local Vietnam antiwar rallies whenever he and his friends could. The crowds were huge, and there was always excitement in the air. They would make it a point to hit the nearest liquor store on their way to the Washington Monument, where oftentimes there were rock bands performing, such as Jefferson Airplane, the Beach Boys, Arlo Guthrie, or Phil

Ochs. The people seemed like one big, happy family while smiling and sharing cigar-sized doobies.

Unfortunately, the rallies were looked upon by the US and DC governments as subversive, and therefore dangerous. That attitude caused dissension and "the pigs," whose intolerance was backed by the lawmakers, and seemed eager to club the first demonstrator who stepped out of line. That caused anger and frustration among the antiwar protestors, and it increased after the killing of four students at Kent State University. In light of that, there were more signs and chants designed to bring the Nixon administration down. As National Guardsmen and DC police would always unite with tremendous force to disperse the large crowds, the protester's efforts often appeared to be hopeless.

On Saturday, May 1, 1971, Bub attended a May Day rally that swelled to nearly forty-five thousand demonstrators. There was supposed to be a great party and concert that night, and Bub and his friends weren't about to miss it. After watching the rally while in the limbs of a huge tree, they joined a long march of protesters. They were headed to West Potomac Park, which was located by the Tidal Basin. That was where the party was supposed to be, so Bub bought some more beer along the way. The organizers had their permit revoked, but they finally said to hell with it, and that meant there was going to be trouble!

When they arrived at the park, someone on the stage announced that they'd begin Sunday's rally by blocking bridges that crossed the Potomac River. That was followed by some loud antiwar cries, and then one band after the other began to play. The party lasted longer than sixteen hours, and even Bub was stunned by some of the outrageous characters, who in their drug-crazed state would strip naked while smearing dirt or paint on their bodies and dance like wind dolls. Sleeping seemed impossible, except for those who were shit-faced on downers, or booze, or both! People were pack together so tightly, they were tripping over one another, and many couldn't lay down. After drinking all his beer, Bub tried to relax by smoking a joint. As he got stoned, he felt awe in being a part of the human drama. Then he wondered, *How are these people going to have the strength to demonstrate in the morning? Will they just crash once they get on the bridges? I guess I'll find out, soon enough!*

Just before the crack of dawn, the crowd had finally calmed down. Bub was drifting into a deep sleep, when Joey nudged him awake. As Bub wearily sat up while rubbing his eyes, he tried to comprehend what he was seeing. There was a line of troops in full riot gear, standing elbow to elbow, and they were surrounding the entire encampment. Then he perked up as a cop took control of the stage and let out a blaring noise with his bullhorn. He announced that the protestor's permit to demonstrate had been revoked, and therefore everyone had to leave the area immediately, or they would be arrested! Not wanting to get clubbed or gassed, Bub and his friends struggled to their feet and stretched before wandering off in the cop's prescribed direction.

As they were herded north past the Lincoln Memorial, Bub observed several policemen applying masking tape to the glass of their patrol cars in preparation for trouble—none of which he wanted! As he observed some of the other protesters, many were still half naked while trying to get dressed. Meanwhile, a lot of girls were tending to their hair while the guys were spitting and adjusting their balls. Nope! They were hardly in the mood for confrontation, either.

Bub and his friends were starved by now, and they wanted to get something to eat. After a long walk, they finally found an open cafeteria on C Street. As they waited in line to get their trays, they saw a young, long-haired man pass out on his feet. He fell straight backward, and as he did he slammed his head on a metal guide rail on his way to the floor. That caused Bub to think, *That railing must have hurt, but it probably saved his noggin from hitting the floor really hard. Wow—everybody's wasted—what a fiasco!*

The following day, the DC antiwar organizers had planned an event in Georgetown. Bub was told it was called "An Evening of the Celebration of Life," so while planning to attend, he split a white blotter of LSD-25 with one of his friends. As he and his friends rode from McLean to Georgetown, they smoked soft, moist, and moldy hashish all the way. The hash was so strong that even a small toke would expand in their lungs, and they would cough violently. After a while it became apparent that the entire portion of the synthesized ergotamine was on Bub's half of the blotter. That made him wonder, as his friend reminded him that it was extremely potent!

By the time they parked on O Street at dusk, Bub was totally stoned and tripping wildly on the acid. As they got out of the car, they heard "rolling thunder" echoing off the storefronts on Wisconsin Avenue. Then they watched in amazement as a long line of chopped motorcycles rolled past. They were ridden by leather-clad and tie-dyed riders who were screaming as they threw bottles and bricks through storefront windows.

Bub saw a half-naked man running up the street toward him. He appeared to him as a blond-haired Native American with a colorful headband and war paint, but in actuality, he was a member of the May Day tribe. Just as Bub was about to jump out of his way, the wiry anarchist turned abruptly and mounted a large Dumpster. With a quick, violent, rocking motion, he managed to bring the Dumpster crashing on its side with a thunderous boom! Bottles, cans, and sordid sludgy waste spilled out on the street, and, as Bub gazed at the oozing filth, the cobblestones in the street looked as if they were oozing too!

Then, to Bub's utter dismay, an army of cops in full riot gear came zooming down Wisconsin and up O Street toward him and his friends. They were riding shielded Honda 50s, and they were fast. Bub instinctively turned to run, and as he did, he noticed the yippie had already vanished.

With his adrenaline pumping, Bub bolted down a side alley. He didn't have time to see which way his friends went, because in instances like that, it was everyone for themselves. After a short sprint, Bub darted left between two brick buildings. It was a narrow passageway, and his shoulders rubbed the walls as he hurdled over A/C units and window wells, before he finally stopped at Wisconsin Avenue.

As he peeked back down the passageway, he was confident that he'd eluded the cops. He crouched down and closed his eyes in order to calm his pounding heart and heaving chest. As he pondered his next move, the acid was wildly distorting his perceptions, so he rubbed his eyes while hoping to get a grip on his circumstance. Then he spotted a small hamburger restaurant across the street, so he ran toward it. He was hoping to find safety there while trying to figure out what to do next.

Bub tried to enter the restaurant, but the door was locked. When he looked up, a burly man was staring at him through the glass. He was wearing an apron and a white hat—the style that sergeants wear. The man drew a scowl as pointed his finger.

"*Go away!*" he yelled. "You and your kind are *not* welcome here!"

Bub did his best to ignore him as looked at the customers with a total look of fear and desperation. As he met their stares, their facial expressions mirrored his own. *They look so scared,* Bub thought, and that temporarily changed his fear to sadness.

It was getting dark fast. Glass was breaking and sirens were wailing, as people and police ran through the streets in total chaos. Bub ran low along the busy street while ducking into the dark recess of doorways. As he ran from one door to the next, he thought, *Now I know what war is like!*

Bub made it to M Street, where he spotted a young man who'd managed to lower a wrought-iron fire-escape ladder by standing on a trash can. Bub ran up behind him, and, after kicking the trash can away, they both scooted up to the safety of the second-story landing. Once there, the ladder retracted with a loud bang! Bub thought that noise would have attracted attention, but as he looked up and down the street, he realized just how busy everyone was.

The two young men lay there on their bellies while exchanging stories and watching the melee continue. Every now and then, they'd see someone who was confused and scared underneath them. If that person wasn't hauling ass, Bub and his new friend would get his or her attention and lower the ladder. It wasn't too long before the landing filled up, and it was no longer possible to lay down.

From their elevated position, everybody watched the spectacle play out like a major sporting event gone wrong. Whenever demonstrators got the upper hand, they'd cheer, and when the police would retaliate, they'd boo. All the while, they were smoking pot and having a good time, now! Most of them were students from Georgetown University and American University, and that surprised Bub. He hadn't realized how many of the protesters were "tomorrow's leaders," and that suddenly made the future look a little brighter to him.

The police finally managed to secure the Georgetown business district by corralling the protesters onto M Street. As they began pushing them east of Wisconsin Avenue, tear gas and other projectiles filled the air. At the same time, the loud chanting of the demonstrators continued. "ONE, TWO, THREE, FOUR, WE DON'T WANT YOUR FUCKING WAR!"

As the force of the National Guardsmen and police slowly pushed the large crowd of demonstrators east on M Street, they walked beneath the fire-escape landing. Then a policeman with a bullhorn shouted.

"YOU PEOPLE—UP ON THE FIRE ESCAPE! COME DOWN, NOW!"

The jig was up, so everyone on the landing nervously descended the ladder in single file. After they were all down, the police opened their line, permitting them to join the other protesters. Loud cheers erupted as they were welcomed with wide eyes and clenched fists. Then, as quickly as the police line had opened, it closed, and the chaos continued. Bub was extremely relieved that he'd avoided being clubbed and arrested up to that point, but he still had a big problem. *Where are my friends, and how am I going to get home? It's dark and it's getting late, and now I'm in this huge crowd, getting pushed the wrong damned way!"*

After noticing that there were no cops on Thirty-First Street, Bub ran toward the Potomac River. Having successfully escaped the large crowd of corralled protesters, he headed west along a poorly lit path next to the Chesapeake and Ohio Canal. As he continued on, the path became darker, as people were lurking in the shadows of nearby buildings. He realized that he was behind the police lines now, so he was worried. He could still hear the chanting of the protestors echoing off the opposite banks of the river. As he looked at his watch, he was amazed to find that nearly four hours had passed since his wild adventure had begun. *Man! I've enjoyed acid in peaceful surroundings and those experiences were fantastic, but tonight? I was freaking out!*

He finally arrived at a point where he was able to climb the hill to M Street, and then he walked across the Francis Scott Key Bridge. The river air was chilly, but it didn't take long for him to catch a ride at the entrance to the George Washington Parkway. After laughing and sharing stories with the driver, who'd also experienced the "Celebration of Life," he got dropped off at Dolly Madison Boulevard.

As Bub made his way up to the Boulevard, he heard "*Pssst.*" To his utter dismay, it was his friend Joey. He was just calmly sitting there, smoking a cigarette under the dark concrete overpass.

"Where did you guys go?" Bub asked. "Where's Sam and the rest of the gang?"

Joey just shrugged, so Bub sat down and lit up a cigarette. Then he said, "Those cops freaked me out! I guess you hauled ass too." Then Bub couldn't resist telling Joey about his weird night.

Joey just laughed and crushed out his cigarette as he stood up, as if to say, "Let's go." It was in that quiet way that Bub thought Joey best reflected his true nature.

*   *   *

Washington, DC, was indeed the epicenter of debauchery, and most might agree with that assessment to this very day. If the young adults of McLean wanted to enter a world of lower-caste bestiality, all they needed to do was fall in with a junkie who knew the DC connections that could assist them in killing their spirit. Junk was sold in tinfoil packets, and it was always "stepped on." Although it was blended with any number of unknown substances, to increase the volume and weight, there was a never-ending demand for it.

Bub knew a lot of junkies by now, and some of them had turned to major crime to support their habit. For those who got caught, the powers that be had created poorly designed rehabilitation programs to wean them off their habit. Whenever that happened, some of them would call Bub, to see if he could give him a ride into DC to pick up their "script" of methadone or Demerol. He figured that to be a legitimate cause, and, even though he'd been ripped him off by many of them, he understood their dire situation. Besides, they would usually give him "a taste" for his troubles, and he liked that.

"Getting down" was always eagerly anticipated. As soon as a script was picked up, any gas-station restroom would provide the temporary privacy they needed. As Bub would prepare to inject a narcotic, he liked to have a cigarette ready, holding it between his lips. As the drug caused a warm sensation to loom up in his throat and head, he'd light the cigarette and smoke it with a calm satisfaction.

On one occasion, a junkie asked Bub to buy his whole script of Demerol. Since the junkie didn't have any money, Bub agreed, while making it clear that he wanted only a couple of pills. He understood the desperation of his friend, and he didn't want to take advantage of him.

Upon returning from DC, Bub took his friend to a junkie house that was only a few blocks from the peat-moss bags. Once inside, it suddenly looked like *The Night of the Living Dead*, as other junkies filed out of the bedrooms and came pounding down the stairs. They were all bellying up to the sick man to beg for some pills. No sooner had Bub's friend nervously screwed off the lid on the vial, someone bumped his arm, and the little white pills spilled to the floor. That caused a ruckus as everyone except Bub dropped to their hands and knees and began grabbing this way and that. Lamps were knocked over, and furniture was toppled as heads bumped with a thud! As Bub watched with mixed emotions and utter dismay, he realized he wasn't going to get his "taste," so he just shook his head, as he turned away and left the house.

5. THE SCHOOL OF HARD KNOCKS

At the end of April, 1971, Bub graduated before his former classmates. He was extremely glad to be done with high school, and, while his overall GPA reflected an average education, he figured he'd actually learned quite a bit, despite his debauchery. Therefore, he jokingly considered himself to be summa cum laude in the "School of Hard Knocks." At the same time, he was bummed to have to rush into college just to avoid the military draft, because he wanted more time to figure out what his specific interests were.

Parties had remained the central focus for Bub and his friends, so if there was even the *hint* of a party, they were there. If there were no parties, he and his friends would make one at one of their favorite nature spots. The Peat-Moss Gang had grown into a large clan by now, attracting people from Langley, Great Falls, Falls Church, and Arlington. If they had no money, that was no problem, as far as Bub was concerned. He liked to joke that he was on the "Ways and Means Committee," which meant that if there was a will to get beer, he would surely help to find a way.

That type of instance occurred one night after the cops broke up a huge party. No one was in the mood to call it quits, but Virginia's law prohibited the sale of beer after 2:00 a.m. After some brainstorming, the large group of friends devised a simple plan to get them plenty of beer before going to The Maze. They went to an all-night drugstore where they knew the beer case wasn't locked. Then two guys went as far away from the beer cooler as they could get before staging a loud fight. That drew the attention of the managers as the rest of the guys quietly filed in and absconded with two cases each.

While that kind of behavior seemed bad to Bub, he figured it wasn't as crazy as some of the criminal behavior that he'd seen on the news. Besides, the sale of alcohol was restricted to people who were twenty-one or older, and he didn't think that was fair. In the eyes of the law, he was old enough to die for his country, but he wasn't allowed to drink beer? Absurd! So while one side of his brain feared that some karma might come back to haunt him, the other side told him he was justified.

Bub would still be confronted by rowdy partiers who liked to raise hell at parties by pushing people around. Sometimes he was able to reason with these rowdies, but usually they'd be too drunk to give a damn. An indication of his growing anxiety came to a fever pitch on the night when his former classmates were celebrating their senior prom. There were plenty of parties that evening, and he went to one that started out just fine. However, as the evening progressed, the party was interrupted by the arrival of some drunk and violent young men, so he left. He decided to go to another party, and, while he was still mad, he cruised by his former school.

As Bub passed by the front of the school, he saw three young men dressed in tuxedos. Bub figured they'd stepped away from their prom dates, since they were catching a smoke. He didn't know if they were bored or having too much fun, but he was angry just the same. He leaned out of his car window and yelled *"Penguins!"* That wasn't well received, so the young men hollered something back. That caused Bub to slam on his brakes and get out of the car just to give them the old double-eagle salute. Seeing that, the three gents threw down their cigarettes and started stomping toward him.

Suddenly Bub experienced a lapse of sanity, whereupon he ran to a payphone and ripped the receiver out. Then he grabbed the stretched and twisted end of the metal-covered wire and started swinging the receiver in circles high above his head. As he did, he started charging at the young men while screaming bloody murder! That caused the three men to stop in their tracks while Bub thought, *What next?*

Bub threw the receiver down as he quickly hopped back into his car and sped away. As he drove along, his hands were sticking to the steering wheel, so he turned on the interior light to get a better look. He was bleeding profusely from cuts caused by the twisted metal. Not wanting to alarm his parents, he drove to the local fire department, where he knew a former chemistry classmate might be working as an EMT. Sure enough, he was on duty, and he bandaged Bub's hands while asking him how he got his wounds. Bub said, "Please don't ask," but his friend could tell that he'd been drinking. He advised Bub to go straight home. Then he said, "It's my duty to call the cops, Bub, but tonight we'll just pretend you were never here—okay?"

The next morning Bub thought about his lapse of sanity and equated it to a perfect storm. The rowdy guys at the party hadn't been the only reason that he'd snapped the night before. In fact, he was never in the mood to party in the first place! Now he realized he was feeling anger toward his old school, because he didn't get a big graduation ceremony, and prom night had suddenly exacerbated those feelings. He knew he was lonely for a regular date, so he'd merely been jealous of the young men who were dressed up in their fancy tuxedos. After that revelation, Bub had thought about his notions of rejectionism again. *Did I do that out of self-pity and spite? Good God, I must be fucked up in the head!*

A few weeks later, Bub enrolled in liberal-arts classes at the local community college while struggling to pinpoint his academic interests. That was due to a lack of forethought, of course, since his credo had been to live day to day. Finally, he enrolled in a liberal arts course-load that included accounting, economics, history, and art. Since the parking lot was located far away from his classes, and he was usually late, Bub stole a parking pass from one of the teacher's cars. As stupid as that was, he eventually outdid himself when several months later, he got stoned on his way to school and parked in a "Security Parking Only" space. Oops—busted! Bub went to court over the matter, but the charges were later dropped by the victims, who understood that he was to be placed on a strict disciplinary academic probation. Of course, that was a total embarrassment to the ever-frustrated Bub.

Bub didn't enjoy his visits with the dean very much. After one late appearance, the dean had told him that his academic career at the college was tarnished, so he dropped out. The military draft was no longer a concern, since it was now 1972. Only one-half of the men who were born in 1953 and were randomly selected by way of their birth dates were being called to serve. Since Bub's birth date put him out of harm's way, he correctly figured that he was safe to leave college. Later, he reasoned, *Like my former schools, some of those instructors bored me to sleep! Besides, they only served "near-beer" at their functions, so why bother, and why worry!*

While Robbie was serving in Vietnam, Bub occasionally hung out with an old family friend of his from Vienna. His name was Jasper, and he was at least five years older than Bub. He lived at home with his brother and his mother, who was the widow of a military officer. Jasper was an awkward young man: skinny, with large hip-bones, and he was addicted to sinus inhalers. Still, he was a fun-loving sort, with a crazy sense of humor and an insidious laugh that made everyone take notice. Besides drinking, he also had a penchant for guns, which Bub considered to be a good form of entertainment.

Bub and Jasper often looked forward to taking trips to the mountains of Virginia while taking plenty of guns, ammo, and cold beer. They liked to explore old mill roads and grown-over driveways in search of new places to shoot—or shoot up. If there was an abandoned structure, they'd riddle it full of holes while blasting away at any furniture or appliances that were left behind.

On one such trip, they turned up an old mill road, which seemed to go on for miles. Becoming leery, Bub decided it was time to turn around, but the forestation was very thick, and it grew all the way to the road's edge. After finding what seemed to be the most advantageous spot, Bub backed his "faded, powder-blue, butt-ugly Rambler" into a tight little clearing. The only thing that blocked his progress was a small tree with a two-inch girth.

"Don't sweat it—just take it down, son," Jasper urged.

Jasper always called his friends "son," and it just embellished his quirky personality. That made Bub laugh as he put the car in reverse and revved the engine before popping the clutch. When contact was made, the little tree shuddered, and then it began to bend, but then a bang was heard, and the engine revved freely.

"What the fuck just happened, man!" Bub yelled.

He fished to find reverse, thinking that it had just popped out of gear, but to his amazement, there was no reverse gear. Then he tried first gear, but that was gone too! Nervously, he went for second, but nada.

"Shit! You have *got* to be kidding me," he cursed.

Finally, he tried third gear, believing that the whole tranny was shot, but—

"YES!" he shouted.

Third gear was all that was left, and it would have to get them from Spotsylvania County to McLean. "Holy shit!" Bub exclaimed while realizing that fact. "Help me push this thing, Jasper, so we can get the hell out of here!"

Although their situation seemed dire, they were lucky on three counts. First of all, the car was light, weighing in at just over a ton. Secondly, the mill road was on a slight grade that favored their circumstance. Finally, they'd brought a cooler full of wide-mouthed Rheingold Chug-a-Mugs, and they'd prove invaluable whenever nature called.

Once the car began to roll down the narrow and rutted road, Bub jump in and hollered, "Haul ass, son!" Jasper gave a tremendous effort and dove through the passenger window, and Bub started to ride the clutch. Then they saw that the end of the mill road was fast approaching, so they gritted their teeth and crossed their fingers as the car bounced out of the woods, and Bub turned onto the road with a stuttering squeal. A couple of hubcaps popped off, but Bub laughed and said, "Sayonara!" As he drove along, Bub anticipated stop signs and traffic lights. Meanwhile, beer bottles were emptied into their bellies and later refilled, whereupon they became "urine bombs!"

When Bub finally made it home, he told his father of his unfortunate exploits, to which his father responded negatively.

"Sorry, Riddick. I can't help you with your car. You should have been saving some of your own money by now!"

Bub was frustrated by the whole affair and pissed off about having to drive such an ugly car in the first place. He promptly went outside and picked up a concrete cinder block before hurling it through the windshield of the Rambler. Then he walked off his steam while heading to the peat-moss bags. He figured he could always depend on someone being there, and, for the price of a couple of beers, they would laugh at his crazy exploits.

*   *   *

Getting a different car meant going to work, so Bub found a part-time evening job at a Tyson's Corner gas station. It was the usual full-service type facility, with three repair bays, and Bub pumped a lot of gas while performing small repairs. One evening, while he was working alone, an old, flat black Chevy van appeared at the gas pumps. As Bub and the two occupants struck up a conversation, they came to realize that they knew some of the same people, who happened to be junkies. Then the guy riding shotgun asked Bub if he was interested in buying some really good heroin. Bub told them that he'd been out of that scene for some time, but, as he continued to pump their gas, he dwelled on their offer. Finally he said, "What the hell," and purchased a nickel bag while receiving a brand-new syringe.

Soon after they'd left, Bub was in the restroom, cooking up his shot. He wasn't a regular user, so he never injected more than a than a small amount. However, the heroin was unusually strong, and it surprised him. He spent the rest of the night sitting on the small island that separated the repair bays while nodding in and out of consciousness. As he did, angry or confused customers had to pump their own gas, and then they'd either throw the money at him or set it at his feet.

Soon after that night, Bub received a mysterious call at home. It was the same guy in the black van who had sold him the dope. His name was Terrance Smart, aka Smarty, and Bub had since learned that he was a hard-core junkie.

"Hey, can you hook me up, man?" Smarty asked.

Astonished and perplexed, Bub instantly said, "No way!"

Still, Smarty persisted. "Come on, man! I'm hurting! Just this once," he begged.

"I don't know," Bub replied. "How in the hell did you get my number, anyway?"

"One of those guys we both know told me your last name, and I got lucky with the phonebook. So, please—just this once? Check around, and I'll call you back, okay?"

Before he could respond, Smarty hung up the phone. That caused anxiety as Bub thought, *What the fuck! I'm not a drug dealer!*

Over the course of the next few days, Smarty continued to call. Finally, Bub had enough. His parents were becoming aggravated by the calls, and they sensed that something strange was taking place. Since Bub had been easy to persuade when it came to helping sick junkies, and he was trying to abate his parent's suspicions, he decided to call Sam. He knew that Sam was always looking for ways to get his next shot, and he figured he might kill two birds with one stone.

Bub had already told Sam about Smarty. He told him who Smarty said he knew, and that's when Sam realized who he was. Sam had seen him hanging around Falls Church, and, after making some inquiries, he learned that he was an unpopular junkie who lived near Seven Corners. Sam figured he was probably hurting for a new connection, so he told Bub it was okay to set up a deal.

The next time Smarty called, Bub asked him what he needed. He still sounded desperate, so Bub set a time and place for later that night.

"Okay, I can hook you up with a couple of spoons. Just come to the gas station at 10:00 p.m.," Bub told him.

Sam and Joey were still tight with each other, and by now they knew how to hustle as a team. They'd invited Sam's new girlfriend into their world, and the three of them had become inseparable. They would usually go to DC to score dope from an old black woman they only knew as Mama. If they were going to sell some, they'd take a good cut for themselves before stepping on the rest with baby laxative.

It was getting close to 10:00 p.m., and Sam looked plenty nervous and agitated. Since he had to buy the dope on such short notice, Bub figured that he hadn't had his shot.

"Do you think this guy is cool?" Sam asked nervously, pacing back and forth.

"I think so, but I can't be sure. I told you that I barely know him," Bub responded, and then he added, "To be sure, why don't you stash your dope behind the soda machine?"

"Aw, fuck it!" Sam quickly retorted. "Let's get it on!"

Just as Joey and Sam's girlfriend were emerging from Sam's car, their worst fear manifested. Marked and unmarked police cars came speeding into the gas station from different directions. As they screeched to a halt, pistols were drawn along with the commands to "Freeze!" and "Put your hands up in the air, now!" As the four stunned, long-haired youths reluctantly complied, more sirens wailed as backups arrived to secure the area.

The plainclothes detectives were quick to have them stick out their tongues and empty their pockets before handcuffing and separating the three of them. It was very surreal for Bub, who couldn't believe his utter stupidity. He was ushered into the gas-station office by a narcotics detective named Guzzi. Once inside, Guzzi used the usual fear tactics to get Bub to open up.

"You know you can make this a lot easier for yourself, Kellow, if you just tell us where you got the dope."

"I don't know a damn thing," came Bub's lame but honest reply. "I was just pressured into this thing, and I'm guessing that Smarty is one of your snitches!"

Guzzi stared at Bub for a moment, probably believing him while figuring him to merely be a flunky. Then he looked at the uniformed cop who was holding Bub from behind.

"Okay, search him again, and take him in," the detective snapped. With that, the uniformed officer swung Bub around and pushed him over the desk.

"*Hey, man!* Who's going to lock this place up? *I'm* responsible, you know!" Bub hollered.

Guzzi was already out the door and walking toward Sam, when the uniformed officer spoke up.

"Don't worry, son. The manager's being notified, and we'll be searching this entire place until he gets here."

Sam was also arrested, since he'd held on to the smack. However, Joey and Sam's girlfriend were merely questioned, before they were released.

Bub spent the rest of the night in jail while talking briefly with his bewildered parents. Finally, after his bail amount was set the following morning, and his dad had secured a $100,000 bond, Bub went home totally devastated. To date, that was unquestionably the worst thing that had ever happened to him.

Bub figured that since he was twenty years old, he'd be tried as an adult. His friends would surely doubt his story, and some would figure him to be an informant. Of course, he'd lost his job, and his parents were at a loss as to where his life would go from here on. Then Bub started thinking. *Life's a bitch, man! People between the ages of eighteen and twenty-one aren't considered to be adults when it comes to drinking, but they are when it comes to getting busted, and that sucks! No wonder I've copped a damned attitude!*

Bub's newly retained lawyer didn't want to fight the case, based on entrapment, because Bub had flunked a polygraph examination. During the test, he was asked if he'd ever sold drugs, and that sent his mind reeling. Prior to answering, he recalled selling some orange vitamin C pills to some young kids. He'd done that because the kids had approached him while asking him if he knew where they get some acid. After saying no and then thinking about it, he stole a few of the pills from the drugstore. Then he sold it to the kids, saying they were "orange sunshine," so he could buy some beer. Therefore, his "no" answer had registered as false, and his frustrated lawyer had gone away thinking that an entrapment plea was hopeless.

When Bub later learned that he'd flunked that all-important question, he objected, but his lawyer snapped. "It's purely hearsay, now!"

The lawyer suggested that the best way to go was to plead nolo contendere. He explained to Bub that was Latin, and it meant "I will not defend it." Bub was already familiar with that term, since Spiro Agnew had just copped the same plea. So now he knew he'd be at the mercy of the court.

During his court hearing, Bub blurted out the possibility of entrapment, whereupon the prosecuting attorney scolded him to keep his answers short and not convey conjecture. Despite Bub's reprimand, the circumstances of a troubled and naive young man who'd been used as a pawn by the narcs were probably a common occurrence. Therefore, the wise judge figured that Bub was of little danger to anyone but himself, and that no "kingpin" would be brought to justice as a result of his testimony. At the end of the hearing, Bub was given a three-year imposition of sentence and the judge briefly explained what that meant. "You will undergo three years of probation, before I will render a final decision on the matter." Bub was bitter about the outcome, but his lawyer argued that he didn't know the significance of his disposition.

"As it stands, you're hanging in the balance of being a convicted felon, which means that you could lose some important rights. If you don't straighten up and fly right, you'll never be able to vote, possess a firearm, or travel to another country, among other things. However, if you satisfy the terms of your probation, your case might be dismissed, and that means your life as a free and productive citizen would continue."

After hearing that, Bub felt a little better, but still, he worried. *That's all fine and dandy,* but *I don't know if I can change my ways, and I can't stand the thought of people probing my mind—especially, the damned government!"*

*   *   *

Even bad situations have fruit to bear, as Bub's drug bust proved to be a pivotal point in his life. At his mother's beckoning, "Riddick" cleaned up his appearance and went in search of white-collar work. As it turned out, the Washington area was filled with entry-level positions. That was due in part to it being rich with businesses, lobbying organizations, and government contact houses. It was also due to many young men in the area serving in Vietnam. That made it easy for Bub, who landed a mail clerk position with a major oil corporation located near Tysons Corner.

As Bub became familiar with postal procedures, his duties included running to the post office, purchasing office supplies, and acting as the Xerox key operator. On special occasions, he was expected to take the company car to pick up or drop off big shots at Dulles Airport. He loved that responsibility, because, when he was alone, he'd often drive their black Chevrolet Impala, with its 454-cubic-inch, four-barrel engine, over a hundred miles per hour. As he did, he knew the access road was privately owned and only patrolled by rent-a-cops who lacked radar equipment. For that reason, and others, Bub liked his new job a lot.

Bub was now rubbing shoulders with "normal" people who like to have fun in moderation. As they got to know Bub, he got invited to their parties. Many of his coworkers liked him because he seemed to be easygoing, and he was their office supply connection. To that extent, he would order them such things as fancy chairs and calculators, and his boss didn't seem to mind.

Although he seemed more at rest while working with sensible, easygoing people, he still drank copious amounts of beer. Sometimes he'd drink a quart of beer while making a run to the post office, and oftentimes he'd knock off a pitcher during his lunch break. He figured that was the best he could do to get high, since he was being forced to undergo periodic drug tests.

It was during that period of employment that Bub lost some close-knit relationships with his original friends. Thad's father had unexpectedly passed away, and it crushed both him and his mother. That was the third time that Bub had witnessed an only child losing a parent at a tender age, so he was already familiar with the devastating effects. He stayed close to Thad, while Thad's mother sold their house and made plans to move to Virginia Beach. Thad had bad feelings about moving again, but, when the time came, he knew he had to go.

Joey, on the other hand, pretty much disowned his old friend Bub, while holding him responsible for the whole drug bust thing. After all, it had changed Joey's world, since Sam was also being forced to attend a drug-rehabilitation program. Bub took the time to think about the growth and decline of his relationship with Joey. After weighing in all the circumstances, he figured that the parting of their ways was inevitable.

Of course, Sam was angry at Bub, too. To that effect, Bub figured that they'd both been stupid, and now they shared a mutual disdain for each other's ignorance. They still had to see each other at their scheduled urine tests, and since they were at a state-owned facility, civility was maintained.

Since the drug bust, the rumor mill had been churning. The word on the street painted Bub as being either an informant or a full-blown narc. As different friends would tell him what the rumors were, he'd laugh and tell them about lies and fish-tales. At the same time, those rumors greatly affected his feelings. Just as he'd predicted, he was now feeling the pangs of a harsh new reality, and there was little he could do about it.

As 1972 ticked away, Bub heard some stories about his former friends participating in muggings, burglaries, and rip-offs. He didn't know who or what to believe, but in any case he figured that their lives were merely proceeding as it had for many hardcore drug addicts. Joey, Sam, and Sam's girlfriend continued to make their regular trips to DC, and Bub would see them every now and then. As he'd observe them, they looked as if they were very nervous or heavily sedated, and that made him sad in many ways.

On a better note, Bub's brother had returned from Vietnam during the summer of 1972, now the Kellow household was buzzing with joy. Bub had grown to five feet ten and 160 pounds, so when he'd first seen Robbie, he was eager to wrestle him to the ground. It was in that way that Bub wanted to rekindle the spirit of the raucous and obnoxious behavior that they'd once enjoyed. However, Robbie wasn't in the mood for the same old games, so they just settled into a long and serious conversation centered on recent local happenings.

Bub was surprised by Robbie's cooler attitude. It seemed to him that his brother's experience as a military policeman had made him understand more about the complexities of life. Robbie had seen the lengths to which soldiers would go in order to get discharged from military service, and that included getting strung out on heroin. Now Robbie was sad to see that his younger brother had become a victim of the drug scene in America, and he humbly asked Bub to "take it down a notch."

Bub was captivated by his brother's stories, and, since he understood Robbie's new perspective, he readily agreed. After that they hooked up the elaborate stereo equipment that Robbie had brought home from Vietnam. Then they proceeded to celebrate his homecoming as they rocked the night away.

* * *

Bub moved out of his parent's home and moved into a house with some of Robbie's past acquaintances. To say that they were interesting people would definitely be an understatement. The young man and woman who held the lease were into check-cashing schemes, and they'd hustle or trade anything of value. Aside from dealing porno, guns, and other hot items, they'd even go so far as to set traps in the woods, so they could sell baby squirrels and raccoons. They were also into humorous antics that would freak other people out, such as their pretending to be engaged in oral sex while sitting at a stoplight. For those reasons, Bub found them interesting, and that caused him to gravitate toward their seemingly harmless, free, and fun-loving lifestyle.

One day, his landlords asked Bub to participate in a prank that required his uncanny knack for making real fart sounds. He'd demonstrated that by biting the inside of his cheek while holding his hand against the other side. He agreed to give it a shot, and, as he made blubbery, flatulent noises with his face down in a toilet, they recorded the sounds on a cassette tape after a thirty-second gap. When the recording session was complete, they all rode to a department store, whereupon the cassette was put into a demo player. As they pretended to browse through the isles, thirty seconds passed, followed by, "PHHHhhht ... PHt ... PHHhhHHT" at high volume. They made every effort to hold back their extreme laughter, but it was the store employees who laughed the loudest as they came running to shut the cassette player off.

As an extension of that acquired behavior, an incident occurred when Bub and his brother went to a fast-food hamburger restaurant. While Robbie ordered their food at the counter, Bub was busy bumming a match from a stranger to light his cigarette. Next he found a table to sit, whereupon he pulled a small smoke-bomb out of his pocket and poked the fuse into the side of the cigarette. Then he felt under the table, and sure enough, there was a wad of bubble-gum, so he stuck the smoke-bomb to it. When his brother came to the table, Bub said, "Hey, man. Let's go outside and eat. It's too damned smoky in this joint."

As Bub and Robbie ate their food in Robbie's car, they became engrossed in a heavy conversation. To their surprise, the parking lot suddenly filled with people, while yellow smoke was pouring out the doors of the restaurant. It was then that Bub confessed to his brother what he'd done, and, in that same instant, the stranger who'd given him the match came marching up to his door. Bub couldn't contain his laughter, and that caused the angry man to spit at him. That in turn prompted Robbie to jump out of the car before hopping up on the front hood of his car. He was preparing to pounce on the man while threatening to kick his ass, but the man instantly backed away. His retreat allowed Bub to get out of the car, and, as he did, he feared the worst. In that same instant, the restaurant manager appeared. He looked nervous as he found himself in the midst of what appeared to be a very volatile situation. His upper lip was twitching, as he opened his arms to make a plea.

"Please stop it—all of you! Please leave now, or I'll have to call the police!"

Alas, it seemed that Robbie was always defending his crazy-ass brother!

*   *   *

By the end of 1972, Bub's boss became hip to his severe drinking habit. Without the desire or the ability to change his ways, Bub landed another mail-clerk job with a large lobbying organization on K Street, in Washington, DC. The long bus rides were entertaining for him, as he observed women tending to their appearance, while the men tried to look like James Bond. He also found DC to be an exciting place, with all the hustle and bustle creating electricity in the air. Since he was back to dressing like a collegiate; he was attracting the attention of some high-class legal secretaries. He was still a virgin, but now he was hoping that was about to change.

Bub quickly made friends with a good-looking black guy, named Devon, who had a big Afro and drove a bitchin' 1970 Olds 442. Together they smoked weed in the stairwells before making their daily rounds while shooting the bull with the secretaries. After a while, they could tell which girls were easy and which ones weren't. Of course, Bub liked the hard-to-get type of girl, but, after realizing that he was facing stiff competition from the lawyers, "easy to get" seemed a more likely catch for him.

One evening Bub went to an Alexandria high-rise where Devon was going to rendezvous with one of the "easy" secretaries. Bub had been told her roommate was a charming young woman who was worldly and wise. Therefore, he envisioned a hard-to-get and intellectual type of girl. However, when they got there, he was suddenly surprised by a cute little Asian woman who ran toward him and clung to him like glue! Although he wasn't sure if she lacked the personal traits he desired, he'd never thought about getting involved with a girl of another race before. Being flustered, Bub tried to ward her off, but the aggressive little woman didn't speak English, and, he found it difficult to be rude while she was being so friendly, and all. Since it was Friday night and Bub had a tendency to party, he started guzzling down cans of beer. As one thing led to another, he came to realize that oral communication wasn't necessary for two humans to jive, and that's the last thing he recalled thinking about.

The glare of sunshine coming through a window woke Bub up, and his head felt as if it was on fire. His throat was dry, too, but those weren't his only problems! His "new friend" was lying beside him, and she wanted to fool around some more. Bub wasn't sure if they'd done the wild thing, since he'd drunk himself into a blackout, but he was in no mood to do it now. He escaped her grasp before quickly getting dressed, and he then said good-bye with a promise to return, but he never did.

A couple of days later, Bub realized the true extent of his sexual encounter when he discovered a little critter crawling on his thigh. After exiting the men's room, he approached Devon in the mail room.

"Hey, man. Check this thing out—I found it crawling around my thigh, and it looks like a tick of some sort."

As Devon examined the creature on the end of Bub's finger, his eyes suddenly bulged, and he took a few steps back.

"Brother, you got the crabs! Get that nasty thing away from me, and go see a doctor, ASAP!"

Bub's situation was hilarious to nearly all who later learned of it, and even though he laughed with them, he was bummed. After all, he'd been saving himself for Miss Right, and that made him think. *Oh, the irony—I had all those opportunities to have sex during high school, but I didn't cash in! I guess God has a sense of humor, after all—or maybe it's vengeance!"* One again, adversity opened Bub's eyes to how he thought and who he'd become. Of course, he realized that God had nothing to do with it, so he started to blame his bad behavior on his drinking.

* * *

In 1973, Bub came across a popular book titled *I'm Okay, You're Okay,* by Thomas A. Harris. It was instrumental in Bub's first introspection regarding the suggestion that a trichotomy of the mind controls human behavior. The three categories of intellect, as the term suggests, were referred to as the child, the parent, and the adult. From what little he'd read, Bub figured his "child" had been in too much control of his life, while his "parent" and "adult" had been stifled by his drug and alcohol abuse. In the absence of his old friends, and in that moment of clarity, "he" (the adult), decided to call on "Riddick" (the parent) to begin a transformation of his life in a role of responsibility and dedication. He imagined Riddick as his parent, because his inner mind referred to himself as Riddick, just as his mother had always addressed him. He figured that Riddick was the part of his mind that could be strengthened in order to tame "Bub." Then he shut his eyes and wondered. *Just imagine who Riddick could have been, or yet, who he could be!* Then he opened his eyes, and Bub said, "Yeah, right!"

It was in that instant that he knew his adult was the arbitrator of two distinct personalities, the weaker of which was definitely Riddick, the parent. Then he recalled a cartoon he'd once seen on television when he was just a child. The cartoon character had an angel on one shoulder and a demon on the other. As he tried to make a moral decision, the demon would always poke the angel in the ass with a pitchfork and make her disappear. Then Bub recalled laughing, even though he knew the angel would wind up being right in the end. After that fond recollection, Bub figured that the book had at least opened his eyes and caused him to realize just how unbalanced his screwed-up mind had become!

*   *   *

Bub's new job was paying him better wages, and, since he'd been away from his old friends, his drinking lessened. As a result his bank account had grown, and now he was focused on buying the car of his dreams. He searched the classified ads for a muscle car, and, after reading the description of a 1969 Ford Mustang Mach 1, he urged his mom to take him to see it. His dad was through with that scene, and besides, he didn't think that Bub was mature enough to own a car that might kill him. While his mom mostly agreed with her husband's assessment, she wanted to believe that Bub had finally gained some wisdom from his past experiences. After all, his recent behavior had given her the impression that he was finally maturing. In light of that, she wanted him to experience the rewards of his hard work and efforts so he would maintain his good behavior.

The fire-engine red Mustang with gold stripes was owned by a White House Secret Service Agent who was assigned to protect President Nixon. It was between two protective concrete pillars in an underground parking garage, and, with only twenty-eight thousand miles on the odometer, it looked like new. As the agent showed his mother his new Porsche, Bub stared in amazement at the Mach 1. It was nearly identical to his brother's old Mustang, except for the fact that the interior was red instead of white. It had a 351-V8 and a factory four-speed, and, although Bub later ground a few gears while getting it home, he finally mastered it.

A short time later, Bub was cruising the streets of McLean in his shiny red car, and life was good! He'd spent hours washing, waxing, and detailing the car, and with its white-lettered Goodyear Polyglas tires, it looked sweet. He was eager to show it off, so he drove to the peat-moss bags, where he revved the engine in front of his old party friends. Of course, they were amazed at Bub's sudden rise to success, and they were curious, too. Since most of them were eager to share in his good fortune, Bub started hanging out with them again. Unfortunately, that caused him to return to his old behavior, and he started drinking and partying excessively.

Bub ravaged the Mustang on the streets. Eventually he bought a pair of cheater slicks to use at various drag strips in the area. He also bought a bigger carburetor, traction bars, and list of other goodies. His wild street escapades cost him his first DUI. Needless to say, his parents, his probation officer, and his insurance company were not happy about that! Shortly thereafter he got arrested for doing 110 mph on the Beltway in Maryland, with two cases of beer in the back seat. After that, his probation officer became extremely concerned, telling him, "You're skating on very thin ice! The only reason that I'm not requesting another hearing is because you reported all of this to me, immediately—and I appreciate that," she said. "Still, it's a major concern to me, and, since it should be a major concern to you as well, that type of behavior has got to stop!"

Shortly after that probation meeting, Bub went to a party in the Manassas countryside and tied one on. After running low on beer at the party, he and a friend Phil took his car into town to buy some more. After buying the beer, Bub spotted his friend Barry, so he pulled in behind Barry's Corvette in order to shoot the shit. When Phil got out of the car to talk with him, Bub decided to pull up alongside Barry's car. In his drunken stupor, he didn't realize that his passenger door was open, and it hit Barry's bumper, leaving a large dent in the door.

After looking at the damage and drinking a few beers, Bub and Phil said, "Happy trails!" to Barry. By that time, they were so drunk that they became lost while trying to find the party. Phil suggested pulling into a fire station that they were passing, so he could ask for some directions. While Phil was in the fire station, Bub passed out temporarily, and then he woke up. Wondering where he was, Bub put the Mustang into gear and drove aimlessly into the night.

At 3:45 a.m., Bub was awakened by the screeching horn and loud roar of a freight train. In his sudden astonishment, he honked his horn, quickly discovering that his head was stuck inside the steering wheel. His drool had dried, and his cheek was sticking to the hub. After getting it unstuck, he tried to turn on the headlights, so he could see. Then he realized they were already on, and that meant the battery was dead. "Where the fuck am I *this time*!" he raged. Then he thought about his old habit of saying, "What the fuck just happened, man," and it suddenly made him feel sick. As he looked about, he realized he was in a corn field. Then he imagined the train engineer saying, *"It's time to wake up, dumbass!"*

While totally bewildered and still drunk, Bub exited the car. As he stumbled back, he saw that it was mired deep in mud, and it wasn't more than ten feet from the railroad tracks. Then he frowned as he saw the passenger-door dent, now covered with splattered mud. As he strained to recall what had happened, he wiped his eyes and gazed about. He saw a farmer's house in the distance, and there was a light on, so he trudged through the muddy field and knocked on the front door. It was only four, but the farmer was up and eager to hear Bub's plight. Since he was a friendly sort, he made Bub some coffee while letting him use his telephone.

After waiting for his father to get out of bed and answer the phone, Bub sheepishly told him about his predicament. His father sighed, and there was an awkward silence. Then his father asked to speak to the farmer, who gave him directions. While the two men conversed, Bub knew that his father's silence had replaced, "I told you so, and I told your mother, too!"

When his dad arrived, Bub led him to the Mustang. Meanwhile, the farmer obliged them by bringing his tractor over with some jumper cables. Once the car was started, his father began rocking the car while slinging mud up into the air and the open driver's door. He rammed the floor shifter from reverse to second gear while turning the steering wheel back and forth and pumping the throttle. He finally managed to get the car out of the deep ruts, and then he moved it onto the farmer's access road.

After a menacing look from his bewildered father, Bub drove the battered and filthy Mustang home and went straight to bed. Later, his brother removed the inside panel of the door and popped the dent out, leaving only a slight dimple. Sadly, it seemed that Bub was back into his old groove, and he wasn't about to slow down.

* * *

During the summer of 1973, Bub and his friends decided to sneak into a community pool. It was a hot and humid night, and they'd been drinking at The Planet with nowhere else place to go. They made a plan to meet at the end of a dead-end road behind the pool, so some of them rode there in a VW Beetle, while some rode in Bub's car. Once they got there, they hiked down a wooded path to the back of the pool and scaled the protective chain-link fence. Bub joined some of them in skinny-dipping, while others swam in their underwear. Then they started getting loud, and suddenly two squad cars approached from the main entrance, and panic ensued!

While some of his friends quickly grabbed their clothes and climbed back over the chain-link fence, Bub swam fast to get out of the pool. As a policeman with a flashlight hollered *"Halt!"* Bub raced to the fence and scaled it like a monkey. He ran through the woods and found his passengers waiting by his car. As he reached for his keys, he realized that, in his haste, he'd forgotten to take his clothes! He stood there, naked and dazed by his stupidity, while everyone else crammed into the Beetle. He thought, *Hey! That looks just like one of those marathons that I saw some college kids do!* Then he thought, *Holy shit! I've got to hide! I don't want to get busted while I'm naked, for crying out loud!* With that, Bub took cover behind a clump of bushes in someone's front yard.

As the Volkswagen sped away, Bub thought about what he had left behind. He was relieved when he recalled that he had a spare set of car keys, and that he'd left his wallet at home. Then he thought about his Led Zeppelin T-shirt, burgundy slacks, and red suede Adidas. *Damn!*

Perplexed but not defeated, Bub began his one-half mile walk toward his home. Luckily for him it was late at night, and the streets were empty. As he darted from bush to bush, he soon discovered that his friends had gotten pulled over at the next intersection. The cops had everybody out of the Volkswagen, so Bub had no other choice but to wait behind some bushes, until the coast was clear. Eventually he made it home with only a few mosquito bites and one tick.

The following morning, Bub took his spare set of keys and went to retrieve his car. Later his friends told him that the cops had let everyone go, except for his good friend Frankie. As the story went, Frankie had been merrily back-floating in the pool while naked and oblivious to the sudden ruckus. That is, until the cops ruined his peaceful swim!

Later that summer, while his parents were on vacation, Bub lost control of his Mustang. He was driving home from a late-night party, and his passenger had fallen asleep. Bub started to doze off too, and when he hit some gravel on a turn, he became startled and overcorrected the car. As it slid sideways toward a bridge going over a creek, it jackknifed into the end of a guardrail.

After the crash, Bub ran to a house to get the occupant to call for an ambulance. When it arrived, he rode with his injured friend to the hospital, where they treated him for a fractured collarbone. Bub's dream car was totaled, and he was charged with reckless endangerment, but, he didn't argue with the police. At the time, he was more concerned with having hurt his friend than anything else.

The following day Bub was worried about the reaction of his probation officer, but he was more concerned about buying another car. His parents were returning from their cross-country trip in their new Oldsmobile, and he didn't want them getting involved in his purchase. The insurance investigator insisted that his totaled car was not a Mach 1 but a regular Mustang. When Bub argued with the man, the investigator lost his cool and yelled in Bub's face. Subsequently, he wrote Bub a small check and told him, "Take it or leave it!" Bub was angry and flustered, but he took the check.

After seeing what he could get for his money, Bub settled on a red 1971 Mustang convertible with a 351 four-barrel and automatic transmission. It was a beautiful car with a white top and interior, but it was not as nice as the Mach 1. Even though it had high mileage, it ran well. Still, the engine wasn't strong enough for Bub's liking, so he installed a high-performance intake and exhaust to make it go faster and sound louder.

While his parents were still on the road, a large, drunken fest ensued in the Kellow home. Robbie and Barry were locked in the lower-level bathroom, and they were raising holy hell! With towels stuffed under the door and in the toilet, they'd turned on the shower and sink with all the drains blocked. They kept flushing the toilet so the water would overflow and help flood the entire bathroom.

Bub had come home drunk and high from partying all day, and he heard the commotion. He ran to the back of the house and peered through the bathroom window. Suddenly it slid open, and the two laughing drunkards pulled him in by the arms! Bub was immediately stripped of his clothes by the two men, and now the three of them were thrashing around in the water, naked. As they did, the water rose to a level of three feet. It contained beer cans, clothes, shoes, towels, toilet tissue, and a rug. Yes, while the cats are away, the mice will play!

It wasn't long before his sister Darla and Robbie's girlfriend managed to push the door open. To their sudden amazement, about a thousand gallons of water and debris whooshed down the hallway and into the family room! The two girls just stood there, stupefied, as the three naked drunkards fought their way through the doorway in search of more beer, and, while they did, they were bellowing in a joyous and uncontrollable laughter. In Bub's absence, he later took the rap for the entire incident, which his parents believed without a doubt.

Great bouts of fun and drunkenness took place at the Kellows', day and night, and didn't matter whether the parents were away or not. Since they were usually in their upstairs bedroom, watching TV, they didn't see and hear it anyway. Although their sons' behavior was a concern to them, they thought it was better to allow them to have a good time at home rather than taking their rowdy fun elsewhere. Besides, if Bub was with his brother, they knew he wasn't on the streets.

The beautiful Virginia summer nights were enough to make any person drunk, without imbibing, and the days were splendid too. As Bub, Robbie, and their friends would work on their cars while boozing it up in their parent's driveway, neighbors would often complain about the noise. Loud laughter and yelling, along with sound of glass bottles breaking and engines revving, disturbed them. On one occasion, Barry power-braked his Corvette and sizzled the rear tires long enough for Bub to scrape up a fresh four-inch rubber ball. That noise angered one neighbor, who came out of her house to complain, only to get caught inside a drifting cloud of thick, blue, rubber smoke! As she raced back into her house coughing and sneezing, the young men toasted, as they bellowed with outrageous laughter.

Sometime later, Bub appeared in court on his reckless endangerment charge, and his dad went with him. That was fortunate for Bub, because somehow his dad managed to get the judge to find him guilty of a lesser offense. Although he didn't go to jail, Bub was severely reprimanded by the judge, who said the police report indicated the presence of alcohol. Bub was relieved that he didn't get a DUI, and he considered himself lucky to just be paying a heavy fine.

Even though the police report had indicated the presence of alcohol, his probation officer couldn't prove him guilty of drinking. Therefore she reasserted her warning that he was skating on very thin ice, while further warning him not to take her for a fool. "No more beer in the car, or you, while you're driving! *Understand?*" She scolded, and with that, Bub had somehow managed to avoid falling through the ice once again. After that meeting, Bub got serious about going straight again, so he decided to sober up.

*   *   *

While working for the same lobbying organization in September of 1973, Bub spotted a computer school across the street. After he checked their credentials and reputation, he enrolled in their computer programming curriculum. His boss told

Bub that he had plans for him, but since programming was his newly discovered interest, his mind was made up. After all, he had completed an IBM logic test, and his score indicated that he would make a good programmer.

Bub attended all his classes at night. As he took them one by one, his grades were at the top of his class. Then the time came when he only had one course left to take, and that was computer operations. Lo and behold, the school administrator told him the mainframe computer was being replaced, so he offered Bub a temporary contract job at NASA. Under that guise, the man went on to tell Bub that he couldn't be issued a certificate until he completed all his courses. At that time Bub couldn't know that the school was going belly-up, and IBM was repossessing the mainframe computer, so he was delighted to take the job.

In November of 1974, Bub arrived at NASA to be assigned as a computer operator. Although it wasn't the position he'd hoped to fill, and, it seemed ironic to him that that he was taking a position for which he hadn't yet been trained, he was fascinated none the less. His duties included a scheduled collection of satellite data using worldwide tracking stations and program-controlled monitors. As the data was received, Bub would initiate data-collection programs, and then he'd print the output to be distributed to scientists. He found the job and the atmosphere to be extremely interesting, and, he was equally excited about his new career path.

Upon returning to his school two weeks later, Bub found the doors locked. As he peered through the windows, he noticed that the interior was empty, except for the telephones, which were sitting on the dirty nylon carpet. He didn't know who to call, or what to do. He only knew that he'd been screwed! He'd already paid for his education, but the school had given him nothing but a receipt to prove it.

6. THE NOT-SO-GREAT ESCAPE

Although Bub had learned a good deal about programming, he figured it would be nearly impossible to get a programming job without a certificate. It was a shame, too, because he'd taken to all the technical courses like a duck to water. All the while he'd been dazzled by the system architecture and software and how it related to the human mind. He'd dreamt of using that knowledge to develop unique and efficient programs that would integrate, process, and report all types of data. *What happened to my dreams?* he wondered. All things considered, Bub thought he could have gone far in that field—a field of study that had yet to be taught by the less-expensive community colleges that he could afford. Now the only computer-related jobs that he could foresee landing would be limited to operations, and since Bub lacked the virtue of tenacity, that's all that he'd get.

In April of 1974, Bub was a lonely and dejected man. He was only twenty-one years old, but he'd come to believe that all of his positive efforts amounted to a fiasco. He had no steady girlfriend, and that was understandable, due to his wild and self-destructive nature. He'd been naively stung by the law in a clear case of entrapment, and now he was under the scrutiny of the law. He wondered, *What next!* He knew that his life had turned better when he avoided his party-loving friends, but, since it seemed as if life were working against him, he turned his anger inward once again.

As Bub was finishing his contract job at NASA, he attended a party in his neighborhood and was spurred into a fight. He was enjoying the peaceful party, which was attended by mostly younger kids, when he decided to make his way up the crowded basement staircase in search of a bathroom. Suddenly, he was pushed backward as other people began falling against him. As Bub hollered, "What the hell!" he looked up at the top of the stairway to see Jake and his rowdy sidekicks. Evidently they'd just arrived, and now they were having fun at the doorway to the basement, pushing the kids out of their way. Bub noticed that his old friend, Manny, had decided to hang with them, and that made him even angrier. Of course, they were just having fun bullying the younger crowd, but Bub wasn't in the mood to be empathetic. He pushed his way through to the top of the steps, where he butted into Jake.

"You think you're tough shit, pushing the young kids around! Well, let's go outside, and we'll see what you're all about!"

Jake was surprised by Bub's sudden appearance, and he warned him to stand down. He didn't know why Bub was so angry, but he was not about to back down. As Bub continued to make it clear that he was fed up with Jake's constant bullying, Jake finally agreed to settle the matter on Bub's terms.

Once they were out on the driveway, Jake pulled a knife on Bub, and when Manny saw it he walked toward Bub and pleaded with him to stay the hell back. That only made Bub angrier, so he punched Manny in the mouth while yelling, "Get away!" The force of the punch sent Manny to the ground, and, as the gathering crowd reacted to the violence, Bub instantly regretted hitting his good friend. Then a surge of adrenaline gave Bub a strong alcohol rush, and, as he attempted to turn his attention back to the knife-wielding Jake, Manny sprung up from the ground and tackled him.

As Bub attempted to rise to his feet, Manny got him in a rear naked choke hold before pulling him back to the ground. Bub gasped for air, and his mind raced as he tried to break Manny's firm grip. Then he squinted as his vision behind his eyelids went from a bright-red glow to a bright white glow, whereupon he slowly went limp. As he did, Bub thought, *I can't feel any pain, and I feel—peaceful!* Within seconds his pain returned, because a friend of theirs had urged Manny to loosen his grip.

"Manny! You're killing the poor bastard," was the first thing Bub heard.

As Manny got up and walked away, Bub slowly regained the full use of his motor skills. When he finally stood up, he saw the damage he'd done to Manny's lips. Jake and his friends were already tending to him, and that bothered Bub, since he couldn't get a word in edgewise. As far as he was concerned, the party was over, so he went home.

Although Bub was often obnoxious when drunk, it was never his nature to be malicious. He was simply interested in fun and games, but it wasn't easy for him to have his way all the time. On those occasions he would simply be forced to deal with other people's attitudes toward him, while he tried to protect what little honor he had. At the same time, his lack of self-respect was becoming more apparent to others, and as a result, threats and insults aimed toward him were becoming increasingly common. Still, with his dark attitude, he didn't care what came his way, and, as he would emerge from bouts of extreme drunkenness, he would vaguely remember what happened anyway. Those bitter experiences, in addition to his failures, were causing him great despair, and, as he started to drink more beer in an attempt to drown his sorrows, he was becoming a morning drinker to calm his shattered nerves.

Bub's maniacal penchant for drinking and driving had earned him a dubious reputation, so there weren't many people who were willing to ride in his car. While he knew that to be true, he didn't care anymore. He was now seeing himself as a virtual loner, and he embraced his new reputation as a reckless outlaw. He figured he could always hang with his brother and sisters' friends, anyway. They all had fast and fancy cars, and they liked to have fun and race.

On one such occasion, Bub drag raced a local hot-rodder on Georgetown Pike. They started near the entrance of the CIA, at Langley, and the other fellow got the jump, but Bub slowly caught up. As they raced past a gas station and came upon a high school, Bub started to pass on a hill marked with a double yellow line. After seeing that, the other guy quickly hit his brakes because Bub didn't seem fazed by what might have become a grim disaster.

That same evening Bub unbolted the exhaust pipes from his headers and terrorized the local streets in search of parties. All the while, he laid noisy whole-shots everywhere he went. Finally he found a party where he challenged anybody to race who thought their car was faster than his, and that started a fight in the process.

That day was typical of Bub's increasingly cynical attitude. He was now seeing his better nature as an inherent weakness in his personality, so he was determined to become more rambunctious and daring. His aim was to act like the people he'd always detested. *After all,"* Bub thought, *they always seemed to get the girl and the upper hand!* With that new attitude, Bub was forming yet another personality, and that meant he was as far from his true nature as he'd ever been.

* * *

Although Bub had become a fairly smooth talker, his probation officer was beginning to see through his bullshit. Since his drug bust, he'd been cited for public drunkenness, driving while intoxicated, reckless endangerment, and speeding. He also seemed to switch jobs a lot. And recently, after Bub had made a verbal slip, she realized he was going to Maryland beaches without telling her! Of course, all those matters were required to be reported at once, and now she was tired of Bub's ignorance. As for Bub; he had just sat down in front of her, and all he could think about was getting the hell out of her office and drinking a cold beer. Then she spoke up.

"I should confine you to the custody of the law, before you do something stupid again, but I sense that there is good in you!"

Bub looked away and squirmed in his chair. The last part of her statement touched his soul, and he was trying to formulate some kind of intelligent response. At the same time, his probation officer was reading his body language, so she continued.

"I could do it just like *that*!" as she snapped her fingers.

The silence was deafening for Bub, and then she continued.

"You have a lot of potential, and you've demonstrated that, but you seem—no; you *are* hell-bent on self-destruction!"

More silence followed, as Bub figured he better let her run her course, and she frowned at him as she continued. "What do you want me to do with you? Or, better yet, what do you want to do with *yourself!*"

That question struck one of Bub's nerves, and it sounded as if she wanted some type of answer. Her frown had turned to a look of hope, and after seeing that he struggled for words as he started to wing it. "I know you've been very fair with me—"

"More than fair," she interjected.

"Yes, *more* than fair," Bub quickly agreed. "You see, my life has been hard since my school shafted me, and now, just having talked with you, I realize how it's been affecting me lately. Please allow me to continue at my job, and I promise you that I'll snap out of my doldrums—I've just been going through this damned awful phase, and I really want it to stop!"

Bub paused while realizing that he was spewing the same old bullshit, so he called upon "Riddick" to feed his squirming mind. Then Riddick looked up at her eyes, and he continued. "What you said gives me hope, and I love that about you! I've been hearing the same thing from my parents, but to hear it from someone like you only reassures me."

More silence.

"I know I can be a better man—a better person. I promise you! Please, just give me one more chance."

With head down and arms folded, her eagle-eyed stare evaluated his sincerity. She figured that he was either being sincere, or he was a damned good liar. So far, he hadn't lied to her, so she decided to give him one last chance. Maintaining a stern look and holding up one finger, she began her conclusion. "I'll give you one more chance, but it will be your last. I don't know if you're a professional bullshit artist or not, but know this! You need to find a way to get over your personal problems—if you can't, and you screw up *one* more time, you won't get anything out of me except action. Am I making myself crystal clear?"

Bub's head was perked up like a pooch now, and he quickly nodded as he nervously twiddled his thumbs.

"Go on now, get," she continued. "But I want you to return to me in one month with nothing but good news and a good disposition, or you'll discover what hell is really like! *Understand?*"

Her words echoed through his head as he drove home. He'd told her the truth when he said she gave him hope, and he loved her for seeing the good in him. *Why can't I find a woman like that?* he wondered. As he thought about her angelic face and the mature wisdom behind it, it filled an empty place in his soul. Then he thought, *Even though she has a duty was toward society, she also seems to have a duty toward lost souls. "I see something good in you," she said. She truly seems to care about me.* As Bub recalled her eyes and her mannerisms, her womanly graces and attributes loomed larger. Then he became aroused, just like he did whenever he encountered an intelligent woman. Suddenly he felt guilty about his tendency to give way to fantasy, and his anxiety increased as he began to dwell upon the shortcomings of his character. After thinking about that, he thought, *While I'm mature in some ways, I'm extremely immature and naive in others. Up to now, my life's been filled with all sorts of dreams and fantasies. Meanwhile, other people my age are already realizing theirs!*

That last thought pissed him off, and now he gripped his steering wheel tighter. *Here I am, mired in my sickly thoughts, and I need a drink just as badly as I want it! Shit! It's become a part of who I am! It's what I see, it's what I think, and it's what I fucking do!* Then Bub remembered the question that had affected him the most. *What do you want to do with yourself?* After realizing the root cause of his recent behavior while in her office, Bub knew the answer, and he figured the probation officer did too. He needed to find help with his lust for drinking, and, if he couldn't find it, then she would! As he dwelled on her possible interpretations of help, he thought of the stories he'd seen and heard regarding prison life. *Prison would sober me up, for sure, but I don't want to be an ex-con for the rest of my life, and I don't want to get screwed in the ass, either!*

Soon thereafter, powerless over his hard addiction, Bub and a group of Falls Church desperados found themselves in dire need of alcohol, and no one had any money. They'd all congregated at an apartment of an acquaintance who'd recently been given a dishonorable discharge from the US Marines. Since Bub had a fast car, he was elected to go with a volunteer who would shoplift some beer. Bub didn't like the plan, because it wasn't foolproof, and he was on probation, but despite his objections, he was overruled. Well, since Bub was short on friends, he finally agreed.

Twenty minutes later, Bub found himself parked beside a grocery store. He'd lowered his convertible top in order to facilitate a faster getaway, and just as he thought about covering his license plate with a paper bag that was blowing in the wind, his accomplice came running from the store with three cases of beer. As Bub heard his friend approaching, he turned to discover that there were two store managers in hot pursuit, and, at the same time, his desperate friend threw the beer in the backseat while yelling, "*Drive!*" That didn't seem like a wise idea to Bub, though, since the managers were now standing right beside the car, so he threw up his hands and smiled.

Knowing that it would be foolish to drive away and risk going to prison, Bub decided to put the car back into park and shut off the engine. Instantly, he went into bullshit mode as he asked his friend, "I take it you didn't pay for the beer?" Then, without hesitation, he quickly turned in his seat to do some fast talking.

"I'm sorry, guys. If he didn't pay for the beer, we'll take it back inside right away. You see, a good friend of ours just returned from the service, and he is a highly decorated Vietnam vet! My friend wanted to surprise him; that's all! If there's any way that I can beg your forgiveness, please let us take the beer back, and we'll be on our way. If you prefer, I'll give you a copy of my driver's license, and then I'll go right home to get some cash!"

After exchanging glances, one of the irritated store managers reached into the backseat and snatched up the beer. Then he told them if they ever came back, he would pummel them with a baseball bat before pressing charges. That was an embarrassing and humiliating experience, so Bub and his friend didn't utter a word as they returned empty-handed to the apartment.

After entering the apartment, Bub and his accomplice related the series of events. As they began arguing in front of their thirsty friends, it became the consensus that Bub had blown it. That riled Bub, because no one seemed to care about his dilemma, and, after calling his accomplice a fool, he was quickly challenged to a fight. As the young man stood with his fists clenched in rage, Bub was embarrassed and frustrated while realizing the hopelessness of the situation. That caused Bub to turn red while wisely backing down from the fight. Then he quickly left the apartment, hoping to never to see any of them again.

As Bub drove home, his anger was replaced by the relief of his narrow escape. He figured that someone upstairs was giving him yet another chance. He recalled the expressions of those who'd watched him back down from the fight, and that made him think about how pathetic his life had become. *Whatever happened to the good old days? Everybody's messed up now, just like me, and we're all going down—but down to where and what!*

* * *

In May of 1974, Bub's probation appointment went better than the last, since it appeared that he'd been a good boy. He was upbeat, as he explained to his probation officer, that he'd taken on a new friend named Danny. Danny was a young mechanic who Bub had met at the local auto-parts store, and, since they shared similar interests, they enjoyed working on their cars together. Finally, Bub explained that Danny was good for him, since he wasn't a member of his old gang of friends. For that reason, plus the fact that he'd move back into his parents' house, he told her he was having more success avoiding trouble.

Later that month Bub was driving through Arlington when he spotted a tricked-out yellow 1971 Mustang Mach 1. It was up on the display lift of a small-time used-car lot, and man, did it look sweet! After a closer inspection and test drive, Bub managed to make an even swap for his 1971 convertible. Both cars had high mileage, but Bub's rear shock towers had all but rusted through, so he figured the banana-yellow beast was a godsend. It had a 351 Cleveland with a big Holley double-pumper and a factory Hurst four-speed. The body style was long and sleek, and it rolled on fat white-lettered tires mounted on polished aluminum racing wheels.

After drinking while polishing his new "used-up" car all day, Bub was intoxicated and on the hunt for someone to race. The car seemed fairly fast to him, but he could only be sure by testing it against some of the cars he'd raced before. While driving through McLean, he finally pulled into the Jack in the Box, looking for admirers and takers, but since no one was there, he decided to call it quits for the night. He pulled a hole-shot as he left the parking lot, unaware that a policeman had been watching him from across the street.

As he made his way toward home, he didn't let up. Instead, he winded through the gears while speed-shifting down Old Dominion Drive, oblivious to the fact that a cop was now in full pursuit. Since he was traveling at such a high rate of speed, he missed his normal turn and elected to take Kirby Road. He knew it had a triangulated median for easy right-hand turns, and he loved to rip that corner!

As Bub downshifted and hit the brakes hard, he veered onto Kirby Road and prepared to punch the throttle once again. It was in that instant that he noticed the dreaded and familiar flashing of a red light in his rearview mirror, but when he looked again, it had disappeared. Curious now, Bub hit his brakes and looked into his side-view mirror, where he was amazed to see a cop car sticking out of the ditch on the opposite side of the road. Without hesitation, he backed up and put on his emergency brake. Then he ran across the street just in time to see a police officer squeezing out through the window of his car.

"Are you okay, man?" Bub asked, whereupon the officer fumbled with his holster and finally pulled out his gun.

"*Freeze!*" the policeman yelled.

Just after that, another cop car arrived, coming to a screeching halt. Moments later, Bub was arrested for DUI and taken to jail.

The cops were peeved as they told Bub he was responsible for wrecking a government-owned vehicle.

"Not hardly," Bub was fast to reply. "I can't help it if you cops don't know how to drive, man!"

That only angered the cops even more, but Bub didn't care as he continued his rant. "I could have *easily* ditched your asses and gone home to bed, but in the kindness of my heart I pulled over to see if you were okay!"

At the police substation, Bub refused the Breathalyzer, reminding the officers to "Stick it, man." He figured that he was in enough trouble as it was without further incriminating himself. After being thrown into the drunk tank, he wondered how long it would take for his probation officer to learn of his arrest. *Sooner or later she'll find out, and that will be the last straw! What am I going to do now!*

It was June of 1975, and Bub had been working in Reston, Virginia, which was blazing a trail to become one of the fastest-growing and trendiest townships in America. He had been hired to operate a Burroughs L5000 computer, which was housed in a spectacular little building constructed with huge, smoked-glass panels. He was happy while working there, because he had an unobstructed view of a beautiful golf course. What turned Bub off about the place was the fact that there was a pharmaceutical laboratory next door that tested drugs on large primates. He shuddered every time men dressed in white jumpsuits, gloves, and face masks would carry out a dead animal. That happened about once every other week, and, as he watched them, he wondered where they'd found the magnificent beasts and what they were testing on them. The thought of their fate made Bub melancholy, as he now considered his own. Ever since he'd been charged with his most-recent DUI, Bub had been getting antsy. To add to his consternation, soft rock was now filling the airwaves, and the nation appeared to be in a decline. The Vietnam War had ended without honor, and since then the DC scene had become dull, leaving Bub to feel as if the party had finally ended. Notorious people such as Timothy Leary and Charles Manson had underscored hard discussions about substance abuse, while great musicians such as Jimi Hendricks, Jim Morrison, and Janis Joplin had tragically died. All the while political leaders had taken their lumps, after waging an ugly war against those who'd fairly opposed the status quo. Now the demoralizing effects of those events overshadowed his generation of baby boomers and left some with a sadly complex and confusing legacy. To that extent, Bub wondered if the protesters of the sixties had ever made any difference at all! Then he thought about the disco scene, and he couldn't stand the new direction the country was taking. Substance abuse was still at an all-time high, and the cost of fuel was steadily rising, as the economy had taken a dire turn for the worse. In addition to that, new government regulatory agencies had been formed, and as a result cars were being produced with big, butt-ugly bumpers; more plastic; and significantly less horsepower. With all of that running through his mind, Bub seemed to be suffering from self-afflicted circumstances and a 1960s-era PTSD.

I have got to get the hell out of here, Bub thought. *I need a change. Shit! Once I'm convicted of my latest DUI, I'll be headed for prison anyway!*

While continuing to work in Reston, Bub came up with a plan to escape the DC area. His father had given him a whole life insurance policy when he turned twenty-one, and it had a cash value of $250.00. Since Bub's dad had only recently done that for him, he wondered if his dad suspected that he would meet with an early demise! Nevertheless, it was his now, and he planned to go to Minneapolis, Minnesota, where his dad bought it, so he could cash it in. From there, he figured he would head west. His sister Jessie had recently moved to San Diego, California, and he thought she might welcome him there. After getting his next paycheck, he dropped in to see his young friend Danny. While talking to him, Bub filled his mind with visions of a care-free life.

"The first stop will be Minneapolis, Minnesota!" Bub exclaimed. "That's where we have to go, so I can cash in my life-insurance policy. Then we'll hightail it to sunny San Diego, California, while having fun along the way. It'll be bitchin', dude! Just think about it—we'll be living the good life while chasing *las chiquitas bonitas* around the sunny beaches!"

That sounded great to Danny, so without informing anyone they quickly packed their gear and hit the road.

The open road was immediately home to Bub, because he felt as though he was born to keep on moving. All the while, he and Danny drank lots of beer and listened to eight-track tapes. They made it all the way to Gary, Indiana, before pulling over for some much-needed rest. Although Danny held a valid driver's license, Bub never let anyone drive his car, because alcohol had taken its toll on his nervous system.

Upon arriving in Minneapolis, Bub learned that the face value of his insurance policy would take ten to fifteen business days to process. That greatly concerned him, because his cash was disappearing fast, and he had only his dad's Standard Oil credit card as a backup plan. Realizing their circumstances were dire, he told Danny that they were going to take a ride up north to see his old friends in Forest Lake. He explained to him that if they hung out there long enough, they could just snatch up his insurance check hot off the press and be on their way.

Once in Forest Lake, the pair quickly wore out their welcome, since Bub had imposed on his old friend Jackie without prior notice. After all, Jackie still lived with his parents, and they thought Bub looked as if he had grown up to be wild. With nowhere else to go, Bub and Danny opted to camp out under an old fifth-wheel trailer that was located near some woods.

They managed to get a job at a local motorcycle-helmet factory after getting a tip from Jackie's sister. Bub was okay with their new job, but, since Danny was a mechanic, he quit on the second day due to the monotonously boring assembly routine. Not wanting to work alone, Bub followed his lead, and shortly thereafter they got pulled over for speeding through the middle of town.

The small-town cop was savvy, and he detained them for possessing a dope pipe and having open cans of beer. He made Bub open his trunk, whereupon he discovered Bub's .22 caliber rifle with a high-powered scope. Luckily for Bub, the chief of police turned out to be none other than an old boyfriend of his sister Darla. After inquiring as to her welfare and the rest of his family, the chief looked Bub square in the eye and said, "Head straight out of Forest Lake, and don't come back!"

Some eighteen hours later, Bub and Danny found themselves entering the Eisenhower Tunnel, heading west through Colorado. Bub was extremely tired, since he'd done all the driving, and now he was ready to stop for a long rest. When they came out the other end of the tunnel, the view was magnificent! The light green aspen trees and tall, dark pines adorned the snow-covered peaks and the little town of Dillon, with its pristine reservoir, glistened in the sunlight below.

"This is where we'll stop," Bub said thoughtfully.

After making some inquiries, they found a rustic bar at the base of a mountain road that led to Breckenridge. There was a payphone outside, so Bub dropped a dime after getting up the nerve to speak with his father.

"You're where? Colorado! What in the hell do you mean by quitting your job and running off across the country with my credit card! What in God's name are you doing, Riddick!"

Bub tried to assure his father that he'd pay him back, but his dad was no fool.

"Hey, Dad, calm down! You'll have a heart attack! I'll pay you back as soon as I get my insurance check."

That only made matters worse. "What insurance check are you talking about? Do you mean to tell me that you cashed your life-insurance policy? Just head straight back here, and don't use that credit card for anything, except gas! Do you understand me? If your probation officer finds out you've left the state without permission, you'll become a fugitive from the law!"

Bub had forgotten about that condition, again, and now he was getting really nervous.

"Look, Pops. I don't need a lecture—what I need is support! I quit my job four days ago, and I didn't report it, so I'm screwed anyway!"

His father was silent, but Bub knew what he was thinking.

"Listen, Dad—I know I fucked up, and that's because I *am* a fuck-up, okay? Just let me breathe, and give me some time to think about things. I'm going to hang up now, and I'll call you back."

Bub hung the phone up before his father could respond, and then he went into the bar to drink his fill. He told Danny how his father had reacted, and, after rattling off his life story, Danny shook his head. "Man! I had no idea…"

"Well, life's no picnic!" Bub interrupted. "Isn't that what they say, Danny boy?"

Then he smiled before chugging the rest of his beer.

After using his father's credit card to check into a motel, Bub and Danny got a good meal, and then they slept until dark. Upon awakening they got cleaned up and ventured back to the tavern. Bub loved Colorado for its rustic and glorious surroundings. The mountain air made his animal nature swoon, and the saloon-style tavern, with its swinging doors and wooden porch, made him want to belly up to the bar like the cowboys depicted in the movies.

It wasn't too long before they met three young men from Denver, and for Bub and Danny, it would prove to a fateful encounter. Their names were Christian, Chance and Cody, and they seemed genuinely nice while offering to pay for all of the beer and pool games. Then they made Bub and Danny an offer they couldn't refuse. They told them that they'd put them up at their place and feed them if Bub and Danny helped them with a condominium roofing project near the Dillon Dam. As Bub and Danny looked at one another in disbelief, they figured that was a no-brainer!

The days that followed were spent having lots of fun. After working through the early-morning hours, all five of them would hike up into the upper regions of the mountains. On one journey, they came upon a porcupine that seemed oblivious to them, since it was in no particular hurry. Then they quietly mounted a mossy bluff, so they could watch beavers as they built their dams. After that, they came across old encampments, where Bub and Danny learned the term *turkeys*, given to "assholes who leave garbage in their wake," as one of the young men put it.

Of course they drank copious amounts of beer, and they toted firearms "just in case." That caused Christian, who was now familiar with Bub's circumstances, to laugh as he remarked, "Hey man, did you know that it's illegal for you to possess or carry firearms?"

"Well, I forgot, man—just like leaving the state. In fact, I went totally berserk, and I needed to get away. Should that be a crime?"

At night, they all pigged out on hamburger mixed with packets of blended spices. That caused them to let loud farts, and they roared laughter while telling silly jokes and funny stories. It was in that setting that life seemed sweeter, and it gave the troubled mind of Bub some much-needed relief.

The owner of the Denver-based company had sent the three-man crew to Dillon with enough food to feed them for two weeks. Since Bub and Danny joined on, the food disappeared after only nine days, and now they were faced with hunger.

"Food is not a problem, Danny," Bub said. "Since I brought my rifle, we'll just hike up that mountain trail tomorrow morning and shoot us some breakfast. Okay?"

Danny was looking a little worried, but he slowly nodded in agreement. That caused Bub to give him a reassuring smile, but as he drifted off to sleep, the look on Danny's face haunted him.

The following morning, Bub and Danny set out to hunt, but on the way they stopped at a country store to buy a six-pack with their last $1.50. Once inside the store, Bub passed the meat department on his way to the beer cooler and smelled fresh corned beef being sliced by the clerk. That proved too much for him, and he couldn't stand his hunger pangs any longer. So, with a quick glance about the store, he stuffed a pack of hot dogs down the front of his pants!

As it turned out, the meat case had a two-way mirror behind it, so Bub was apprehended after leaving the store. The police were called, and after they arrived they searched Bub and his car. As they confiscated his rifle, Bub begged the police to let Danny take the car. He explained that he couldn't afford an impound fee, and Danny had no way to get home. The police were okay with that, but Bub was only mildly relieved as he was put into a squad car and taken to jail.

That night in the jail was tough for Bub. He contemplated the fact that he was going to be incarcerated for *who knows how long!* Then he wondered if Colorado would find out that he was on probation in Virginia. *Will they extradite me? I'm sure I'll get fined, and that means I'll have to call the insurance agency, so they'll send my check to this jail!* It was then that the full gravity of his grim reality hit him. He wouldn't be going to California, after all—at least not in the foreseeable future! *Oh, damn!* Bub shuddered. *That means I'll probably be heading back to Virginia, where my fate will be decided by my probation officer!*

The morning came too soon for Bub. He'd only just fallen asleep when he was startled by the loud noise of a baton dragged across his jail-cell bars.

"KELLOW, UP!" the cop bellowed. "You're due in court! Let's go!"

Bub went before the judge as a common criminal with an open-and-shut case. He wore full shackles and striped jail garb as he begged for the court's mercy. Even as he did, he knew better, as the judge's reputation had preceded him. Still, Bub put on his best whimpering act, to no avail.

"Two weeks," came the shrill verdict of the small hunch-backed man, dressed in a black robe, "plus a $250.00 fine!"

Bang! went his gavel.

As Bub was led back to his cell, he recalled the judge's enunciation in slow motion: *"plus a teehoo-hunndred-and-fiffftceee dollar fine"—Jesus! That was supposed to pay for some food, at least!*

Of course Bub had no choice but to accept his self-imposed fate. Even though he was worried, his time in jail seemed to pass in relative comfort and peace. The jail cells were clean, and Bub was given a mop and a paint can and a brush to keep it that way. He learned he wasn't the only guy to have stolen something out of that store. According to the cops, a lot of hungry drifters had been arrested, and they mopped and painted, too. Given that fact, he figured that he wasn't the only destitute soul to have buckled to hunger, and at least, for the time being, he was sober, and they fed him three square meals a day. They also let him choose some books to read, so he was happy about that. After cleaning and painting the jail cells, he was rewarded by washing patrol cars in the fresh mountain air.

Danny had visited Bub in jail only one time, and that was just after his sentence had been imposed. Bub was concerned about Danny getting enough to eat, and he worried about his car.

"Just drive it to the condos and park it!" he had pled.

Danny told him his mother was sending him some money by way of Western Union. "Don't worry, Bub, I got it under control!"

"What a saint," Bub said. "Listen, man. I'm sorry about everything, and you know that, right?"

Danny just nodded, and then he did a quick drumroll on the metal screen divider before he got up and left.

As fate would have it, Bub received his insurance disbursement just as he got two days off for good behavior. Upon getting out of jail, he realized that Danny hadn't been informed, so he walked seven miles to the condos. When he found Danny, he figured that he'd driven the car, because it had broken down with a seized bearing on the right front axle. Bub wasn't mad, though. All he could think about was getting the damn thing fixed, so he could go home to face the music. All the while, his new Colorado friends pleaded with him to reconsider. "Fuck Virginia," they said, but Bub's mind was made up. After all, his parents lived there, and he loved them dearly.

* * *

After fixing his car and arriving back in Virginia with Danny, Bub took the heat from his parents before seeing his probation officer. When he entered her office, she picked up her phone, and he was immediately arrested. While he'd been expecting that, he was stunned by the reality of it all. After all, the process seemed too abrupt as he suddenly thought, *What... no phone call? No time to buy a carton of cigarettes? No good-byes to anyone who might give a shit? This sucks!*

As he had sat stunned before his exasperated probation officer, she just shook her head. Then a uniformed police officer entered her office and handcuffed him before taking him directly to jail. Once he got there, he had to check in.

"What about my phone call, man?" Bub asked.

"You aren't being arrested, son," the jailer said, "you're just serving out the sentence that the judge issued in the first place."

That didn't sound good to Bub, and he looked as if he'd just taken a big gulp of cheap whiskey. "No, no—not three years!"

Bub was placed in cellblock C. It occupied about a quarter of the second floor of the jailhouse. He entered through the mechanically operated side door, which led to the daytime area. The length of the entire cell area was approximately fifty feet. To the left were six small cells whose combined width equaled the length of the daytime area. Each cell contained a metal sink, a metal toilet with no lid or seat, and two bunks, which were welded to the walls and contained filthy, stained mattresses. These individual cells were to be locked shut at night. In the center of the daytime area, opposite the cells, stood a metal bench and table, which were also welded to the bars. Above the metal table, a ten-inch TV was mounted for viewing until lockdown at 8:00 p.m.

Bub was about to get educated by the total experience of living in a large county jail. Of course, the range of that experience would better be described as limbo, rather than the hell of a "big house" prison. The general population consisted of all types of characters, ranging from fairly decent to extremely vile and demented. Bub was told by a guard, "If you're on the first floor, you're there for a short while. However, if you're on the second floor, you're probably awaiting a more serious disposition. That is to say, you might have already been found guilty, and you're either awaiting transport to a state penitentiary, or you're here from a state penitentiary and awaiting further trial. The third floor is mainly used for small-time county prisoners and second-floor overflow."

Bub's cellblock was full, since he'd filled the last vacancy. He was assigned to bunk with a fellow who had no personality or teeth, which was fine with him. All he wanted to do was to immerse himself in books or some other diversion, which might soothe his troubled mind.

Unfortunately, jail life wasn't that simple, as Bub soon found out. He found himself confronted by a man with the craziest eyes he had ever seen! The man wanted to know all about him and who Bub *thought* he was! Then he wanted to lock hands with him, in order to see who could bend the other man's hands back first. Bub was overwhelmed by the man's persistence and begged the guy to leave him alone, but it was in the nature of this man to get his way. Finally, Bub couldn't stand the harassment anymore and obliged the crazy-eyed man simply to end his relentless harangue. As they went to lock hands, the man seized Bub's grip with sudden fury and quickly bent his hands back. Bub instinctively dropped down to his knees, in order to lessen the strain on his fingers and wrists.

"Are you happy, dude?" Bub asked, wincing and fighting back just enough to keep his wrists from breaking.

The crazy-eyed man smiled, revealing bad teeth and gums, and simply said, "Yes—*I am!*"

It didn't take long for Bub to consider himself to be a saint compared to most of his cellmates. There were bad eggs in his cellblock, and to his amazement he learned about some of them on the TV. One guy was awaiting trial for rape, and he had only one testicle. He blamed his alcoholic father for his rape charge, saying he was always razzed by him about his natural defect while growing up, and therefore he'd been too ashamed to seek a normal relationship. Bub thought that was a very sad situation and it made him think about his own father's gentle and understanding nature.

There was a huge black man who, while serving time for murder, was brought from a state penitentiary to go to trial for murdering his cellmate. Bub almost became his next victim! Upon receiving his cigarettes from the canteen, Bub took them out of the paper sack they came in, blew it up, and popped it. The black man, who happened to be standing next to him, lurched with fright. As laughter ensued, he quickly became embarrassed, so he threw Bub up against the bars and threatened to break his neck! Later, after the illiterate man apologized, Bub read him the newspaper as a mutual gesture of good will.

Bub learned the evil methods of "paybacks." On one occasion, he witnessed the crazy-eyed man's chili getting mixed with feces, before he was awakened to eat it. Bub dared not say a word due to the threatening stares from the perpetrators.

Bub also learned just how far men would go to escape reality. As the guards rolled cans of insect spray under the bars, some prisoners would scurry like ravenous hyenas to grab them. The "lucky" ones would scramble back into their cells, grab a roll of toilet paper, and spin some off to cram it into the middle of the roll. Then they'd spray the insecticide directly into one end of the roll while sucking their lungs full though the other. Those actions horrified Bub. Of all the drugs he'd done and the desperate people he'd seen, that had taken the cake. Experiencing that was beneficial for him, though. As he lay in his cell that night, he meditated on his intense and misguided passions. *Was I meant to see that freaky free-for-all in order to make me face my own reality? With all the drugs I've done, aren't I just like them? I'm perverting my life while cutting it short, and if I don't change, I'll experience a miserable death! If there's a God in heaven, please help me to help myself from this day on!*

Coffee and other precious commodities were smuggled to inmates by way of the trustee who operated the library cart. It was during those "better times" that Bub learned how to heat water by taking two pieces of wire from the edge of his mattress and taping them to opposite sides of a piece of wood. He'd carefully place the other end of the wires into a power outlet while the wood was submerged in water and voila! That was called a stinger, and Bub realized it was just one of the nifty tricks that inmates learned while trying to make the jail feel like home.

Six weeks passed before Darla, Robbie, and Barry came to visit Bub. Other than his parents, they were the only people who'd bothered to visit him! Still, it was a great relief to him, since he had a lot of stories he wanted to tell them. He started with the chili episode and how he worried that he, too, might get duped while adding, "The inmates told me that the cooks screwed the raw chicken meat!" Then he told them that the summer temperature inside the jail had been in the upper nineties with high humidity, and how his bed sheets always turned yellow from his sweat penetrating through to the filthy, stinky old mattress. Those terrible conditions had caused a riot one night, when the inmates got so hot, they raised hell on purpose, just to get the fire department in there to hose them down! He said it was a terrifying experience but, once it was over, "the temperature in the place had dropped a good ten degrees, and it didn't stink quite as bad."

The three captivated listeners experienced mix emotions while listening to Bub's stories. They finally concluded their visit by telling him that he needed to straighten up and stay away from jail! Of course, that was a forgone conclusion to Bub, and he told them so. The question remained "How could Bub do it?" but that only evoked a myriad of answers that he'd already tried. Just before they left, Bub asked them if any of his old friends had asked about his whereabouts, and the answer was no.

One evening, shortly after that visit, the jail guards were performing their lockdown procedures when Bub stuck his head outside of his cell to ask the guard if he could see a doctor. He felt as if he was going to have the stomach flu, but he hadn't thrown up, and his pain was getting worse. To his sudden surprise, he was jerked backward just in time to keep his head from getting crushed by the heavy weight of the mechanical slide-door. After thanking his cell-mate, he paced back and forth in their tiny cell, late into the night. All the while, he was doubled over and groaning with intense pain.

"Shut the fuck up," everyone began yelling, and soon a guard appeared who echoed their sentiments.

"There's no one you can see until the morning, so shut the fuck up!"

As morning came, Bub was still in intense pain. The guard who came to open the cells had apparently taken turnover from the night shift, because he immediately called for "Kellow" to "come forward." It was just as well, because one of the inmates had promised to punch Bub in the stomach, so he would "throw up and shut up!"

"Let's go, Kellow," the guard ordered, "you're going down to the infirmary."

Once Bub was in the infirmary, the doctor examined him and noticed that he looked a bit jaundiced.

"Lay flat on your back and touch one toe to the ground," he ordered, which Bub did.

"Okay, let's take some blood samples," he said, and he stuck Bub with a large needle and withdrew two vials of blood. Then he told Bub that he thought it might have been an attack of appendicitis, but if it had been, Bub wouldn't have been able to put his toe on the ground.

Bub objected. "It might very well be appendicitis, because it hurt like hell when I tried to follow your orders!"

Still, the doctor scoffed and returned him to his cell.

During the next twenty-two hours, Bub hunched over in agony while rocking back and forth in his bunk. The cellmates, who'd long lost their patience, still threatened to punch him in the stomach, so he promised to be silent. After that, he forced himself to handle the pain throughout the day and night without so much as a peep!

The following morning, a jail guard and a state trooper entered the cellblock, ordering Bub to come with them right away. As it turned out, his white count was off the charts, and he was being chauffeured to the local hospital. As the trooper gunned his cruiser and wailed his siren, Bub appreciated his concern and commitment to duty. After conveying that to the trooper, he told him that it was the first time he'd ridden in a cop car without being handcuffed!

The operation to remove Bub's appendix was done immediately after his arrival. After the usual miserable post-op recovery period, he finally got some sleep and awoke to the bliss of a strong painkiller, fresh-cut flowers, and smiling faces. While his physical condition was still bleak, his mental status had taken a tremendous turn for the better. To him, his nurse looked like Marilyn Monroe, and the hospital food tasted like cuisine. He had his own remote-controlled nineteen-inch TV, and he had a *Reader's Digest* as he sat on a toilet that actually had a seat on it. In addition to those contrasting amenities, his sixth-floor room was clean and sterile, and it had large windows that offered him a grand view of the Capital Beltway and beyond. Only his immediate family was able to visit him, since he was considered a criminal, but that meant he had the room to himself. For those reasons, it seemed as though Bub had gone from hell to heaven, and he dreaded the thought of going back to jail.

When Bub's parents came to visit him, his dad relayed the latest news. He told Bub that his most-recent DUI had been handled in his absence, and the lawyer managed to get the charge reduced to reckless driving. While Bub didn't exactly figure that to be great news, his father suddenly became sullen as he told Bub that a long-time friend of his, from Falls Church, had apparently overdosed and died. His name was Frankie, and he was the young kid who'd gotten busted on that warm summer night for swimming naked in the community pool. He was a good friend who had often made Bub laugh, so he was devastated!

As Bub would later learn, the Peat-Moss Gang had thrown a huge party after some of them had successfully burglarized a pharmacy. To celebrate, they rented two connecting hotel rooms, where they whooped it up on pharmaceuticals and booze.

Evidently the pills that were passed around proved to be fatal for Frankie, who, after drinking, had vomited and choked in his sleep. Out of all his friends, Bub had found Frankie to be one of the most genuine, warm, and loving people whom he had ever met, and now he wondered, *Why him!*

For Bub, Frankie's death, along with his own bleak circumstances, caused him to dwell on the sadness of wasted lives. Now that he'd been sober for some time, he was thinking clearly once again and realizing the importance of breaking away from his past and starting anew. *If only I could leave this area*, he thought. With that in mind, he knew his life had become a major dilemma, because his love for fun and alcohol made it extremely difficult to change within the confines of his old stomping grounds. While he wanted desperately to become the man whom his mother hoped him to be, he knew familiar streets and faces would surely plant the seeds that would cause him to stumble. Then he considered his lack of will power as he thought, *Even as I lie in this hospital bed, I'm yearning for the taste of a nice cold beer! How am ever going to overcome this tremendous urge without the continued support and watchful eye of someone who will love and understand me!"*

Realizing his thoughts had run in the same old circle, he now felt that familiar crushing sense of hopelessness. That made him wonder how he could ever escape his seemingly endless and futile quest. Once again, he realized that changing his ways would require a deep desire and a sharp focus on the minute details of his thought processes. *I'll have to continue to educate myself, in order to identify, understand, and respect the better nature within me.* While his inner child was still whining, *Shit—that'll be the day*, he knew another, more intelligent voice was becoming stronger.

When Bub went back to jail, he was relieved that he'd been assigned to a first-floor cellblock. According to what the guard previously had told him, he figured that meant he would soon appear in court and learn of his pending fate. During that period he was in the company of a more civilized crowd, and he made some friends. Together, they would attend Mass on Saturday nights, just to get out of their cellblock. They also shared stories, watched TV, and played gin rummy and poker for cigarettes. Oftentimes, they sang songs, such as "Another Saturday Night" and "I Shot the Sheriff," which were current hits at the time.

One day an old friend of Bub's was escorted past his cellblock. It was a young man who, once handsome and bristling with confidence, had gotten his face blown off by a shotgun-wielding man in a drug deal gone bad. Bub tried to call out to say hi to him, but the man's mind was too preoccupied with his present fate and called out for Jesus to save him. As his old friend was escorted upstairs, Bub could hear other inmates whistling, screaming, and howling about his grotesque appearance. Bub later learned his friend had gotten strung out on cocaine and alcohol, and that led Bub to believe the sudden withdrawal had no doubt had a profound effect on him.

Bub spent two weeks on the first floor before he was called to court. As he stood in front of the judge, he realized it was the same judge who had presided over his original case. The judge peered over his glasses at Bub and cleared his throat.

"Jail is not the place to be, is it, Mr. Kellow?"

"No, Your Honor," Bub said sheepishly.

It seemed to Bub that the good judge had not only been informed about his attack of appendicitis but also was aware of the sordid conditions of incarceration. At the same time, the judge tagged one year on to Bub's probation before declaring him released as of the following Sunday morning. Bub bowed his head, as stress flowed out of his shoulders. He thanked the judge, with his hands held in prayer, before leaving the court room in shackles but smiling. Once he was back in his cell, his cellmates congratulated him, but when a trustee passed by his cell and learned of his good news, he simply shrugged his shoulders and said, "You'll be back!"

When Sunday came, Bub was released at 6:00 a.m. sharp. No one in his family had been informed of his disposition, so no one was there to pick him up. That was fine with him, though, because all he wanted to do was walk and smell the sweet Virginia air! The morning sun was shining brightly, and, feeling like a free man, he couldn't recall feeling any better than he did at that particular moment.

* * *

Although Bub was try to avoid the agony of his past, he was eager to look up his old friends. He wanted to find out more about his dearly departed friend, Frankie, while wanting to share his recent exploits. At the same time, he wanted to understand why no one bothered to visit him in jail. As he soon discovered, no one was willing to talk to him about Frankie, or the pharmacy heist, since they still feared he might be a narc. As far as Bub's recent exploits went—no one seemed to care.

After learning Bub was back on the streets, some of his favorite Peat-Moss Gang friends treated him with caution, while others went so far as to threaten him. That misunderstanding of his character and hardships affected him, overshadowing his recent desire to forget about his old friends and his past. As a result he developed more spite while experiencing feelings of self-pity. As a strong urge to suppress those feelings returned, he started to drink alone. As he sunk back into his former state of depression, he thought, *I'll just have to keep a low profile and bide my time. Hopefully, I can stay out of trouble until I'm done with my probation, and then I'll boogie on out to California.*

After about six weeks of drinking, Bub decided to walk up to a bar in McLean one night. His yellow Mustang had since been sold to pay his debts, and he was feeling like a wayward bum. Once he arrived, he noticed some of his old friends down at the other end of the bar. As the night rolled on, he was invited to play darts with them, and all seemed fine, but as they had more to drink, one of them became belligerent. His name was Lonny, and he was a "program" junkie who had acquired had a chronic liver disease. Still, he was drinking hard liquor, and Bub told him that seemed like sure suicide. Lonny was incredulous that he was being reproached by the likes of Bub, so his anger grew as he started yelling out to everyone in the bar that Bub was a narc. Well, Bub figured that the party was over, so he got up and left the bar, with Lonny chasing after him to fight. Luckily for all, some of Lonny's friends followed behind him, and, when they got outside, they held him back. Bub apologized to them all and thanked them for having been his friend. Then he turned and walked away with the intention of never seeing them again.

While walking home, he stopped at a fast-food restaurant and got in line to order. As he read the overhead menu, three teenagers in front of him started to mutter curse words in his direction. Bub, who'd simply had enough bullshit for one night, told them to watch their mouths, but the young men acted as if they didn't hear him. Their antics continued, until finally Bub raised his voice and said, "Shut the hell up, or I'll kick all of your asses right now!"

Just then a security guard nudged Bub from the rear to get him to calm down. Bub told him to butt out, and that's when all hell broke loose. The security guard quickly reached around the front of Bub's face and sprayed his eyes with mace. Bub reacted by going after him like a blind man having a panic attack, but, as he chased after the guard, all he could find was heavy, cast-iron tables and chairs to throw around. While running short of breath, he finally gave up and found a chair, whereupon he calmly sat down and covered his swollen eyes.

The police quickly arrived and arrested him, and one officer remained behind to take a report. As Bub was booked and led to a drunk-tank cell, he learned that the teenagers' cursing had actually been directed at the security guard and not at him. Still, the damage was done, since the security guard had pressed charges for being drunk in public and disorderly conduct.

Bub was scheduled to appear in court a week later, after having been sprung by his dad once again. While taking the bus on his way to court, he remembered the words of the jail trustee: *"You'll be back!"*

With that grim prophecy rolling around in his head, Bub decided to tie one on at the Vienna Inn before his scheduled appearance. As he drank, he wondered if he shouldn't just make a run for it and rejoin his Colorado friends. Then he said, "Screw it," as he realized the thought of such a sudden flight seemed like a futile and absurd fantasy. Indeed, Bub was nearly broke, and so was his spirit as he paid his tab and left the bar to go face his grim and uncertain fate.

When his name was called, the security guard was nowhere to be found. That made the judge mad, and he cited the security guard for contempt of court. He'd been drooling over Bub's thick rap sheet, and after seeing that it became obvious to Bub that the judge didn't want to let him go free. Nevertheless, without the accuser to testify in person, the judge had no choice, so he banged his gavel and shook his head, declaring, "Case dismissed." That was music to Bub's ears, and he was all smiles as he quickly left the courtroom with a kick in his step.

7. HELLO, AA!

In January of 1976, Bub turned twenty-three years old. He was avoiding the use of all but two drugs: alcohol and pot. He wasn't nearly as reckless as before, but, since he was still in the grip of uncontrolled passions, he was still prone to get in trouble. Therefore, his self-esteem remained low, even though he'd acquired a decent computer job, and his driving privilege was restored. He bought an old, beat-up Mustang, and he was using it to get to Georgetown. The disco scene was hot there, and that's where he searched for the female companionship he so desperately needed. Of course, Bub was still shy and nervous around women, and he was finding it hard to conceal his depression. He felt like he needed to get revved up with a few stiff drinks to get loose and break the ice. Although that worked, and he landed some one-night stands, it wasn't long before he was arrested for driving while intoxicated.

That was Bub's third DUI, and his probation officer was stunned! Still, she was steadfastly determined to root out Bub's behavioral disorders. Since he was arrested in her county this time, his name was flagged on her computer terminal, so she quickly had him held in detention. Alas, Bub was certain that he was on his way to the penitentiary this time. In fact, she had ordered him moved to solitary confinement, were his mind raced with thoughts of total despair. His isolation seemed like an eternity while he was suffering from a hangover, and, to make matters worse, he had nothing to read or smoke. As he lay on his back and stared at the ceiling, his mental state was bad, and as he thought of a dark future loomed in his mind, he just wanted to die.

After a couple of days, a peaceful-looking gentleman with a mustache came to visit him, along with his probation officer. As Bub stood on the other side of his jail door, his probation officer gestured toward the man.

"This here is Sam, and he runs a halfway house for alcoholics. We think—no; we *are sure* that we know what your problem is."

Bub instantly knew where this was going, and boy, was he relieved!

So, "yes … yes ... yes," was all that came out of his mouth, and, after a firm handshake, he soon found himself being driven to a farm for alcoholics, somewhere in the beautiful Virginia countryside.

The main lodge house was just like something you'd see in the movies. Except for the shower/toilet area, it consisted of one huge room finished with knotty pine and a vaulted ceiling that rose high above the axe-carved trusses. The room was lined with bunks set perpendicular to the wall, and there was a common area out in the middle for eating, reading, or just plain socializing. The compound also included a cook house, a chapel, counselor offices, and a large maintenance garage.

After orientation, Bub took long walks, ate satisfying meals, and attended regular AA meetings, where he learned the Serenity Prayer and twelve-step process for recovery. He also learned that he must let go of his ego and let his "Higher Power" take control of his life. *Hey, why not,* Bub thought. Even though he'd already come to that conclusion, he was eager to be further enlightened by the wise old men who ran the place, and he was also happy to come in contact with others who suffered from his affliction. He figured that, through them, he might finally be able to conquer his desire for the drug that was the cause of all his problems.

During his stay Bub had plenty of time for reflection. He found a tattered paperback about ancient Greek philosophy, which included a chapter on Socrates, who once stated, "The unexamined life is not worth living for a human being." He also, found a book on psychiatry which he found to be very interesting. Aside from Bub's reading, which included *One Flew Over the Cuckoo's Nest*, he shared his wild stories with other alcoholics while listening to theirs. He also volunteered to help build another outbuilding, and in doing so he learned the proper use of wood tools. All those experiences calmed his spirit and gave him a sense of purpose, and since he realized that he was feeding his "better side," he hoped for the best.

After a week had passed, he received some more bad news from home. His old friend, Joey, had overdosed on "Mexican mud," leaving his grieving parents childless. That caused Bub to stew as he reflected on the various musical groups that had glorified the use of drugs in their lyrics. Joey had grooved on the blues and honky-tonk that made it seem cool to get strung out, and while that only seemed natural to Bub, he wondered, *"Natural" for what? What purpose did his life serve?* Then he scowled as he though, *I wish Joey had been busted, too! Oh, yeah—I wish to God!* That led him to wonder, *Why me? Why am I alive? What's the purpose of my life, and why aren't I with Frankie and Joey, and all the others who have gone—who knows where?*

The counselors were very impressed by Bub's steady progress, since he was exuding a healthy state of mind and humbling himself to their way of thinking. Bub had told them everything they wanted to hear while quoting the Big Book and the Bible, so, as far as they were concerned, he appeared to have his head screwed on straight. He was also the youngest man there, so they treated him as if he were their son. They felt that his grasp of his own dilemma, combined with his willingness to help others, had earned him a spot at the lecture podium, where he would address the new arrivals. As Bub rose to the challenge, he often spoke of the truth of his condition, but, as he gravitated toward his memories of good times, he began to sense skepticism in the eyes of some of the newbies. Perhaps his ability to deceive himself was duly noted by the intuition of others, he concluded. After all, he'd been there only a short while, and, with his better health, he was exuding more passion. Nevertheless, his counselors were impressed and felt that Bub was ready to rejoin the ranks of society.

During the long ride to his new residence at the halfway house in Arlington, Bub meditated on the root cause of his self-destructive nature. His deep thoughts took him all the way back to his adolescence. In his earliest years, he recalled being greatly affected by the natural reactions caused by his peculiar names, since they had been the focal point for his classmates' taunts. Then he thought about the nuns who had called him a doubting Thomas. *Where have the reactions to those experiences taken me? Was it all meant to be? Certainly there must be a reason and purpose for living—to think otherwise would be absolutely absurd!*

While those elements of profound thought boggled Bub's brain, they were a result of the philosophy he'd digested while at the farm. Now he was seriously contemplating them in his search for a greater truth that might cure his suffering. As for his initial definition of truth, he'd read about epistemology and finally concluded that empiricism would be his divining rod. *God only knows how much I've experimented!* he'd thought while making that determination. While he'd read that there were great debates regarding the definition of truth over the centuries, they seemed trite to him, since everyone is so different. His newly formulated theory for establishing his *own* truth was a combination of logic and common sense when applied to his observation of natural phenomenon and their reasonable causes. He figured that if he became baffled by one of life's mysteries, he would simply try to use an analogy as a means to figure it out.

As the van continued down the highway, Bub wondered, *What's in store for me next? The Jekyll-and-Hyde thing they discussed during the AA meetings seems simple enough to describe the changes in a personality, but, they didn't mention Harris's theory of a trichotomy in which the mind observes and analyzes the brain.* After further considering that theory and thinking about the psychiatry book he'd read, Bub figured his intuition was the voice of his subconscious and that it was telling him to changing his brain's cyclical patterns of thought behavior. He thought about Freud's theory that also explained how the mind can be divided into three parts: the id, the ego, and the superego. That made him think about Freud's interpretation of the superego, whose moral concepts conflict with the basic instinctual desires of the id. *That battle of two opposing forces of thought seems like it's meant to be,* Bub thought. *Nevertheless, I agree with Carl Jung that the superego is our soul, which is a part of the collective unconscious of all human experience. I also think that it's a lack of love and understanding that's driving my emotions, and not sex.* Of course Bub desperately wanted to get out of his mess, but all of those profound thoughts were driving him nuts! Therefore, he deferred to the notion that maintaining his focus on the pain that drinking had caused him, one day at a time, would lead him to overlay his bad memories with new and better experiences. As Bub dwelled on the simplicity of that notion, the transport van pulled up in front of the halfway house, and he was ordered to get out and go check in.

* * *

In May of 1976, a judge ordered Bub's license suspended for one year, while showing leniency for his willingness to participate in the AA program. That being the result of his drunk driving, he was forced to either take the bus, hitchhike, or ride his newly acquired and formerly owned ten-speed bicycle. Although the spring weather was certainly a factor, he preferred to ride the bike. It was a long ride to his computer job near Tysons Corner, but he slowly came to appreciate the effect it was having on his coordination and strength. He had a few bad experiences, such as the day he was run off the road by some rednecks, but since he was sober and in a new frame of mind, he could handle situations like that without losing his cool. After being at the halfway house for two months, he felt as though he'd finally attained total control of his passions. That is when he asked permission to take his roommate, Billy, with him on an overnight trip to Ocean City, Maryland.

"Don't worry," Bub told his counselor. "I've got my drinking under control, and I'll be sure to keep a watchful eye on Billy."

"Okay," his counselor responded, "but you know what'll happen to either one of you if you slip up! Just remember that, and stick with coffee or soda, okay?"

Upon receiving his counselor's blessing, Bub called his probation officer and humbly asked for permission to go. He explained that he would be a passenger, along with two girls and Billy, and that one of the girls would be driving. He also told her the address that they'd be staying at, which was an upper duplex that the driver's boyfriend had rented. Finally, he told her that they were all straight shooters, trying to assure her that nothing bad would happen. Although his probation officer was leery, she figured that the trip sounded harmless enough, so, in light of his truthfulness and continued sobriety, she let him go.

The outset of the trip reminded Bub of *One Flew Over the Cuckoo's Nest*, since he and Billy were like two nutcases that were rendezvousing with two free-spirited girls. The girl driving the car, whose name was Wanda, was the girlfriend of one of Bub's old river pals, named Dave. The other girl, whose name was Amy, had formerly expressed an attraction to Bub. However, just as many girls who had known him, she was cautious. As they rambled on toward Ocean City, Bub nodded to Billy as they enjoyed drinking some cold beer. Meanwhile, he did a good job of pacing himself, but he wasn't counting the beers Billy was consuming. When they stopped at a restaurant, Bub was concerned because Billy wouldn't eat, but he also realized that was par for the course for many alcoholics. When they finally arrived at his friend's place, they partied until they went to sleep, around two in the morning.

Unfortunately, Billy soiled his underpants during the early-morning hours, and, after an unsightly accident in the bathroom, he got kicked out of the duplex. As Billy explained it, "I was taking off my undies, and my big toe got stuck in the damned waistband. I started to lose my balance, so I tugged at the sons-of-bitches, and they flung dung everywhere!" To make matters worse, Billy had tried to clean up some of it, but he did a poor job in the process. That pissed off Dave, who had discovered the mess before kicking Billy out into the cool night air, and, Bub and Amy went outside to console him.

After Billy blamed Bub for his own unsightly transgression, he climbed into the backseat of their car to crash. That left Bub and Amy with little to do, so they strolled along the empty boardwalk before finding a bench that was facing the ocean. The trip had been an unexpected experience for Bub, and now he had time to reflect upon his present conditions.

A new guilt welled up inside Bub, as he realized his friend was right. That made him distraught, and he barely noticed Amy, who was leaning on his shoulder while watching the sun rise. Instead, he dwelled on the fact that he'd led Billy astray by trying to convince him that he could control his drinking. When he'd told Billy that the word *alcoholic* was nothing more than a word, that was actually "the alcohol talking," and now he realized that. It was in sharp contrast to his AA speeches, where he'd divulged the root causes of his deep addiction and how they always haunted him. He'd made perfect sense to all who listened and won the trust and admiration of those—including his friend—who also struggled to overcome their nightmares. So now Bub's dream of partying and making love to the girl by his side resulted in his new surge of guilt, fear, and depression.

On the way back from Ocean City, the group was eerily silent. Once again, Bub's mind was focused on solving his drinking problem. He figured that he'd learned from AA and the philosophy he'd read, but while that'd made him a little more intelligent, he realized he was slow to become wiser. Even though he'd managed to stay clean for two months, he was still at odds with his recurring transgressions, and that made him think. *It's the same old shit! Every time I get to feeling strong, I feel too good! In fact, I feel like a caged animal right now, and there's nothing I can do about it! Raising hell while drinking is what I love, since it's a part of my personality, but getting myself into another damned state of worry and depression is pure hell, and it's getting to where I can't stand myself. What a damned paradox that is!*

As Bub continued to dwell on his problem, he figured he'd milked AA for all it was worth. His counselors told him that he'd have to attend meetings all his life, but whenever he thought about going every day, he also thought, *Forget about it!* The meetings had become redundant, and he felt he wasn't getting all the stimulation he needed to escape his dilemma. While a lot of the newbies and "retreads" had interesting personalities, some of them seemed, to Bub, as if they'd been lobotomized. They surrendered their egos, he figured. Then there were "the weirdoes," as Bub put it. One guy invited Bub to his home, and, without any warning, he tried to kiss him. On another occasion, a guy became agitated while telling Bub that he was damned to spend eternity in hell! That occurred after Bub refused to partake in a religious ritual to be reborn, and therefore he seemed unwilling to be saved.

The last recollection caused Bub think about Jesus, who said, "And ye shall know the truth, and the truth shall make you free." That made Bub think about the probability and necessity of being physically reborn, because he didn't believe that all people were capable of attaining enlightenment in one lifetime. That made him wonder, *Was the fact that they took reincarnation out of the New Testament because people behaved like me? I'll bet they wouldn't have removed it if they'd walked a mile in my shoes! After all, who wants to be reborn and experience this shit again. Maybe the notion of reincarnation was seen as a threat to the churches power, while using fear of hell as a motivator to keep the people in line. Shit! Fear seems to steer me straight whenever I think about going to prison!* After chuckling, Bub thought about some of his Christian peat-moss friends. Since their behavior was just as bad, or worse than his, he figured that religion, alone, wasn't saving them either.

By the time they reached the halfway house, Bub had made amends with his sad friend. He had convinced Billy they needed their bad experience, just to see the error of their ways. After that, they made a pact to keep silent about their weird little trip while agreeing to start a new period of uninterrupted sobriety.

*　　*　　*

With the end of his probationary period in sight, Bub began to read books that expounded on the proper use of thought while avoiding alcohol and drugs. Meanwhile he'd been allowed to leave the halfway house, and now he was back at his parents' home, in McLean. Prior to that he had started working part-time for a moving company, so he was looking strong and fit. He was glad about that, because he wanted to make a good impression on the judge during his final hearing.

After four years of probation, Bub went to have his final court hearing. He'd been sober for several months, and he was fortunate to have some fine character witnesses testify on his behalf. Even his probation officer gave him a thumbs-up before the hearing. Her big hug seemed to further indicate all would go well. The same wise judge conducted the hearing, and he must have also figured that Bub was worth saving. He gave Bub a quick smile and a wink just before declaring, "Case dismissed!" All those involved made a big impression on Bub that day. In the midst of his efforts to change for the better, he hoped to "keep on truckin'!"

A short while later, Bub got his driving privileges restored. Since he'd enjoyed riding his bicycle, he decided to buy a tried but true 1965 Honda 305cc Super Hawk motorcycle. Although it was considered to be a beginner bike, he thought it was a blast to drive. He also thought it was ugly and so was the white half-helmet that came with it. Nevertheless, they were his, and the motorcycle was cheap to insure.

One day he had decided to drive his motorcycle to lunch, and a police officer walked out ahead him and waved him to the side of the road. As Bub pulled over, he realized he had been caught in a radar trap. As the cop wrote him a ticket, another cop began to examine Bub's bike as well as Bub himself. He started to chuckle and when Bub asked him what was so funny, the cop looked at the other cop, and they both burst into laughter.

"Here's your ticket, Rid-*dick*," the county cop said, waiting for a reaction.

Such a blatant show of disrespect usually caused Bub to come unglued and maybe get arrested, but this time he slowly smiled as he carefully folded the ticket and put it away. He was calm because he'd just finished reading a book that expounded on the tendency of people to take things personally while failing to realize that the offenders would show the same disrespect toward most anyone who was unfortunate enough to come their way. To that effect, he realized that any display of frustration would only cause the cops to increase their agitation while justifying their actions. He figured that their attitudes would eventually cause dire circumstances, and he hoped that the outcome of those circumstances would teach them one, or more, of life's all-important lessons. Therefore, he continued to smile as he kicked his little motor bike into gear and sputtered away.

In the fall of 1976, Bub traded in his little Super Hawk for a new 1977 Yamaha 650 Special. He had previously purchased subscriptions to two motorcycle magazines, and both had written glowing reviews on the bike. It was styled after, and tested against, the popular Triumph, which also had a vertical twin-cylinder design. Since the Yamaha beat the Triumph in every category, including the retail price, Bub was proud to own one. He drove the bike whenever he could, and he enjoyed maintaining it and keeping it spotless. Since the Yamaha had a tool kit under the hinged seat, Bub took delight in setting the valve clearance, adjusting the cam-chain tension, and doing other maintenance. He was so happy with his new "joy ride," he'd always take a moment to admire it before slipping on the factory cover.

While Bub was staying sober, he focused on his perceptions of society and thought further about his notion of rejectionism. After recollecting some of his childhood experiences, he realized that he'd always stood firm in his own perception of God while facing opposition from those who either had blind faith or who couldn't care less. He figured that it was a combination of that, plus others' adverse reactions to his peculiarities, that had caused him to develop a self-defeating complex. He thought of his early adolescence, when he'd developed spite toward those who failed to understand and bully him. At first he'd stood proud to be who he was, but, as his family moved from one place to the next, the monotony of having to defend himself became arduous. That's why he'd changed his game plan when his family had moved to Vienna, Virginia. In an effort to fit in with the "cool kids," he did what was necessary to win their favor. As smart as Bub thought he was being in doing that, he now realized that he'd unwittingly created a personality who was not in alignment with his true nature. To make matters worse, he realized he had developed a series of sub-personalities, so he could relate to different types of people. Although a good shrink could have explained that to Bub some time ago, his books pertaining to the human will and psyche were beginning to open his eyes.

After reaching those conclusions, Bub better understood the causes of his present dilemma. In regard to sub-personalities and putting on airs, he realized that people could see that he was less than genuine. That was enough to make them cautious—they sensed that he had some type of problem. He also understood that the shame and effort of having to adjust his personality caused him to gravitate toward using drugs and alcohol. That made his problem only more complex, as he used those crutches to cope with his confusion, loneliness, and despair. Of course, he knew he had other reasons for taking drugs. Other than just plain liking them, he was introverted because he was always preoccupied by the way in which his mind worked. Bub realized how rejectionism had effected his actions, which had formed habits that were deeply engrained in his character. Still, the question of how long it would take to eradicate them and become a better person remained.

As Bub remained steadfast in his desire to change, the overload of too many self-revelations began to take its toll. He'd learned a lot about himself while reading, but eventually he started to get bored while thinking he was becoming insane. In the AA meetings, they discussed the importance of setting the ego aside, but he'd always been reluctant to do that since he thought it added color to his character. Now he was becoming aware that his ego was taking a pounding, so he decided curb his profound thoughts and give his mind a rest.

*　*　*

After the first snowfall and with the holiday season fast approaching, Bub began to succumb to his old behavioral patterns associated with festivity and cheer. That tendency was something that he hadn't anticipated, but, as usual, he thought he might have his problem under control. He knew that "sinking to the level of the beast" meant that he'd quit reading his self-help books, but, at the same time, he tried to reason through the use of an analogy. *I guess this higher-power thing is going to take longer than I expected. It's as if I were a crooked tree, and, in my attempt to straighten myself, I pulled too hard and broke the damned rope! Oh well! No one really gives a damn, other than my family, and besides—I can always reattach the rope, if I have to.*

By the time the summer of '77 rolled around, Bub had made friends with two men who had motorcycles. Oftentimes they'd take long rides through the Virginia countryside while stopping at bars along the way. That summer was hot, and the pavement was steaming, so the cold beer they drank went down easy. All the while, Bub was trying to pace himself by smoking some pot, since he figured it would reduce the amount of beer he needed to get a good buzz. During that time, he'd laugh whenever he thought about his old AA meetings and mottos, such as: "It's the first beer that gets you drunk." His "better side"— the angel that he'd once imagined as a little boy—knew those mottos were true, but now he was choosing to side with his devil, and ignore them.

A girl passed through Bub's life during that time. Her name was Angela and she'd come between a married couple whom he considered to be among the best of his friends. Angela was being persistent with her affections toward the husband, so Bub quickly befriended her. Of course, he had mixed intentions, and some made him feel less than honorable. After all, Angela was only eighteen, and—with her big, brown eyes and long, dark, silky hair—she was a cutie! So, even though Bub wanted to save his friends' relationship, he was just as interested in having some fun while putting an end to his constant loneliness. However, Angela was smart, and since she couldn't take her mind off of Bub's good friend, she used Bub to learn more about him. As her ploy became apparent to Bub, he felt foolish at his getting caught up in his own game. As time went on, he gave winning her mind one more shot before realizing he was wasting his time. Finally, he drifted away from her, and in his solitude he felt bad, as he wondered what his friends thought about him. After all, he'd never shared his plan with them, and, since it hadn't worked anyway, his good friends were now separated.

After that relationship Bub landed a job as an accounting clerk in a retirement trust division of a large worker's union. There was a pretty blonde who worked in the cubical next to his, and he grew fond of her. Even though he knew that he needed a good woman, Bub still became terribly nervous and shy around the type of women he really wanted. Therefore, it took some time, but he finally got the nerve to ask her out. He was surprised when she simply said "Sure," and now his hopes were soaring.

He took her to a nice dinner, and then he asked he where she wanted to go. She suggested that watching TV at her place would be fine, and that's when Bub's hopes soared higher. As they drove to her home, he thought, *This is it! If she returns my feelings of love, I'm prepared to make a commitment that just might save my soul!* Just as they got to her townhouse, her telephone rang, and she took it in the other room then talked at length. After the call, she apologized for the interruption and told Bub that her caller was a Vietnam Veteran who was a friend of her brother. She said that he was suffering from PTSD, and, since she'd recently comforted him, he was getting sweet on her. When Bub asked her if her feelings were mutual, she deliberated for a brief moment, and then she nodded. Having gauged Bub's involuntary facial expressions, she told him it would probably be best if he left, before she "raped him." That brought about a moment of awkward silence. Even though Bub knew her joke was well intended, he was caught off guard and speechless. Knowing that she could see he was hurt, while feeling anger toward his bad luck, he simply said, "Okay," and then he left.

Soon after that night, his former "dream girl" got promoted to regional director. Bub was stunned when he realized that she would be his boss! While he was happy for her, he knew that working closely together would be an awkward situation for them both. After all, even though he was still infatuated with her, he'd shown pangs of rejection, and reaction had since left her to wonder about his attitude.

Just as Bub had figured, it wasn't too long before she drew her own conclusions and became perturbed. Even though he was trying to be more friendly, he finally realized that their relationship had spiraled out of control. He subsequently quit his job after landing a second-shift computer operating job, deep in the heart of Washington, DC.

*   *   *

As the summer of 1977 gave way to fall, and the cold winds began to blow, Bub figured that a new plan was at hand for getting to work. He scoured the classified ads and bought a 1966 Caprice Classic. It was silver with a black top, and it had a warm, nylon-stitched interior. The V-8 was smooth, and it had an AM/FM radio with a front and rear speaker, and power windows, brakes, and steering. He'd negotiated with the original owner and gotten a great deal, so he was happy with his new "winter joyride."

Bub worked alone on the seventh floor of his building on Pennsylvania Avenue. During the night he'd routinely finish the daily processes before starting the lengthy backup process. After that, he always had a great deal of free time to read and work puzzles. Once in a while, he'd peer through an office window to gaze upon the empty streets and a haunting view of the Old Executive Building. Since he could also see the north lawn of the White House, he'd usually look there, and sometimes it appeared as if the Secret Service agents were surveying the place while catching a smoke. Occasionally after work he would stop at a bar that was on his way home. He didn't have too much time, since it closed at 2:00 a.m., but he thought he might get lucky someday and find a girlfriend. As he would discover, though, most of the bars were frequented by college girls who were cautious when it came to "the loners," whose only intentions might be a one-night stand.

On one particular night, Bub had a question regarding month-end processing, so he called his boss at home. It was late, and the big man sounded as if he were very drunk while Bub was describing the problem to him. As his boss became confused, he also became very belligerent, and finally, he told Bub to, "figure it out for your damned self!" Well, Bub did figure it out, and at the end of the processing routine, all the numbers balanced. The following day, Bub apologized to his boss for bothering him, but the manager was apparently so drunk that he had "no recollection of a phone call, whatsoever." That led Bub to realize just how stressful life was for people who usually appeared to be normal, and that made him happy that he wasn't the only one with deep personal problems.

It was soon after that little incident that Bub received some more bad news. The younger sister of an older junkie friend had died from a drug overdose. Her name was Alice and she was the kind of girl who always greeted everyone with a warm, sweet smile. If it wasn't for the fact that she was already dating one of her brother's acquaintances, Bub would have asked her to hang out, but as he was quickly learning, things are meant to be the way they happen.

As the winter of '77 gave way to the wet spring of '78, Bub was still resorting to the warmth and comfort of his old Chevy. Since his job was normally a simple routine he'd occasionally run down to the liquor store and buy a pint of hard Whenever he did that, the liquor would fill his senses and cause him to stop by the same-old bar after work. After all, he was lonely, and he figured that something was bound to happen!

8. A DREAM BEFITTING BUB

It was during that same wet spring that something did happen. After striking out again, at the same-old bar on M Street, Bub was driving home through Arlington just after 2:00 a.m. His foot was always heavy on the accelerator when he'd been drinking, and, as he made a right turn, his rear tire started to spin. To his dismay, the familiar red light of a police car suddenly appeared in his rearview mirror. As he yanked back on his steering wheel, he cursed in utter frustration. He was all too familiar with the drill that he was about to go through, and he knew he'd wind up losing his license again.

After his sad, sympathetic, and bewildered father sprang him from the hoosegow, Bub immediately sold his car. With the proceeds, he instantly paid his father back for the bail money and banked the rest for the retention of a good lawyer. He figured he'd have to ride his motorcycle from McLean to DC, rain or shine, but that was the least of his worries.

The following day Robbie gave him the name of a good traffic lawyer, so Bub decided to ride his motorcycle to the attorney's office. It was a gorgeous spring morning, and he felt that he couldn't ride far enough to satisfy his frustrations. He gunned the bike from a stop light, and it accelerated so fast that he had trouble loosening his grip to shift into second gear. As he quickly hit third gear, the power surge shot tingles through his body and put a grin on his face. As he raced through the remaining two gears, he dwelled on the irony of having received a ticket for speeding on his old Super Hawk. He also thought that his emotional state while riding the bike scared him, but, since it was counteracting his grief, he never wanted to let it go.

The lawyer was just emerging from his BMW when Bub arrived at the parking lot of his firm.

"Boy, I liked that bike!" he told Bub.

Then he stared at the bike long enough to give Bub the impression that his fee was going to make a down payment on one just like it. After all, Bub's former attorney had once told him that he had scored a new set of golf clubs as a result of Bub's probation violation. So, after unstrapping his helmet, Bub introduced himself without a smile, and then they went into the lawyer's office.

The lawyer continually snorted and adjusted his tie as Bub gave him the details of "the night in question." Meanwhile, Bub noticed that the man never took his eyes off of his desk. When Bub was through, the lawyer finally perked up and looked up while clearing his throat. Then he mentioned the matter of a healthy retainer, as if expecting Bub to object. That made Bub think, *If he expects me to object, he hasn't seen my rap sheet yet.* Indeed, Bub knew all too well the high costs involved in these matters, and, although he was resentful, he didn't flinch. After writing a personal check, he left the lawyer's office, never to see him again.

In the days that followed, Bub discussed his misfortune with his friends and family. It was their opinion that, since it was his fourth DUI, the judge would undoubtedly throw the book at him. That meant that there would probably be a huge fine and perhaps some jail time. Then there was the probability of his having to attend more AA meetings. Of course, those discussions only brought about more anxiety, as Bub thought, *Dear god! When will my nightmare end! I was doing so well, but then I fucked up again! Now I guess I'm stuck just in a never-ending cycle of getting sober then getting drunk. Damn! I reckon I'll just keep on drinking until I die!"*

The thought of impending doom at the hands of an angry judge proved too much for Bub. He loved his new bike, and he didn't want to miss out on a summer of riding it. *I'll just have to leave the state and start anew,* he quickly concluded. He realized that conclusion was the result of his desperation, but he rationalized that it made perfect sense. Bub had been wanting to get away from everybody and everything that reminded him of who he was, and now he realized that the time had finally come. After getting busted in Colorado, he learned that prior driving offenses didn't matter if they had occurred in states that didn't have reciprocity. That made him swoon as he thought his trip to California was likely meant to be. He also thought about his sister Jessie, who lived just outside San Diego, and then he remembered that his uncle James lived there, too. That made him feel even better, and he was excited as he thought, *Hey, I'd be riding to San*

Diego on my motorcycle! I heard the weather is wonderful and— far out, wow, and hell yes! Then he thought about the rides that he and his friends had taken to the mountains. *That would definitely be the trip to end all trips! Damn! I wonder how many miles it is?*

Bub knew that switching environments had played a large part in his behavior, and, as he thought about California, he started dreaming again. *Once I get there, I might find love, once and for all, and who knows! Maybe that'll be a good reason to settle down and finally develop a purpose in life. And at least no one way out there will know about my past!*

Bub thought he had to keep his plan totally to himself, because someone might tell his mom. She loved him dearly, and he figured she'd do anything to keep him out of harm's way—*especially something as crazy as this*, he thought. He knew his mother had done her best to raise him properly while trying to steer him toward a good education. Up to this point, he'd let her down, but now he felt that the trip might save his soul and finally make her proud of him.

On the following Friday, Bub awoke with a lump in his throat and a queasy feeling in his stomach, as he thought, *Today, it's do or die; California or bust!* As he scoured his room and selected clothes for the trip, he also packed a cheap plastic rain suit, in case of soggy weather. Then he gathered his toiletries and crammed everything into an old crumpled and mildewed Boy Scout backpack that he had worn back in the early sixties. Finally, just before he left for work, he snuck out the back door to hide his backpack under his motorcycle tarp. Then he went back into the house to give his mom a huge hug and a big kiss on the cheek.

"Good-bye," he said, while trying to act normal. "I'm off to work!"

His mom looked at him with a mother's intuition of suspicion, because he was acting peculiar. She noticed he seemed to have the same mannerisms that she'd seen before he was about do something strange!

"You be careful, boy," she said rather sadly, and then she watched him leave.

Bub was filled with trepidation but firm resolve. He felt like he was in dire need of a drink to calm his nerves, but he knew that was out of the question. As he drove his motorcycle toward DC, he was stricken with the irony and the reality of what was he was doing. *I'm riding toward Pennsylvania Avenue and then Pennsylvania, the state. Wow, man—is this crazy, or what!*

When Bub arrived at work, he parked on the wide sidewalk in front of his building, and then he made his way to the elevator. As it took him to the seventh floor, he thought about the job he was about to quit. *I'm going to miss this job. It's simple, but it also has potential. I've only had two people to deal with, and besides that— where else am I going to run into George McGovern, like I did the other day? Ha! Oh, well.*

He made his way into the computer room to discuss the nightly shift turnover, as planned, and he collected his paycheck. Since he was early for work, he excused himself to run down to his first-floor bank to cash his check. After he cashed the check, he headed straight for his motorcycle, and, with his wrinkly backpack still strapped on, Bub was on his way.

It was June of 1978, and since it was 4:30 p.m., rush hour flowed at its usual snail's pace. Bub had chosen to get to San Diego by way of St. Louis, because that way was more familiar to him. He took Pennsylvania Avenue to M Street, and, as he rode through Georgetown, the eerie memories of his past caused chills to run up and down his spine. He glanced at the fateful fire escape, on which he'd once sought refuge. Then he surveyed all the bars in which he'd blown his paychecks. As he continued to roll along, he saw the long stairway where they'd filmed a scene for *The Exorcist*. That made him think of the time when he and his friends had sat upon the high concrete arch that traversed that stairway. *We were fucked up that night, and we could've easily killed ourselves,* he thought while shaking his head. As he rolled on faster, he was glad to be done with those days and getting as far away from those memories as he possibly could.

Faces of his family and friends ran wildly through his mind as he passed the Chain Bridge, but by the time he hit the Capital Beltway, he was all business. From there he slowly made his way to I-270 North, and as he rode the traffic thinned out, and the sun sank lower in the sky. *This is it,* he thought with a lump still in his throat. *There's no turning back now!* As he climbed the Allegheny Mountains, the sun disappeared behind the treetops. The rushing air became colder, and his muscles began to ache from the tension he felt. "Hard ride ahead," he said aloud, just to hear his own voice.

Bub rode until midnight, before stopping in Washington, Pennsylvania, to check into a room for the night. His nerves were frazzled, and his butt was numb, after the hard 240-mile ride. As he got off of his bike and stretched, he thought about the sanity of what he was doing. *Frickin' Pennsylvania is a long damn state, and it's colder than a well digger's ass up here in the mountains. Hmm—Washington, DC, to Washington, P.A. Jiminy Christmas— that's just too much irony for one day.*

It was a strange feeling for him to check into a motel room all by himself, because it was something that he'd never done. Even though he was twenty-five years old and used to feeling alone, the thought of riding so far by himself gave him the willies. He'd always lived with his parents, or very close to them, but now he realized he was going to put more distance between them than he had fully anticipated.

When Bub got settled in his motel room, he called his parents. Then he became apprehensive, as he waited for the operator to announce the collect call to his mother.

"Where did the operator say you are, Riddick?" she finally asked, in her usual Australian accent.

"Washington, Pennsylvania," Bub answered with a wavering voice.

"What on earth are you doing there?" His mother's tone indicated to Bub that she was very alarmed. After telling her straight-out that he'd quit his job and was on his way to California, his mother pleaded with him to stop and head straight back in the morning. His dad had picked up an extension phone and was listening in. After clearing his throat to announce his presence, he agreed that since Riddick had walked out on his job, he'd better just keep going.

Bub quickly agreed with his father's grim assessment, and he tried to convince his mom that this was just what he needed in order to get a fresh start. His mom was temporarily stunned and confused, but as she recalled him constantly talking about his desire to change and his need to get away, she finally agreed. Bub was relieved, because she was the one person who he felt he needed to comfort the most. When he was just a toddler, she'd taken him to the countryside, where he would lay on the grass and watch the clouds swirl, as she painted. She was also an accomplished pianist and literary scholar, so her music and poems had often filled his mind. She used to take him to St. Paul, Minnesota, where she turned in her commercial art to a large department store before taking him to the eye doctor. During those times, she'd often tell him he had a good, strong name, and that someday he would make his mark. As a result of those fond recollections, Bub felt a great sense of separation and melancholy when he bid his parents farewell that night, but that feeling subsided as he thought about his new adventure, and he finally went to sleep.

On the second day of his journey, Bub woke up an hour before sunrise. Then he went to the restaurant next door, where he filled himself with pancakes, bacon, and coffee before quickly hitting the road. The morning air was crisp and cool, as the early morning sun laid his long shadow before him. He was feeling a lot better now, since the jig was up, and he felt confident since he thought he was doing the right thing.

As morning turned to afternoon, he began to pass his shadow, and his muscles ached once again as he rode steadily along. As he approached the outskirts of Indianapolis, Indiana, the sky became a weird shade of grayish-purple mixed with shades of green. The air became noticeably cooler, too. As highway litter began to swirl through the air, big gusts of wind threatened to blow him in the ditch, so he carefully made his way to the side of the road as large rain drops began pelting him. As he scrambled to put on his badly wrinkled rain suit, another hard gust of wind tore it from his fingertips and sent it flying across the busy interstate. As he crouched down beside his motorcycle, he was dumbfounded and embarrassed. To his relief, a Good Samaritan in a VW bus pulled over and beckoned him to climb inside. As the two men watched torrents of rain dance in the wind gusts, they talked about the turbulent spring weather and the recent Indianapolis 500, which Al Unser Sr., had won. By the time the storm had passed, Bub had nearly related his entire life story to the bewildered bus owner, who finally wished him, "Good luck!"

As Bub continued to ride far that day, he stopped only to fuel and eat. Meanwhile he avoided his strong desire for a brewski, knowing that it would lead to more than one and impede his progress. Finally, he saw the sun set in Illinois, but since he was determined to make it to Saint Louis, aka "The Gateway to the West," he pressed on. When he finally got as far as Granite City, Illinois, he became so weary that he was forced to take an exit and rest. At the end of the exit ramp, he spotted the St. Louis International Speedway, and the place was hopping! He pulled in and found their restaurant, which was located right beside the quarter-mile racetrack starting-line. *How cool is this!* he thought to himself.

Bub spent the next hour sitting on his numbed butt while eating a cheeseburger and drinking a cold draught beer. As he did, he watched drivers heat up their tires and launch from the starting line. Finally, after asking the fellow behind the counter for directions to Interstate 44, he took a brief walk to get his blood flowing. Then he forced himself to continue his journey.

Bub got himself a tour of St. Louis that night, because he missed his exit and continued straight ahead. After realizing his mistake, he finally got steered in the right direction. By that time he was worn to a frazzle, so he stopped at a motel in Fenton, Missouri.

While waiting to check in, a young woman standing in front of him was visibly upset. He could only guess that some man had done her wrong, and, since she looked as lonely as he did, he wanted to hug her. Of course, Bub was shy, and since he wasn't inclined to pry, he didn't ask her what was wrong.

After entering his room, Bub immediately drew the hottest bath water he could tolerate. While the tub was filling, he ran out to buy a cold six-pack of beer. Upon returning to the room, he turned on *Saturday Night Live* and slipped into the bathtub with his beer close at hand. Three beers and a couple of cigarettes later, he climbed out of the tub and went to bed. As the thought about his long, hard day, he fell fast asleep, and his mind raced with wild dreams until he awoke the following day.

Day number three was sunny, and Bub was feeling great. There was hardly a whisper of wind, and he was halfway to California—or so he thought. He'd only glanced at his dad's road atlas while studying the long highway route, and since St. Louis was near the center crease of the atlas, he thought he was doing well. Unfortunately, Bub was high when he'd looked at the map, and since he was so excited, he forgot to look up the overall mileage of the trip!

As Bub, feeling like he was on vacation, whisked along in his ignorant bliss, the scenery quickly changed. Big layers of milk-colored sandstone were now visible where the interstate sliced through hills, and the view of the landscape brought a welcome relief from the boring flatland of the central plains. *So this is the why they call it the gateway to the west,* he marveled. As he continued to study the rugged and beautiful foothills of the Ozark Mountains, he passed some billboards urging him to see the XXX adult shops and a cave that was said to be one of the James-Younger Gang's hideouts. Bub figured that represented a shift to the spirit of the west, and that called for a celebration. Since he had three beers in his backpack, he decided to pull into a rest stop to indulge.

As Bub already knew, drinking would only slow him down, but he figured he was making good progress, so he spent a lot of time pulling over to drink, smoke, and urinate. As a result, he became disappointed when he reached Joplin, Missouri, because he was already intoxicated and too weary to drive any further. Still, he reasoned that he'd done okay, since he'd put in a hard ride the previous day, so he checked into a cheap motel.

As Bub found his room, he noticed a motorcycle that was parked out in front of the room beside his. It was a badass chopper, so he figured that the owner must a badass too. After being disappointed by the hard bed, he turned on the television. As he flipped through the channels, he found nothing to watch except for programs about religion or farming and fishing conditions. Then he wondered, *What the hell is this all that about? I haven't even seen one lake around this damned place!* He looked out a window, and that's when he realized that he'd wasted a good amount of sunlight. That made him angry and frustrated over his lack of self-control, and he moped as he drank his last two beers. After that, he ran out of cigarettes, and he thought about how his beautiful day had turned ugly.

The next morning Bub was awakened by the abrupt and loud sound of a deep rumble. As he fumbled to turn the alarm clock his way, he realized that the noise he was hearing was coming from the chopper outside. *It's just as well,* Bub thought. *That guy probably has his act together, and I should be shaking a tail-feather too.* He didn't get a decent night's rest on the cheap mattress, and his head was still aching from the beer. Although he knew he could've benefited from a hot shower, he just wanted to get moving.

As he returned his key to the front desk, he glanced at a map of their motel chain across the United States. It was only then that he discovered how far he had to go. He was shocked as he exclaimed, "Holy shit! St. Louis looks like it's only a third of the way!"

That aroused the groggy clerk, who suddenly appeared from a back room.

"May I help you, sir?" the man asked.

Bub, looking perturbed, turned to face the clerk.

"Yeah," Bub said, "you can help me. You can start by burning this damned joint to the ground! My bed sucked, mister!"

*   *   *

The Oklahoma turnpike was beautiful, but it didn't seem to have the same convenient exits as Missouri. Bub kept seeing signs that warned Do Not Drive into Smoke. *What smoke?* he wondered. As the day wore on, he rode hard, but the only things that had caught his attention were two big-city cow towns and odd little oil pumps that were bobbing up and down. In his cynical nature, he couldn't figure out what excited him the most! About thirty miles west of "OK City," Bub thought, *I've just got to get a damn beer.* He stopped at a store, where the clerk told him they didn't sell beer. He explained that many of the counties in Oklahoma were either dry, or they just sold 3.2-percent beer. That made Bub anxious, as he realized he couldn't buy any full-strength beer until he reached the Texas panhandle. As he pressed on, he thought, *For God's sake—how stupid is that!* Of course, the upside to that letdown was the fact that he rode harder and farther than he would have otherwise.

The flat Texas panhandle was strangely beautiful to Bub, now that the sun had sunk beneath the horizon. The clear night sky was brilliant with thousands of stars, and it seemed he could see forever. Freight trains and the lights of towns to the far north made him wonder, and he wished that he could share his visions with all of those he'd ever loved. By the time he got to Amarillo, the town was a welcome sight after riding through the dusty wind. His limbs were sore, and his mouth was dry, so he bought some beer. As he guzzled a quart of joy-juice, he stuffed a six-pack of beer into his backpack, and then he went to find a place to put down for the night.

After securing a cheap motel room, Bub threw himself onto the bed and marveled upon his current destination. He'd heard that drinking in Texas was nearly mandatory, and now that he'd just put five hundred miles behind him, he was glad to be there. As the cold beer quickly became a friend to his dire loneliness, he began to remember the good times back home—not the good times with his so-called friends but those spent with his brother. He thought about their camping adventures down by the river at night and all the times they'd spent working together on their cars. *My brother should have seen the Texas panhandle tonight,* he thought, as he drifted off to sleep.

Day number five felt like it was going to be a hot one as Bub realized that he'd gotten sunburned the day before. His tank-top shirt had offered little protection, so now he had a serious case of sunburn. Of course, that wasn't his only discomfort. He also had a serious case of raw, sore, and numb ass! As the prickly heat of the sunshine indicated a hot day ahead, Bub didn't want to find himself in another dry county, so he stuffed his backpack with another six-pack of beer.

As Bub neared the border of New Mexico, he looked to the south. There he saw higher elevations that appeared as one huge mesa, with steep rims that gave way to a sunken desert floor. In the coral desert sand, which appeared to be an ancient sea bed, he could see teal and green cactus-like shrubbery. Bub figured that undoubtedly attributed to the sign that read, Welcome to New Mexico—The Land of Enchantment. That had made him happy, since he knew he was only two states away from California.

The look of the "real" west made him feel as if he was in Old Mexico. Those thoughts moved him, so he started to sing songs such as "Laredo" and "El Paso." As he did, his heart connected with the romance of US western history.

After pulling into a rest stop, Bub was drinking a beer, when he met a trucker who lent him an empathetic ear. Bub told him of his plight and explained that he was getting sick of the doldrums of interstate travel. The trucker suggested that he drop down south and pick up US-60 west, through Roswell. Going that way, he would eventually come to Interstate-10, at Las Cruces. Taking a road off the beaten path sounded great to Bub. He was getting tired of the turbulence and dust of big rigs all day. So, after thanking the trucker, he soon found himself grooving down the little two-lane highway.

The experience of traveling on the hilly highway was at first a fun and refreshing change. He thought it was nice to be heading deeper into the southwest, so he started singing "Well, I'm going out west where I belong...." It was a song called "California Sun," by The Rivieras, and it had long been one of his favorites. After some time, though, Bub began to realize the pitfalls of back-road travel. The towns, if one could describe them as such, were few and far between, and the scenery was becoming repetitious. At the same time, the midday sun was making the blacktop highway scorching hot. As he rode over a high hill, he suddenly spotted a welcome sight. There was a little red adobe cantina on the desert floor, and it looked busy.

The dirt parking lot was jammed with sunbaked cars and trucks, and he couldn't figure out where they'd all come from. As he surveyed the surrounding valley, it looked quiet, hot, and empty, except for the usual scrub, tumbleweed, and rocks. After stretching his sore, burned limbs, he stepped inside, and instantly the cool air of the smoky bar sent a chill up his spine.

Thick cigarette smoke swirled through the bright sunlight of the open door, until if finally slammed shut, and Bub found it hard to see. Sun-wrinkled eye sockets winced under straw hats, as patrons tried to make out the weird stranger who was carrying a backpack. Bub found a stool at the end of the bar, whereupon he ordered a cold draught beer as he sized the place up. Country music was playing, but not the kind he'd heard back east. This music was hardcore country-western outlaw, interspersed with an occasional Mexican or trucker-type song. The people were a mix of white, brown, and red, and there was nothing eastern about them.

Bub wanted to connect with someone's eyes, so he could initiate a conversation and tell them all about his perilous journey. No one was looking at his, so he thought, *I don't appear to be a government agent or a jealous husband, so I guess no one gives a shit!* The first beer Bub drank tasted like liquid gold, and, as he lit up a smoke, he slapped a quarter down on the closest pool table. To him, that seemed a sure way to introduce himself to someone without offending their manhood.

When his turn came, Bub tried to own the table. He'd spent countless hours in his friend's basements and at various bars while honing his pool skills, so his confidence level was high. Of course, there were other good shooters, as well, but that just made his pleasure in winning seem sweeter. Just as he was taking aim to sink the eight-ball and collect his one-dollar bet, a dark-skinned woman suddenly grabbed the cue ball and ran out the door!

Bub and a number of other people quickly followed. Then they witnessed a violent confrontation that was spurned by a jealous rage. The dark-skinned woman hurled the cue ball with deadly accuracy, and it bounced off some guy's bald noggin while he was flirting with another woman in the parking lot. Then she ran up to him while screaming and flailing her arms. As the bewildered man struggled to grab her around the waist, he lost his balance, and they both tumbled to the ground. As the melee continued, the man finally gained control of her arms, and, when the woman quit struggling, she began to cry profusely. Just like that, the two began kissing each other passionately. "Get a room!" someone shouted from over Bub's shoulder, and, as he looked behind him to smile, he discovered that everyone else was already returning the bar. Seeing that, Bub silently retrieved the cue ball while making every effort not to interrupt the couple's passionate embrace. Then he went into the bar, where he finally claimed his one-dollar bet.

It wasn't long before Bub realized that he was late for the road. He was frustrated, because it was often the case that, when he drank, time and money seemed to just slip away. Before mounting his blistering-hot saddle, he bought a six-pack to go. The afternoon sun was still blazing high in the sky, and, while he wanted to stop for the day, he knew he had to keep on moving. As he rode along the hot asphalt, he realized that the desert air wasn't cooling him down, and the heat from his little engine was not helping either! At the same time, the beer he'd drunk was coursing through his veins, so he drove like a madman, passing any vehicles that got in his way. His little motorcycle wasn't a cruiser by any stretch, but in his altered state, while zinging along at eighty miles per hour, Bub didn't care! He figured that if he didn't push it hard while in his present condition, he'd never get there.

As he'd pass cars, Bub envied the people who were in them. They were often laughing and smiling with one another in their air-conditioned cabs. They weren't hot! Their backs and butts weren't sore! Their shoulders didn't ache! They were all snug and comfy while heading somewhere—close to their homes, he figured. As those forlorn thoughts gave way to the desire for another beer, he'd stop to satisfy his craving, only to see the vehicles that he'd passed roll on by.

At sunset, he finally hooked up with Interstate 10, at Las Cruces, New Mexico. As he continued to head west, a car with four people pulled alongside him. As he looked their way, they leaned out of the car windows while holding beers, giving him thumbs up and howling party chants. Bub decided to stay behind them for a while, and, when they exited the interstate at the next rest stop, so did he.

The people were glad to stretch, and so was Bub. They told him that they were from Georgia, and now they were heading to Los Angeles, where they hoped to stay. There were two women and two men, about two years younger than Bub, and sure enough, they had a cooler full of ice-cold beer. They offered Bub one, which he was only too glad to accept, and then they exchanged some stories about their trip. They were eager listeners, as Bub told them about his hard ride, and at his conclusion they expressed amazement and admiration for the desperado on his bike.

After Bub had drunk a couple of their beers, he told them that it was time to ramble. Then the driver of the car showed Bub his motorcycle license and begged him to let him ride his bike, while saying Bub could drive his car. *Well, shit—what the hell,* Bub thought. He was in need of a rest, and he was pretty drunk by now, so he was happy and foolish enough to oblige.

As Bub cruised their big Chrysler at 75 mph, he paid little attention to his motorcycle, which was behind him now. Instead, he was just happy to party and flirt with the girl who sat beside him. Meanwhile, somebody had rolled a joint, and, since Bub was drunk *and* stoned, he lost all track of time. He drove for a long while, and then the guy in the backseat suddenly shouted above the volume of the loud music. "Hey, man—he's back there flashing the headlight, and I'm thinking he wants us to pull over!"

Bub quickly agreed, and, as he wondered what the problem was, he pulled over to the side of the road.

The driver got off Bub's motorcycle, and he looked angry as he stomped toward the car.

"What's the big idea, man! You were driving so fast, I could barely keep up! Couldn't you hear me honking!"

Bub was in his Mister Hyde mode, so he figured that the sourpuss had merely got a good dose of what it's like to be a highway star.

"No, I couldn't—just relax, man! You're the one who wanted to play Easy Rider, and now you know what it's like!"

Of course, that didn't smooth things over. As the men continued to argue, one of the girls got out of the car, while saying that she wanted to ride with Bub for a while.

Bub welcomed her interruption and said that he didn't mind, but the driver strongly objected. Bub didn't care one way or the other, so grabbed his backpack from the car and headed toward his motorcycle. As he strapped on his helmet, Bub noticed the driver whispering something into the woman's ear before telling Bub that he'd changed his mind.

"It's okay if you give my girlfriend a ride, but I want you to pull over within the next ten miles.

"Hey! No problemo, man," Bub responded.

Since it was just the end of a new-moon phase, it was very dark. As usual, the desert air had turned chilly, so, as they rode along, it felt good for Bub to have a young woman pressing against him. That was a feeling that he seldom experienced, and it was causing him to dream once again of a lasting female relationship. It wasn't long, though, before Bub thought, *Either this woman is reading my mind and fondling my ass, or she's trying to steal my damned wallet!* Bub went to feel for his wallet and sure enough— he found her fingers trying to work it out. He quickly pulled to the side of the road and quickly ordered the woman to get off his bike.

As she hopped off the motorcycle and handed Bub his gear, there was no need for good-byes. Bub put on his backpack as fast as he could, and then he latched his spare helmet to the bike while anticipating a fast getaway. Just as he'd finished, the car pulled up behind them. As the men jumped out and ran toward him, Bub leaned forward while revving the engine, and then he popped the clutch. As the rear wheel of the bike hit the pavement with a high-pitched squeal, Bub could hear pebbles and sand hitting the front of their car. As he revved through the gears, he tried to contemplate his next move. He figured that the top end of his bike would be no match for their big old Chrysler, so he'd have to try to ditch out of sight, and fast! *But where?* he wondered. As the highway curved to the right, he suddenly went under an overpass, so he slammed on the brakes, and, with his back tire burning up beside him, he let off the pedal and darted out onto the desert floor. As he quickly turned off his lights and killed his engine, he waited in silence. It wasn't more than ten seconds before his pursuers sped by, and they were flying! The engine of the Chrysler was whining and popping as he watched them go far down the road. Once the taillights on the car had disappeared, Bub eased his tensed shoulders and breathed a sigh of relief. "That car runs badass, but it sure could use a damned tune-up!" He chuckled.

As Bub peered around in the dark desert air, he couldn't see anything but the brilliance of the planets and stars above. It seemed eerily quiet as he wondered what kind of creatures lived in such a place. Because he was drunk, stoned, and extremely tired by now, all he wanted to do was find a place to sleep. He didn't want to ramble on, lest he catch up with his new enemies, so he decided to give the desert floor a try. *Hell—they show them doing it in a lot of the old westerns, so why not,* he surmised.

No sooner than Bub had fashioned his backpack into a pillow while trying to get comfortable, he realized something was crawling up his legs, arms, back, and neck. He quickly lit his cigarette lighter and saw that they were fire ants. "*Shit!*" he yelled. "These little bastards have got teeth!" After doing what appeared to be a hodge-podge of the Mexican hat dance, the hokey-pokey, and the boogaloo, he quickly gathered up his stuff, hopped onto his motorcycle, and sped away.

Without any other recourse, Bub resolved to continue riding, until he could find a motel. The exits were few and far between, and they all led to roads with service stations, but they were closed. As he rode along, he never thought anyone could fall asleep on a motorcycle, but after what seemed like an eternity, he began to feel as if he was going to black out with his eyes wide open. Then he sang songs, slapped his helmet, pinched his legs, and did everything else he could think of to avoid crashing. Finally he came upon an adobe motel that looked just like the one he'd seen on a 1950's Route 66 postcard. It appeared to be dirty and old, and Bub figured that it had to be one of the fleabag motels that he'd always detested. Nevertheless, he was just happy to see a sign out front that flickered *Vacancy*.

The parking lot was dark and empty, and the place was eerily silent. After Bub knocked on the office door, he saw a bent-over old man appear from a back room. As he checked in, Bub asked the man where the closest town was. The man smiled and told Bub that he was close to Benson, Arizona, which is about twenty miles shy of Tucson.

Upon Bub's entering his smelly room, his hunch proved to be correct. *Fleas or not, this place is a godsend,* he thought. He knew it was well after midnight, but he was too tired to care. As he flopped down on a deformed mattress, he summed up his day before passing out. *This has been one of the longest and strangest days of my life. With all of my drinking—I was as reckless and shameful as I've ever been. Damn!*

On the sixth day of his long journey, Bub awoke to the buzzing of a fly that finally landed on his parched lips. To say that he had a hangover would definitely be an understatement. At first, he didn't know where he was, but he was certain that he was in hell. The sun had already heated his smelly little room, and the intruding light made everything look worse than it had the night before. Soaked in sweat, Bub rushed and stumbled toward the bathroom; he didn't know if he was starved for food, or if he was going to vomit. Never before in his life had he felt so much physical pain mixed with mental anguish and despair. As he leaned his weight against the rusty sink, his dry mouth was foul, and his tongue was nearly stuck to the roof of his mouth. He rubbed his tongue along the back of teeth, which felt as if they were one. As he bent down to drink the flowing tap water, he noticed that it was yellow. His head felt as if it had been hit hard with a baseball bat as he recoiled. Then he slowly looked up to the mirror to examine his aching, baggy eyes. He painfully observed that they were unusually bloodshot, and now they were stinging from the sweat of his stubbly and oily face. He noticed that his hair was greasy and flat, except for the ends, which had curled out as a result of the wind against his helmet. As he splashed the same foul water on his face, his throat and chest felt irritated and tight from too many cigarettes. While realizing that he was in desperate need of a shower, he turned around to examine the shower stall. The plastic curtain was stiff and moldy, and the stall looked worse than the one he'd used in the county jail. Then he noticed a small bar of used soap that was infested with somebody's pubic hair. That caused him to shrug as he remembered that all his clothes were filthy and smelly, and, since he'd left his shampoo and toothbrush in Texas, Bub said, "Screw it, man!" He stumbled to find his pants, so he could count what little money he had left. That's when he realized that he was out of cigarettes and beer. As he straightened out some crumpled one-dollar bills a greater sense of despair welled up inside of him. He slumped to the edge of the lumpy bed, and his dismay and confusion led him to thoughts of suicide. The flies still pestered him, and, as he became increasingly agitated, he looked around the room for something to do the job. As he rose to examine a curtain cord, the reality of what he was doing suddenly scared him, so Bub frantically pulled on his pants and grabbed his stuff before running outside into the fresh and cooler morning air.

Having escaped from the dismal effects of the filthy room, Bub's thoughts of suicide slowly diminished. He found it extremely hard to get on his bike, so he just sat on the curb and rocked back and forth with his head between his knees. His nerves were shattered from the hard ride and the binge drinking of the previous days, and, since he had no change to call anybody, his spirit was crushed.

"Who would I call anyway, and why would they be surprised or even concerned?" He scowled.

Then he thought about his motel room again and how it related to the occult books he'd read. It seemed that the motel room had been tailor-made to match his present condition, so in essence, he'd become an essential part of it. *The law of attraction*, he murmured. Then he wondered how many other kindred spirits had found themselves there, and as that reminded him that he wasn't the only person who has suffered, his thoughts finally shifted to the day ahead.

Bub figured he had at least four hundred more miles to go, and last thing he wanted to do was to get back on that bike. At the same time, in his present state of mind, he knew he couldn't spend another night on the road alone. On top of that, he miscalculated the time and money that it would take to make the long trip, so now he was nearly broke.

With a sudden urge to find a store, Bub finally got off his butt and mounted his dirty motorcycle. He rode to a little single-pump gas station where he fueled up and bought some coffee, a doughnut, and a pack of smokes. Although he was still hungry, he wanted to save the rest of his money for fuel, and—"medicine."

With a late start and with a bad head, Bub rode on and on, and all he saw was the great Arizona desert, shortly eclipsed by the city of Tucson. It was another hot sunny day, and the scenery was boring, except for some large cactuses, the shapes of which amused him. All the while, he kept dreaming that the next vehicle coming his way would be his sister in a pickup truck, coming to rescue his weary soul. Of course, he realized it was just a dream, but it helped him to keep himself together.

After Bub got on Interstate 8 and arrived at Gila Bend, he bought a cold quart of beer to relax his nerves and keep him straight in the saddle. At this stage of the trip, it was purely medicinal, indeed, as it helped in maintaining his equilibrium. As he continued along his way, he figured the temperature to be about one hundred degrees. The dry wind parched his lips, and, after what seemed like an eternity, he found himself entering Yuma, Arizona. Luckily for him, his motorcycle was thrifty on gas, because he was nearly starved by now, and he desperately needed another beer.

Bub sat in the shade of a billboard while satisfying his needs. He was sweaty and hot, and he believed the fellow in the store who'd told him that Yuma was the hottest place in the United States! With that in mind, the vision of palm trees swaying in a cool Pacific breeze gave Bub the urge to carry on.

The mighty Colorado River looked more like a lost and confused little stream as Bub crossed the border into California, and he wondered why. As he rolled on, he expected to find lush date palms, orange groves, and wine vineyards, but all he saw were more sand and rocks. He came upon some sand dunes that were nearly as white as snow and wondered, *What in the hell!* As he began the ascent up and over the In-Ko-Pah mountain range, the vegetation remained extremely sparse among smooth and light-colored boulders. They looked to Bub as if they might come crashing down on him at any moment. As he continued to climb one big hill after another, trees began to appear, and the air grew cooler and smelled sweeter. It was then that Interstate 8 seemed like a nice ride for a motorcyclist, and Bub saw a road sign, which indicated that he was coming ever-closer to El Cajon. *Yeah!* Bub thought. *El Cajon! That's the town Jessie said she lives by—hot damn!*

As Bub rode on and on, he was extremely tired, but the beautiful mountain air was filling his senses. Then he noticed that he was going down, out of the mountains, and finally he passed under a sign that read, El Cajon—Santee Exits—1 Mile. "*Yahoo!* I'm going to make it," Bub yelled. He figured he was never so happy to reach the end of a trip in all of his twisted life! He thought, *If approaching the end of my life is similar, dying won't be so bad, after all!*

Bub took the exit and looked for a good place to stop. Ah yes, there it was—a bar on Main Street. Once inside, he ordered a draught beer, and then he headed straight for the pay telephone to call his sister.

Jessie sounded glad to hear that Bub had made it, but it was just his dumb luck that she was heading out the door with some friends to embark on an excursion to Encinitas, Mexico!

"Do you want to come along?" she asked. "If not, I'm sure Bill will come and get you."

Bill was a former resident of McLean who now worked for Bub's uncle. He was Jessie's ex-boyfriend and the reason she had moved to San Diego in the first place. Although Jessie and Bill had since split up, they still enjoyed an amicable relationship while enjoying the San Diego area.

Well, there was no way that Bub was going on any excursion trips south of the border! So, after considering the way that he felt and the fact that he was nearly broke, he decided to take his chances with Bill. He called Bill, who apparently knew he was coming, and agreed to come and get him.

Now that Bub was happy that someone was coming to rescue him, he bellied up to the bar while he waited. As he looked up at the television set, he noticed that the Washington Bullets and the Seattle Supersonics were playing in the final seconds of game seven in the 1978 NBA championship. When the game was over, Washington had won, and Bub erupted with applause while feeling a chill up his spine for all his friends back east. Meanwhile, the rest of the patrons at the bar gazed at him like he was some drunken, filthy bum, who had no doubt lost his freaking mind! That was okay by him, though, since most of them had been loudly rooting for the Supersonics.

About an hour later, Bill entered the bar and smiled. "Gee whiz, Bub! You look like shit!"

"Well, what the hell did you expect!" Bub exclaimed, and their mutual laughter followed.

Bub admitted that was filthier than he had ever been, and he made it clear to Bill that he was mentally broken, too. In consideration of that, Bill offered to ride Bub's motorcycle if he followed him in his truck. That was a tremendous relief to Bub, who gladly accepted his generous offer.

When they arrived at La Jolla, Bub discovered that Bill's apartment was perched high and overlooking the ocean. Since a girl who lived beneath Bill was having a party, Bill suggested that they go down for an introduction and a drink, to which Bub responded immediately. "You've got to be kidding me—*right?*"

No, Bill wasn't kidding, and, since Bub had no other recourse, he followed Bill into the girl's apartment. He could only figure that Bill wanted to show them this dumb freak who had just embarked on a 2,680-mile motorcycle ride, without any clue of what he was going to do when he got there!

As they walked into the girl's apartment, all the people hushed as they stared at Bub with trepidation and disgust. Therefore, it seemed to Bub that they must have known he was coming too! As Bill explained to them what an incredibly desperate thing Bub had just done, he went on to tell them who Bub was, describing some of the details of Bub's crazy past. Finally, Bill concluded by saying that Bub would be his temporary keeper, until he could find something useful to do with himself.

At the outset of that introduction, Bub was very embarrassed, but, as he listened to Bill describe him, he began to accept his fate, so he grabbed a beer from a cooler. He didn't know whose it was, but he figured he was thirsty all the same. As the attentive crowd watched him, he opened the beer and raised it as a toast, just as Bill was reaching his conclusion. After chugging the entire contents of the can, he twisted and squashed it flat while letting out a long and obnoxious belch. *Perfect,* Bub thought. *Here I've come all this way to get a fresh start, and I'm already infamous!*

As soon as that show was over, everyone resumed their chit-chat, whereupon Bub finally got to use Bill's shower. It wasn't the reception he had hoped for, since he wanted to leave his past behind, but now that the cat was out of the bag, he realized he'd likely remain the same old Bub. As he showered and prepared to crash, he also realized that he could never evade his past or wash away his guilt, so, with the crumbling of his California dream, he was getting more depressed. He thought, *I can't blame Bill for what he did. Shit! I probably would have done same thing, had the situation been reversed. Damn! I should have called Jessie to let her know I'm trying to change my ways!* Yes, indeed! Bub should have paved the way for the metamorphosis of his character, and he realized that now. Since Bill was unaware that was Bub's goal, he had no idea of Bub's sincere desire to change. Therefore, Bill had figured that Bub would remain the hell raiser that he'd been in the past.

As Bub dwelled on the further complexities of his shortcomings, he thought about his lack of self-knowledge. The trip had certainly been harder and lonelier than he'd anticipated, and that'd made his "only friend," beer, hard to ignore! So, now that he'd started on a binge, and everybody knew his business, he worried that he'd likely remain the way he was—just as Bill had figured. *After all,* he thought. *I'm in "America's Finest City," and it's known for its wild fun and festivities.*

9. THE LONESOME DRIFTER

Bub lived with Bill for the next couple of months. As he applied for jobs as "Riddick," he had trouble getting back into the computer field. Since he was new to town, and he couldn't use his last job as a reference, he created an aura of suspicion. He didn't have any decent clothes to wear to interviews, anyway, so he finally gave up and went to work for his uncle James.

James was his father's brother, and as brothers often go, they were not alike. Where Bub's father had always been the slow and steady turtle, as depicted in the cartoon, James was a risk-taker. Therefore, he had experienced many ups and downs, and for that reason, he figured he might be more in tune with the wild and impetuous nature of Bub. Although Bub had only met his uncle on a couple of occasions, James conveyed a fun-loving attitude that always made Bub feel at ease.

James owned and supervised a condominium construction project, and he put Bub to work painting. When his uncle had first met with Bub, he applauded him for leaving the East Coast for the purpose of self-healing. After that, he encouraged him to change his "damned nickname." "I'm James," he declared, so Bub figured he couldn't use his middle name. Instead, he became "Rick," since James pointed out that it coincided with "Riddick." While he could have chosen any name, that seemed okay to Bub. He realized that for all who would come to know him through those he presently knew, he would always be "Bub," anyway.

Bub had to sell his Yamaha, because he couldn't afford the payments along with food, utilities, and rent. That was a bad time for him, because he loved that bike just the same as if it were a loyal dog. He liked to joke that he had ridden the damn thing so much that it had literally become a part of his ass. In reality, though, it had become an extension of his character, and now he felt as if a piece of his identity had suddenly died.

After a couple of months had passed, Bill's brother also decided to venture west to California, whereupon Bub was "bumped" out of his room. He thought about living with his sister, but, since her apartment was too small, he decided to camp out in one of his uncle's unfinished condos. That was convenient for him, because it was closer to Jessie's apartment, and he didn't have to wake up early to catch a ride with Bill to work.

As Bub continued to work for his uncle, he was lonely while experiencing a lot of freedom. Of course, he was glad to have a steady job, but the nights were long, and he needed companionship. As Bub walked to neighborhood bars after work, he closely identified with the current Foreigner hits, "Double Vision" and "At War with the World." Then the day came when his uncle arrived at work early and saw that Bub had picked up a one-night stand. As Bub and the woman were emerging from his condo unit, his uncle's face registered his disgust. After the woman left, James tried to make him feel ashamed. That caused an argument, as Bub strongly defended his right to privacy, adding that, as an adult, he should be granted some leeway. While he understood his uncle was merely acting in his best interests, Bub simply said, "Sorry, James! I'm just not able to achieve sainthood, yet!" That flippant remark showed Bub's level of frustration. He'd listened to his uncle, who was remorseful for his past, since he used to be a lot like Bub. James had also turned away from the Catholic faith, but since he'd returned, and it was working for him, he figured Bub should do the same. Not wanting to debate religion, Bub finally agreed that finding a new place to live and work would be the best solution to their disagreements. Of course his uncle was sad, but he stood firm while shaking Bub's hand and heartily wishing him good luck.

Jessie's girlfriends had already became fond of Bub, so one of them let him stay on her couch. She was recently divorced, and other people shared her house, as well. It wasn't long after that when Bub got involved with a girl, named Margarita. She was a lively young Latino who hung with his sister's group of fun-loving friends. He'd met her on more than one occasion, but it was at "The Battle of the Bands" that they finally hit it off. It was the night before the beginning of the annual "Over the Line Tournament," and Fiesta Island was ablaze with bonfires and live music. There were beer trucks lined up bumper to bumper all around the island, and, together with the perfect Southern California weather, it all created an atmosphere that made partying and romance hard to resist. As young couples would walk from one bonfire to the next, they would flirt and kiss in the darkness, and that's how "Bub and Margarita" came to be.

Not long after their relationship intensified, Margarita confessed to Bub that there was another man in her life who was vying for her affections. That led Bub to understand that she wanted to know, right then and there, if he really loved her. He didn't want to mislead her. In fact, he hadn't really thought about the depth of his feelings toward her, so he was tongue-tied. Margarita took his hesitation and confused facial expressions as a no. In an effort to clarify his feelings, Bub explained to her that he needed the test of time to be sure about "true love," but since she wasn't the patient type, she started seeing the other guy.

* * *

Bub had bought a bicycle to get to a new job at a lighting store. The manager was friendly, and he taught Bub how to assembled fixtures before hanging them in the sun-drenched showroom. Bub loved the job, because he worked alone in a back room, and many of the chandeliers he put together came with crystals that broke sunlight into dazzling color spectra. One day the shop owner asked Bub to stay late, and, after they'd drunk a few beers, he pleaded for Bub's affection. That blew Bub away, who said that he had no inclination to have sex with a man, but still his boss begged.

"Rick, Please! I'll roll you and blow you, but I promise I'll never flip you and dick you!"

Of course that made Bub laugh, and, after saying, "Thanks, but no thanks," the manager insisted that Bub let him drive him home.

"If you ride your bike, I'll run you in the ditch!" he warned, and then he smiled.

By that time Bub was a little freaked out while feeling sorry for his boss. Since it was dark outside, and it was a long ride home, Bub finally agreed. As they rode toward Bub's residence, the young boss's harangue continued, but Bub remained adamant while insisting that he could never be gay. Then the man circled Bub's residence while sobbing and making one last plea. By that time Bub had had enough, so he jumped out of the car at a stop sign and said, "I'm sorry, man, but I can't help being who I am."

The next day Bub went to work, and his boss's secretary told him he was fired. His boss wasn't there, and that made him even madder as he fetched his bike from the back room. As he rode home, he thought about the complexities of human nature while wondering where he would work next, and that made him sad and angrier.

The next day Bub went to a restaurant to meet an interstate household-goods mover who'd put an ad in the newspaper. The driver recognized the Doobie Brothers T-shirt that Bub told him he would be wearing, so he motioned at Bub to come and sit at his table. His name was Blake and he was a grizzly man who had a large belly, sunken eyes, and a long, scraggly beard. He told Bub that he was a former Army Airborne soldier and motorcycle gang member who was now making a legitimate living as an owner-operator. As he explained it, one of his gang members got drunk and accidentally shot him in the calf during a party in the desert, so he had decided to leave the gang and do the moving gig. Bub liked the thought of traveling, and, since he appreciated Blake's full disclosure, he told him more about his own experiences. After that, Blake wanted to see what Bub was all about, so they went to load fifteen thousand pounds of household furniture. It was hard work, but since Bub was energetic, and he needed little training, he was hired.

Blake owned a vintage International cab-over with a single sleeper, and it was rough. There was no room for Bub to stretch out, and the bumpy ride became very uncomfortable as they traveled on. Blake told Bub he wasn't allowed in the sleeper, and that made Bub sad, since his seat was hard. After Bub's complaining, Blake suggested Bub could make a bed in the back of the trailer, but to Bub's amazement Blake rarely stopped. Bub didn't know if Blake was on speed or what, but the torture of his sore knees and lower-back pain became almost unbearable.

During the trip, Blake told Bub a few stories related to his trucking, Air Force, and gang adventures. Other than that, he pretty much kept quiet while stroking his beard. Since Blake didn't sleep, they were making incredible time. Meanwhile, Bub would try to rest against a moving pad that he shoved between him and the door. Of course, he wanted to ride in the back of the trailer, but, as would often be the case, it was too full.

On their way to New York, Blake finally stopped in Denver. After catching a few winks in front of the truck-stop TV, Bub became bored and decided to take a stroll. To his delight, he came upon a busy bar that was equipped with pool tables. After Bub's taking control of one of the tables, a well-dressed man entered the bar, and he was carrying a small case. After putting a quarter on Bub's table, the man looked confident as he assembled his fancy cue stick. He figured Bub to be an easy mark, but as they played games of double or nothing, Bub left him deep in the hole. All the while, the man appeared to be cool, as Bub wondered why. Then one of Bub's former challengers acted surprised as he announced that he was "late to be somewhere!" He offered Bub his full pitcher of beer, and Bub was elated. Well, Bub was not wise to all the tricks of hustling, so he drank the beer with gusto while not realizing the generous man that gave it to him was a friend of his opponent. Then Bub started to get reckless and show off as he racked up two more wins. By that time, he was buying beer for all the spectators, and started acting silly. His pool eye, as he called it, became so compromised by his drinking that he started to miss simple shots. After losing several games, he finally quit. He'd lost eighty dollars of his hard-earned money, and, in addition to that, he had to pay a healthy bar tab.

After Bub and Blake finished unloading the New York shipment, they went to a bar called The Squash Inn. While knocking off a few beers, they met a friend of Blake's whose household goods they were going to take to Tucson, Arizona. The man was a lot like Blake, as far as appearances went, but he looked a bit more dangerous. After the long trip back west, with all the goods unloaded, Blake and his friend told Bub to open a cedar chest. Bub opened it, and to his amazement it was loaded with red wax-paper bricks of pot! "Go ahead—help yourself," Blake's friend said through a grin, and with that Bub took out his lock-blade knife and sliced himself a thick chunk of weed. Later, as he smoked a joint, Bub wondered if Blake had really ever left the motorcycle gang.

The road was fascinating to Bub, and he liked big trucks. Parties were always a major happening in the truck stops, and he would tune in the CB radio to find out where the action was. That type of lifestyle was being glamorized in the late seventies, with movies such as *Convoy* and *Smokey and the Bandit*. Meanwhile, truckers were taking it all in stride while enjoying cookouts, taking speed, smoking pot, and drinking plenty of ice-cold beer. Bub always looked forward to stopping at major truck stops, such as Reno's Boomtown, Denver's 76 West, or Tucson's Triple-T. He also enjoyed meeting the families that were moving. If they had kids, he'd try to make them laugh, and, if they were coming from, or heading to some place that he'd been, he'd always share some good stories. After unloading their stuff and finally saying good-bye, he'd always grow melancholy while wishing for a family of his own.

The winter was tough for Bub, but he liked adventure, so he persevered. He was happy to go to places that he'd never been, but as he fought the cold in the back of the trailer, he always wondered where life would take him. He realized that after the winter he would experience better times, but each night, when all was said and done, he was nothing more than a lonesome drifter.

By the summer of 1979, Bub was tired of sleeping in the trailer, so he quit the road. It was one of the longer jobs he'd stayed with, but it was only one of more than a dozen. Since he was back in California, and his sister Jessie had moved to a roomy house, he stayed with her. After that, he had no trouble landing a job with a major moving company in San Diego. The pay was fairly good, and, for the most part, he did all right. He bought a trustworthy 1967 Oldsmobile Delta 88 and made weekly trips to Tijuana to fill it up with cheap gas while buying two bottles of duty-free booze. Other than that, he hung out with Jessie's friends, and, when he wasn't with them, he hustled the pool tables at the local bar. His life seemed okay, at first, but he soon realized he was back in the same rut of living paycheck to paycheck while searching for Miss Right. That made him think about his former relationships and that, in turn, made him sad to think his white-collar career was over. Whenever he started thinking about his old computer jobs, he always thought about Virginia.

As time went by, Bub tried to escape his normal routine. He hated being alone, so he started going to the beaches and the disco bars in search of women. Sometimes he'd get so drunk that he'd have to be picked up by his sister's boyfriend. During that time, the Little River Band had produced a hit called "Lonesome Loser," and it gnawed at him. While realizing that he was unable to control his passions, Bub knew that changing environments alone would never be the means to his new beginning. It seemed his insane behavior would only continue, so he took a moment to reflect. *Every time I go to the bars, everyone seems happy and well adjusted. They're not like me! I need to find a good woman and fast, but where! If only I could find a woman, I'd have a reason to stay at home and maybe have some kids. Then I could go back to school and buy a good car. As it is, I'm fucking dying!*

10. THE EFFECT OF ANGELS

Just after New Year's Day in 1980, Bub got a call from his brother, Robbie. He eagerly informed Bub that he'd spotted a job posting where he worked, at a government contract house. The position involved receiving and reporting worldwide data, just as Bub done at NASA. Then he told Bub that, if he landed the job, Robbie would collect a thousand-dollar finder's fee. Well, that sounded like a good deal for the both of them, so, for the love of his brother and with high hopes of getting back into the white-collar world, Bub headed back to Virginia.

Bub was elated when he got the job, and his brother was happy too. Since it was in Alexandria, and Bub's Virginia driving privileges were still suspended from his last DUI, he needed to find a place to live. He was delighted when he met a coworker who needed a roommate. He lived in a townhouse, and it was just a short walk from work. Unfortunately they had nothing in common, other than the fact that they worked for the same company, and they were both alcoholics! That made Bub wonder if moving back to Virginia had been the right decision, after all.

Robbie was designing military trucks when "Rick" started working on a health contract with the federal government. That required him to go downstairs to the data processing department, where he retrieved his reports. Whenever he did that, he'd always shoot the bull with two good-looking blondes, Joyce and Alice. Bub recognized Alice as a girl who'd attended his first high school, and, since she was single, he set his sights on her. He wasn't sure if she knew who he was, but since he called himself Rick, he thought he was safe.

Both girls were polite and attentive as Bub would ramble on about the beauty and excitement of the western United States. He told them about his long motorcycle ride to San Diego, and since Joyce was from St. Louis, she related to his funny tales while passing through Missouri. When he complained about Joplin and its weird "fishing reports" on TV, Joyce laughed and told him where the lakes were.

As Bub got to know the girls better, he tried to get a lunch date with Alice, but she politely said no. After repeated attempts, he finally learned that she already had a boyfriend, and that deflated his hopes. Seeing that he was depressed, Joyce tried to cheer him up by volunteering to go to lunch with him. Of course Bub realized Joyce was married, but since he was getting lonelier by the minute, he was happy just the same. He'd bragged about west-coast food while anxiously awaiting for Alice to say yes, so he already had a meal in mind. He took Joyce to his place and made her a nice lunch consisting of a California-style salad, barbecued steaks, and a bottle of red California wine.

As Bub cooked and they ate, Joyce told him about her life, and he told her a little more about his while omitting certain facts. As it turned out, Joyce was lonely too. She'd married just after graduating from high school, and it wasn't long before she realized that her young husband was "weird." After receiving a divorce, she had met a sincere gentleman who asked for her hand in marriage before moving her to the Washington, DC, area. As it turned out, she was now missing her family in St. Louis, since "the gentleman" wasn't the man she thought he was, either. That led Bub to think that Joyce truly needed a good man, but, due to his past, he was sure that man wasn't him. After they'd consumed all the wine except for what remained in their glasses, their conversation finally ended with a toast to the future. After a moment of awkward silence, Bub looked up at the clock on the wall and sighed. Then there was another brief moment of silence before Joyce looked into his eyes and said, "Let me make this easy for you." As her stare continued, Bub felt a sudden attraction, so he got out of his chair and gave her a quick but gentle kiss. "Whoops," he said.

Bub's reaction to what Joyce said and the way that she said it seemed natural and wonderful. Even so, he never dreamed of kissing Joyce, and now he was stunned as he slowly sat back down while taking good look at her. The light coming through the window was accentuating her curly, blond hair, blue eyes, and full lips. Her skin and makeup were perfect, and her silk turquoise dress was tapered to show off her shapely curves. She was staring into his eyes as he thought about her maturity and gentle mannerisms. Altogether, she was his very definition of Miss Right, and as he thought, *Mrs. Right!* he flinched and looked away.

After seeing his reaction, Joyce stood up and cleared the table while glancing back at his face. She was no dummy, and she knew he needed time to think. As far as she was concerned, she'd made it clear enough that she was willing to be more than friends, so now the next move would be up to him.

Meanwhile, Bub was busy taking a moral inventory while trying to figure out what to say and do next. He knew Joyce didn't know who he really was, and he didn't want to mislead her. Just as important was the matter of her being married. Even though he'd dispelled Christian beliefs regarding a devil, he still had an existential fear of Hell. In regard to all concerned, he also felt a pang of mixed emotions for the husband he didn't know. In spite of all of that, his attraction to her was suddenly stronger, and, since she surpassed his expectations of finding a good woman, he was terribly confused.

After returning from the kitchen, Joyce saw Bub staring out the window, still mired in thought. As he turned to excuse himself for being aloof, Joyce simply smiled and said, "Come on, buster. We'd better get moving, or we'll be late for work."

As Bub thought more and more about her reaction to his kiss, he became dumbfounded. She'd left him to wonder with her easy-going attitude, as he thought, *What did she mean by "Let me make this easy for you"? Was she talking about the damn dishes? I hope not!*

As time went on, Bub continued to visit with Joyce and Alice, and, when the nights came, he would hit the bars. He was hoping to find another girl, like Joyce, but he already knew that he was kidding himself. He'd clicked with Joyce, just as he'd done with his best friends, and as time passed he wanted to be with her.

Bub's drinking had intensified when, one Saturday morning, he awoke sweaty and hungover while trying to remember the previous night. He vaguely remembered a long, dark hallway that had led to a room with a peculiar woman waiting. She was wearing a black corset with fishnet stockings, and her face was tired and expressionless as she'd asked him for his money. At that point, even in his drunken state, Bub had recognized a new low, so he turned around and left. Then he recalled glimpses of Route 1, as he'd walked miles to his filthy townhouse. Now here he was at home, laying on a ten-dollar Salvation Army couch in the midst of another binge, and he was feeling worried and helpless.

By now Bub realized that a beer was far better than aspirin for his hangover, so he got off the couch and went to get his medicine. Then he spent the day drinking in front of the TV while thinking about Joyce. The following morning, he awoke during a horrific nightmare. He was wide-eyed and cold with sweat, but still his nightmare persisted. The best he could figure was that he was having one of his old childhood nightmares, yet he was fully conscious this time! He sprang out of bed and ran to a window to see if he was truly awake. Then he wondered, *Am I having an acid flashback! This is the whole body feeling and everything!* As he did, his head was spinning with an intense fear that was totally inexplicable. Something terrible had occurred in his dream, and now it was leading him to believe that he'd finally gone completely mad! So, in a supreme effort to regain his wits, he knocked his head against the wall a few times, and then he slid to the floor while thinking to himself, *Joyce!... Joyce!... Joyce!* Just thinking her name repeatedly made him feel better as he imagined her face. Then, as he became calmer, he realized, *Joyce must be the one. I think I love her!*

Bub figured that most everyone he'd ever met had some type of problems, so if there was a chance that he could fix Joyce's problem and his, he wasn't going to let anything or anybody stand in their way! As far as his existential fear of Hell went, he'd just had another nasty taste of what hell on Earth is all about, so he was no longer concerned with the hereafter. From that moment on, Bub spent the rest of his Sunday cleaning his house and grooming himself while remaining anxious and determined to see Joyce.

Come Monday morning, Bub immediately went to see Joyce, and it was then he learned that she'd split with her husband. He was amazed by that news, and now they were both happy and laughing. Then, as one conversation led to another, Bub finally got the nerve to pop the question.

"Hey, Joyce—I know you're going through rough times and all, but so am I. Well, what I meant to say is—would you be willing to go on another date?"

To that, Joyce perked up, and after looking around she whispered to Bub, "I thought you'd never ask!"

Bub's heart skipped a beat, and, in their mutual excitement, they made a plan to call in sick the next day and run off to wherever. Meanwhile, Bub remained overjoyed, and the only thing that filled his mind was anticipation.

The next day, Joyce picked "Rick" up on a back street, and then she drove to Annapolis, Maryland. Once they got there, they bought fresh jumbo shrimp and wine and enjoyed it on a bench facing the Chesapeake Bay. Their time together was precious and wonderful, and Bub experienced feelings of joy and happiness that he had long forgotten.

As they talked, they exchanged stories related to their families and the memories of their early childhoods. They talked about where they were raised, and suddenly they realized that they were both born alongside the Mississippi River and the "Blues Highway." By the end of the day, they had absorbed each other's disparities, interests, hopes, and dreams, as their emotions had run their course. It was then they knew their attraction was leading them to deeper understanding of each other, and that was the seed of their new love.

Many "sick days" from work followed, as Joyce and Bub were eager to be alone together. They visited natural and wonderful places, such as Great Falls, Harper's Ferry, and Bull Run Park, before embracing in passionate love. After those encounters, the rumors began to fly, so Bub quit his job for Joyce's sake. He was only too happy to do it, since he'd gotten his old moving job back, and besides, Joyce let him to move into her apartment.

Joyce's love seemed to be saving Bub. She possessed all the traits that he lacked, and, while he was experiencing an indescribable new joy, she now possessed his heart. So, as far as Hell went, Bub had been surely been there, but now it seemed to him as if he were in Heaven. Together, he and Joyce made careful plans to go to California, where he promised she'd experience a lot of joy and adventure. They bought a puppy, which they named Brandy, and they treated it as if it were their first child. Since love was the nourishment that his soul needed, Bub's health flourished with the woman who knew him as Rick. Nevertheless, his battle with his drinking addiction was not over, and, as Joyce was quickly becoming aware of that, a new battle was just beginning.

At first living together was like a honeymoon, but the more Bub felt at ease, the more he let his guard down. Since he was working as a mover now, he would often get good tips while getting off early. That led to occasions where he'd stop by the local bar before going home. Joyce accepted that, at first, but then she'd express concern toward his consistent behavior, since all the while he was letting her in on his past—a little at a time. She'd also expressed dismay when she'd heard stories from Bub's family, and as she began to realize the depth of the darker side of his nature, she began to wonder who exactly was this "Bub" that they called Rick!

When pressed, "Rick" finally came clean with Joyce and told her that it had all begun with the adversity demonstrated toward his peculiarities. He explained how that, plus moving from place to place, had affected his life. Then he told her about his involvement with drugs, alcohol, and the law and how all his problems eventually caused him to adopt a new name. As Joyce sat there stunned, he summed it up by telling her that she was his saving grace, and that without her he'd be as good as dead.

Bub's full disclosure of his situation and his dependence on her greatly affected Joyce. She worried that she'd attached herself to a hard case, but at the same time, she loved his energy, his dreams, and his willingness to change for the better. Luckily for Bub, Joyce had been able to control his wild nature, while even liking it at times. Therefore, she agreed to remain his girl. Although Joyce couldn't keep Bub from drinking altogether, she did forbid him from looking up any of his old friends. As she put it, "It's simply a matter of who you like best, and I'm not taking a backseat to your drinking, either!" Then she reminded him that she could return to her hometown of St. Louis at any time, if he became overbearing. The thought of that sent a chill up Bub's spine as he promised to always be respectful and faithful—and she had him by the heart.

*   *   *

As 1980 turned into 1981, Bub turned twenty-eight and Joyce turned twenty-seven, with only two days separating their birthdays. Their relationship grew stronger while they both experienced ups and downs during the year. Joyce broke her leg when jumping off the balcony of their apartment, since Bub and a friend did it, and, she, too, wanted to throw their *Frisbee*. Then, when winter arrived, she totaled her car when skidding off of a snowy road and hitting a tree. Meanwhile, Bub continued to party with his moving buddies while overdoing it on occasions, and when he did he blamed his "being human." When Christmas arrived, Joyce went to her parent's home, and Bub went to his, since neither was ready to miss out on their respective family get-togethers. Of course, all of those trials and tribulations were merely normal, and, as they served to bring a greater understanding of each other's faults and emotional needs, these occurrences only strengthened their feelings for one another.

Come the late spring of 1981, their trip to California was exciting and fun. On the way, Rick was introduced to Joyce's family in St. Louis, and they said they were happy to finally meet her mystery man. After they left St. Louis, they followed the same route that Bub took on his motorcycle, so Joyce could better relate his wild tales of adventure. She was dazzled by the rainbows in New Mexico, and, after stopping several times to play with their dog and feed grass to horses, she enjoyed a beautiful morning with Bub at the Alamogordo Zoo. When they finally arrived in Southern California, Bub introduced Joyce to his sister, and then they leased a townhouse in Santee.

Once they'd settled in, Bub went back to the moving company he'd worked for before, while Joyce quickly landed a job at a metal yard by the Coronado Bridge. Of course, they had to buy another car, but, since Joyce had wisely budgeted for that, the cost didn't affect them. On workdays they'd play tennis in the late afternoons, and, since Joyce was an avid bowler, they also enjoyed bowling in a couple's league at night. On the weekends, they had fun as they ventured out to sunny beaches, and, explored Tijuana, Los Angeles, and other interesting places. However, as it often goes, bad times follow good.

As Joyce and Rick enjoyed bowling in their league, the attractions they had for other people their age spurned jealousy. On one occasion, a woman with long hair sat back to back with Bub and threw her hair over his face. On another occasion, a man begged Joyce to go with him to his family restaurant, so she could see his inheritance and meet his parents. Then Bub started drinking with his moving buddies after work, and, with all of those events coming to a head, he finally crossed the line.

There was a topless bar next to Bub's place of employment, and, upon getting off work early, he and his buddies would often whoop it up, with a girl or two, dancing on their table. On one such occasion, Bub left the girlie bar late one night, and, realizing that he was too drunk to drive, he pulled his car to the shoulder of the road and passed out. Shortly thereafter, he was awoken by a state trooper, who, in his mercy and kindness, gave him a ride home. Needless to say, Joyce was not a happy camper when she answered the door to see the trooper supporting Bub! As far as she was concerned, he was offering her little in the way of a happy and secure future, and as she watched him stumble to get undressed, she figured she'd had enough.

The next morning, Joyce kindly asked Bub to help her pack and load her stuff, because she decided she was going home to St. Louis. Of course, she was within her rights to call her own shots, since Bub had exposed his ugly side once too often. That had been their understanding, and besides, Joyce was a Midwestern girl, and she'd been missing the beauty of the change of seasons.

As Bub felt his usual pangs of remorse, he told her that they'd both be leaving. He couldn't stand the thought of being alone again, so he told her he'd deliver her safely to her parent's home, and then he'd continue to Virginia. "That's the least I can do, after all," he explained.

As Bub got busy loading a trailer, he began to strive for Joyce's affections. It took some doing, but after a long day heading eastward, she finally caved in to his dire need for her. So, even though Bub's California dream had gone bust, he was still thrilled to be with his girl.

After visiting St. Louis, again, Bub and Joyce headed to Virginia and settled into an apartment. Bub curtailed his daily drinking, but he still got blitzed on the weekends while working on cars with his brother. After working at steady jobs for a year, they moved into an old house in Vienna and adopted a little Siamese kitten, whom they named Chester.

*   *   *

Joyce finally became tired of their idle affair and told Bub to either marry her, or she was gone! Bub was caught off guard by her ultimatum, but he thought that was a fantastic idea. After all, he knew they were in love, and it didn't seem as though they'd ever split up. Therefore, he said, "Let's do it, woman!"

As Bub's mom began making a wedding dress for Joyce, Bub compiled a list of attendees and reserved a historic little chapel in a state park. They'd preferred to get married in a church, but since Joyce had been divorced, she was turned away. Then there was Bub's list of guests! When his mom and Joyce saw the "derelicts" on his list, they greatly disapproved. Bub cried foul while insisting that their plans were interfering with the central focus of love, so he called the wedding off.

After a few days of feeling sorry for himself, Bub called Joyce at work and asked her to elope. After nearly giving up hope, that was a great relief to her, so she said, "Let's do it, man!" Hearing that made Bub's day, and, since his driving privileges had been restored, he raced to meet her so they could both submit to the required blood test. Then they searched through a phone book and found a justice of the peace who agreed to marry them right away.

The JP was in his nineties, and he was most gracious as he welcomed them into his historic brick home. After Riddick and Joyce registered and made their solemn vows, they celebrated with Bub's parents, who in light of everything that had ever happened to Bub, were very relieved and pleased. When Robbie congratulated them later, he told Bub and Joyce that he and his wife had gotten married by the same man. That interesting fact made Bub wonder, as he thought, *Are we all angels who are helping one another in some mysterious way?*

When Bub had flat-out quit his former jobs, he had effectively burned his bridges, so now his career path was flip-flopping again. In an effort to improve their financial position while keeping adventure in his life, Bub enrolled in a tractor-trailer driving course. First, he had to take a correspondence course, and then he had to finish his final four weeks in Delaware. The separation was tough for the both of them, but Bub finally graduated and got a regional job loading and delivering household goods.

It was just nine months and seventeen days after they were married, when, on Bub's thirtieth birthday, Joyce gave birth to a healthy girl they named Marissa. The hospital had let Bub hold her right after she was born, and when she looked into his eyes for the first time, she smiled. That experience was profound to Bub, and he knew that he was holding another angel, who'd come to help save his life. He now realized he had a purpose as he looked forward to turning his bad experiences into her good fortune.

Soon after that wonderful experience, Bub ran into a carload of his old Peat-Moss Gang friends in Vienna. They were all pleasantly surprised to see that Bub was still alive, so he invited them to his home to see Marissa. Of course, they were curious, so they followed him home. As his old buddy, Phil, held Marissa in his arms, he smiled, but then he looked at Bub and shook his head.

"You're going to raising a child? Man, are you crazy, or what! Does your wife know who you are?"

Since Bub had always kept a lot of his inner feelings a secret to his Peat-Moss friends, he was hardly in a position to argue or disagree.

After their visit, Bub thought about his encounter with his old friends. He worried if Phil was right. Would he ever be a good father? Then Bub remembered what he'd read about "fruit to be gained from all experiences." *Maybe that's the way the world works*, Bub thought. *Phil's remarks hurt, for sure, but at least they've given me a burning desire to do right by my child.* That made him wonder, as he thought, *Was seeing Phil and experiencing his reaction merely happenstance, or was that meant to be?*

*   *   *

A month had passed since Marissa was born, when Joyce's parents came to visit. As they doted upon their beautiful grandchild, Joyce's dad surprised Rick and Joyce by handing them the keys and the pink slip to the new Oldsmobile 98 Brougham that they'd arrived in.

"Congratulations to you the both of you, and good job, Joyce!" her father said.

Then, as Joyce and Bob were both stunned, he made them an offer that they couldn't refuse. He told them that if they moved to St. Louis, he'd give Joyce a bookkeeping job at home, so she could personally attend to her baby girl, and he'd hook Rick up with a job as a lease-operator with a major moving company. That was indeed a no-brainer, so, after some quick planning, Joyce and Marissa flew to Saint Louis, leaving Bub to sell their old cars and pack and haul their stuff.

Bub called his parents to break the news, and, after taking Joyce and Marissa to the airport, he went to visit them. When he went to leave, his father followed him out to his car.

"I want you to know, Riddick, that you're breaking your mother's heart," he said.

That made Bub doubt if he were doing the right thing, but in light of all the advantages and the fact that the deal had already been done, he begged to reason.

"Geez, pops, It's not like we'll never see you again. Besides, nobody in Saint Louis knows who I am, and with Joyce at home to raise Marissa—I don't know—it just seems like it's all for the greater good."

Bub's dad was a man of logic, so he understood Bub's reasoning. Still, he'd expressed his opinion for the love of his wife, and to him that trumped any reasoning based on logic. Bub sensed that now, and he loved his father as he extended his right hand.

"I love you, Dad. Wish us luck."

After obliging Bub, while giving him a serious stare, his dad went back into the house. Bub drove away, and, as he looked into the rearview mirror of the big, shiny Oldsmobile, he was filled with sadness.

Now that he was alone, Bub stopped to get some beer. Then he weighed in on his situation as he drove home. There was a lot of pressure on him, since he was now accountable for the situation he'd created. He was filled with fear and doubt as he drank his beer. *Everyone's counting on me,* he thought.

Upon "Rick's" arrival in Saint Louis, he and Joyce rented the top floor of a duplex. As Joyce became acquainted with the bookkeeping practices of her family's business, Bub took on the frightening prospect of over-the-road driving. Since he'd become dependent on Joyce's love and her watchful eye, he knew he couldn't restrain himself from drinking in her absence.

Sure enough, in the months that followed, "Rick" reverted to the same old "Bub" while driving his eighteen-wheeler over long distances. He'd drink beer and smoke pot while driving, and, after he sobered up, he'd feel scared and ashamed. The long and distant highways reminded him of his days without love, and now he was sorry that he'd painted himself into a dark and lonely corner. Although he was making a great deal of money, that quickly paled in comparison to the torture he was feeling while missing his wife and not being a part of his daughter's life. To make matters worse, his trusty dog, Brandy, would bark at "the stranger" whenever he'd return from weeks on the road.

After months of relentless despair, Bub confessed his drinking dilemma to Joyce, and since she saw that his current situation was hopeless, she urged him to quit. Then he used mere loneliness as an excuse when telling his boss and father-in-law that he was quitting right away. Of course, both men were hard put to understand, but Bub perceived their reactions to imply that he might be less than a man. That was a bitter pill for him to swallow, but at the same time, he knew he was doing the right thing.

It was now the summer of 1983, and Bub was happy to take a new job delivering ice-cream cones within a 250-mile radius of Saint Louis. He enjoyed every night with his family, as Marissa was learning to talk and walk. Before falling asleep, Bub would read more books on various religions, philosophies, and the human mind. As he did, he was building upon his own foundation of spiritual belief while heeding only wisdom that stimulated his intuition. Each morning thereafter he would be mesmerized by new revelations as he drove along his route.

As a means to control his drinking, Bub applied some critical thinking to what he'd learned. One thread of wisdom had told him that two thoughts could not occupy the mind at the same time. Another thread told him that a thought was like a seed, from which actions grow. Therefore, he'd keep his mind focused on his desire for a better future while planting those seeds, and, if his desire to drink came knocking, he would quickly turn his thoughts to those he loved. As a result, his disposition and circumstances greatly improved as Joyce became pregnant again.

Since they would need more living space with the birth of another child, Bub and Joyce searched for a new place to live. As one thing led to another, they became elated when they discovered that they qualified for a home loan. Finally they bought a modest turn-of-the-century house in a western St. Louis neighborhood. It was called Dogtown, because that's where dogs were once kept to feed the Aborigines who were displayed at the 1904 World's Fair. Therefore, it was a few blocks south of Forest Park, and, with a myriad of cultural activities, that location would be ideal for raising their children. Bub always dreamed about having a family and a house, and now he realized he was finally living his dream.

Joyce gave birth to their second daughter, Vanessa, in 1984. It was a joyous occasion, and all the proud grandparents visited to see their new granddaughter. Marissa was eighteen months old, and she was excited, too. To that effect, the little family of four was doing just fine, and, as Vanessa learned to talk and walk, they enjoyed their lives immensely.

As for Bub, he wasn't out of the woods yet. He missed the DC area, and, when he worked on his car in his detached garage, memories of drinking with friends while working on cars affected him. Then there was the friction he was experiencing with his new job. Since the ice-cream cone factory shut down, he'd gone back to moving furniture, and now his coworkers were turning him off. Nevertheless, Bub remained steadfast to his desire to become a good husband and father, so he searched for more books that might help him to transcend his present conditions.

* * *

As Bub read more about the power of the human will, he decided to enroll in another computer school. His new aim was to improve his family's life, while he escaped the lower-caste mentality of his blue-collar associates. All was going fine, until one day Bub learned that his dear mother had developed an inoperable cancer, and now she only had a short time to live. Devastated, Bub took an emergency leave of absence from his work and school and then drove to Virginia, alone.

When Bub arrived in McLean, he learned that his mother had just come out of a post-op surgery. He wasn't able to see her, so after talking with his family, he looked up an old friend. In his bitter despair and in his former surroundings, Bub alluded to drinking, and, when he was finally allowed to see his mother, she smelled alcohol and turned him away. So he quickly sobered up and met with his grieving family again, whereupon he was afforded one last opportunity to visit her before he was scheduled to leave. His mother appeared to be incoherent as Bub sat down beside her, and then he whispered in her.

"I'm so sorry for all the pain that I've caused you, and please understand—I'm trying to improve. God, I love you!"

Then his mother responded in a clear and soft voice.

"I love you, too."

Those were the last words that Bub heard from his dear mother, and now he was crushed.

After bidding farewell to his heartbroken father, Bub started his long drive back to Missouri. Whenever he thought about all the pain that he had caused his wonderful mother, he found himself crying uncontrollably. Then he thought about the rest of his family's sorrow, and that made his trip tough too. As soon as he got home, Joyce hugged him and told him that his father had called to inform him that his mother had finally passed. After that, Bub was stunned by the reality of it all and later, he lay in the solitude of his bedroom while closing his eyes and trying to feel her spirit.

Bub, feeling naked to the world, was later consoled by his in-laws. He knew there were no words that could truly console him, and he didn't like talking about it. His mother had been the driving force of his inspiration and pride, and he was stunned that he'd lost such an angel. He feared it would be harder for him straighten up and aim high, since he was crushed and had one less angel to guide him. Of course, there was no way to convey the full extent his feelings to his in-laws, since they had been kept uninformed about his true past.

After Bub finished school in that same year of 1985, he took a position with a large department store as a lead computer operator on the second shift. Since his mother's passing was still devastating him, he browsed through a catalog of the Theosophical Society. He ordered a book titled *To Those Who Mourn* by C. W.

Leadbeater, and, after reading it, it helped him immensely. The idea it conveyed told him that his mother was in a phase of transition and retrospection, and that his feelings of great despair would only do her harm. Bub accepted that explanation, since it seemed logical to him that life has purpose. It caused him to focus on the strength of love while wanting to give his family a better life and his mother's life a greater meaning.

* * *

As Bub looked forward to a new era, the watershed of his mother's passing caused him to straighten up like never before. He happily accepted himself as Rick, and he quit smoking cigarettes and started jogging. When riding the bus to and from work, he immersed himself in the subjects of history, philosophy, religion, and science. There were a lot of holes in his high school education, and he wanted to fill them all.

In the year that followed, Joyce and Rick managed to get a good credit record while keeping the same jobs. It was then that Joyce saw modern new homes being built in the countryside of St. Peters, Missouri. After driving out and marveling at the great room design of a ranch-style house, they told Joyce's family about it at a get-together. It just so happened that her brother-in-law knew the builder, so he got them a fantastic deal. Then Joyce's brother, who ran the family business, said he would barter with a professional moving service to make their transition free and easy. Of course, Joyce and Rick were stunned, and Marissa and Vanessa were very excited!

In 1987 Jonathon was born, and, as everyone celebrated, Rick was feeling the graces of redemption. When he wasn't reading, or having fun with "the wife and kiddies," he either tinkered with stained glass or worked on his old Pontiac convertible. He also created fun computer programs to help his children learn, and that he found most rewarding. At the same time, he knew he wasn't over his addiction. After experiencing overloads of stress at work, he'd sometimes break down and drink a beer on his way home. Whenever that happened, though, he'd always feel deep remorse the next day and turn to his self-help books.

Whenever possible, the Kellows would travel to McLean to visit with Rick's family, and oftentimes his family would reciprocate. Whenever they got together, it was tender and caused Bub to reflect on his mother's passing. He realized that event caused him to speed up the cycle of his metamorphosis, which resulted in a richer and deeper meaning of life. At the same time, he felt sad, because it seemed as if his mother had somehow surrendered him to Joyce and now Rick needed her love desperately and dearly. After all, she'd bestowed him with three happy and loving children him, and that made humble.

As Bub continued to develop his higher power through continuing his education while using the power of positive thinking, wonderful things continued to happen. That led him to think about James Allen, who wrote, "Men do not attract that which they want, but that which they *are*." The melding of such profound thoughts, observed through experience, oftentimes caused him to gather his three little children together, so he could teach them what he'd learned. As he'd talk about tending to the garden of their minds, or the effects of pressure on coal, they'd roll their eyes. That led him to realize that they had no problems, yet, and they just wanted to play. Of course, he understood that, and he figured he'd talk with them after they gained more experience.

In 1992, Joyce and Rick were still on a roll when they bought a big, two-story house in St. Charles, Missouri. It was designed to their specifications, and it boasted a three-car garage and large swimming pool. That made their family life flourish, as Joyce and Rick were climbing ever higher in their careers. In addition to a home and public school education, their children went to special classes to determine their special interests. They also enjoyed wonderful vacations, as their mom and dad would share the wonders of new experiences. To that extent, the whole family was living the American Dream, but, as bad times often follow good, Rick suddenly experienced the severe long-term effects of Bub's misguided passions.

11. IN MEMORY OF BUB

After complaining of fatigue in 1995, Rick's doctor informed him that he had hepatitis C, which had only recently been given that name. Then he sent Rick to see a gastroenterologist who, after testing his liver, told him that he had about three more years before he'd need a liver transplant. That made Rick spin off in a daze while the doctor told him about anti-rejection drugs, and he thought about someone else's organ in his body! Then she told him he might qualify for a medical study that used an experimental drug to combat AIDS. In either case, she warned him that those procedures would be hard on him, and they weren't always successful. Of course, Rick and Joyce took that prognosis very seriously, and they decided to keep Rick's disease a secret from their children.

Since Rick had gotten his drinking under control, he thought that his body had healed. Sure, he still had a couple of drinks with friends every now and then, but he thought, *I wasn't losing control anymore!* Now, the thought of his liver failing him seemed horribly strange and somehow wrong. After dwelling on that, he accepted his fate and saw his dilemma as one big exclamation point following a hard lesson that would be forever engrained in his soul.

After successfully enrolling in a university medical research program, Rick had to inject himself with interferon. Every time he did, it reminded him of Bub in the old days, and that made him feel guilty. Instead of getting high, he was now feeling the ill effects from a drug that he'd have to use over the course of his one-year program. Nevertheless, he was grateful and happy. After all, he'd always been amazed by the marvels of new scientific discoveries. They demonstrated that mankind possessed the ability to understand the intelligence that creates and sustains life.

As Rick turned gaunt from the drug's effects, his associates at work began to notice. When he explained his condition, most people were ignorant of the cause and condition. The word *hepatitis* naturally scared them, since it had become a conceptual metaphor associated with being contagious. At the same time, some sensed that Rick had done something wrong in his past, and he was probably deserving of his condition. Of course, Rick knew that to be true, and he felt guilty, so once again he delved deep into introspection. As before, he started with the earliest recollections of his youth, and by the time he reached the middle of his teenage years, "Bub" wanted to smoke, take psychedelics, and drink few beers! That made Rick realize the power of regressive thought whereby he'd temporarily descended to the "level of the beast!"

Due to his raw experiences, it was clear to Rick that his life had served the purpose of a greater self-awareness. He knew that was difficult for young Bub to comprehend because he was constantly plagued by ignorance of his social complexities. After meditating on his involvement with all the people he'd ever met, he clearly understood how those attractions came about and why they were necessary in discovering his true self. Of course, his parents had warned him about bad associations and lust, but Rick figured that it's the desire and destiny of all people to experience life's lessons in their own unique way.

After completing his introspection, Rick delved into a deep meditation. He thought about the implosion and explosion of the Sun and how the law of attraction had wondrously formed a planet that manifested a self-awareness of energy. He felt as if his body was merely a tentacle of that energy, and it was used for learning more about itself in the absence of total awareness. In that same physical world, he also felt that everything that exists feeds a vast intelligence—the essence of which the Earth is just a tiny speck within the seemingly endless boundaries of time and space. Then he thought about the distortions of time and space, and how they make it hard for people to understand that every little thing happens for a reason. That that made him wonder about the future of mankind and the fate of the planet. *Will the self-awareness that energy has created through the illusion of a unique identity and free will succeed? Will mankind adhere to the obvious moral virtues that equate to Providence, and realize a full awareness of what, who, and why we are before we destroy the Earth? I guess that's what the collective consciousness has set upon biological organisms to discover—if education and compassion can overcome ignorance and greed before the earth recycles—just as it's done before.*

* * *

In the months that followed, Rick immersed himself in books. He read about nativism (the theory that humans are preprogrammed genetically) versus innatism (the theory that human minds are born with no inclinations, other than those instilled by God). After dwelling on the genotype-phenotype distinction, in relation his past experiences, he thought that both theories were correct. Whereas the physical body caused animal-like appetites and bad behavior, Rick was certain that his better nature came from the energy that most people refer to as the soul. He figured that the highly vibrating energy that constituted his soul was created by the attraction of all the thoughts he'd ever accumulated through experience. *After all, thoughts are composed of energy,* he reasoned, *and the law of conservation of energy states that energy cannot be created or destroyed.* Therefore, he imagined that after the death of his physical body, his soul would meld with the collective consciousness in order to absorb a better understanding of the world it had created. He figured that after the period of reflection and absorption, it would return to another unique form, environment, and circumstances that were necessary in rounding out the experience of life on Earth. At the same time, he believed that the law of attraction would bring kindred souls back together. He figured they shared the common bond of past experiences, and, they're constantly helping each other to learn the lessons of love.

Rick knew that his beliefs pertaining to creation and purpose were metaphysical notions, but he wasn't prone to stifling his intuition or his imagination. He'd used those faculties, along with empirical and common knowledge to create his theories and attitude towards life, and now he was content. He was fascinated by the law of conservation of energy, which states that energy cannot be created or destroyed. He'd also read about such things as the Murchison meteorite, which contains over 15 amino acids. That led him to believe that various combinations of organic elements and planets could create an endless array of life forms. As he imagined those life forms, he wondered if they might include those that could also achieve self-awareness, and, if some of them were superior to human beings. Although most scientists didn't profess to believe in the theory of the soul, he figured it was just their nature and duty to require tangible evidence.

While reading about the advancement of civilization, Rick focused on the socio-political theories that were introduced in the middle of the seventeenth century. The Age of Enlightenment was a name given to a movement to reform society. It had gained momentum by replacing the superstition and intolerance of religion with scientific facts. The result was more compassion and better living conditions for those who'd otherwise suffer. Once again Rick was enthralled by the debates between men and women who were finally able to present their arguments about the means by which to define simple truths and the nature of the human spirit. As he read on, he realized that the notions of liberty and justice that those debates inspired were directly related to the cause and outcome of the American Revolutionary War.

While most philosophers in Europe were merely satisfied to be publishing their observations and metaphysical notions, others were not. Thomas Paine wrote and published an inexpensive and scathing three-part pamphlet called, "The Age of Reason; Being an Investigation of True and Fabulous Theology." It was a best-seller in the United States, and, while it exhaustively attacked the Bible's veracity using reason and logic, it also questioned the "ken" and "credulity" of those who would object to Paine's accepting its contents without question. Although it was highly controversial, it undoubtedly influenced Paine's good friend, Thomas Jefferson, to suggest that a "wall" be built between "church and state," which was included in the first amendment to the US Constitution. Rick liked that wall, because he saw it as a means of defining true liberty and ensuring the protection of free thought when developing the "social contract" with federal, state, and local governments. He also saw that wall as a monument of hope for those who immigrated to the United States to avoid religious prosecution while expressing free thought.

Rick had taken a special interest in transcendentalism, which was a philosophical movement in the United States during the nineteenth century. The literary forces of that movement reignited the theory of the preexistence of the soul while expounding on the belief that all humans are born with inherent goodness. Those ideas made transcendentalists a threat to many Christians, who were seeking to establish their religion within major colleges and military institutions. Transcendentalists argued that archaic beliefs would stifle imagination and literary content, but they were quickly made unpopular by an overwhelming political force. That made Rick sad, because he'd read literary works by such people as Emily Dickson, Ralph Waldo Emerson, and Henry David Thoreau, and their thoughtful expressions caused tingles that touched his soul. They also made him feel good about his natural progression toward spiritual and political beliefs.

After struggling to imagine how the world could become a better place in which to live, Rick realized that would have to start with children. He knew that teaching them about personal identity, human behavior and social philosophy would give them a greater understanding about life and the malignancy of rejectionism. Furthermore, he was certain that young people would mature faster, and, while understanding the need to adhere to Providence, they would someday create a better world. After repeatedly reflecting upon his own life, Rick believed he should have been taught the benefits of a *thorough* introspection during his formative years. He was sad to think that his schools had never encouraged him to identify the root causes of his bad behavior, but, after learning that psychiatrists largely disregard introspection as viable means of self-help, he was not surprised. As he thought about all the people that he'd ever met in jail, and their inability to reconcile their own problems, it made him sad. Then he thought about Joey, Frankie, Jane, and all the other young people whose lives were cut short due to ignorance. *Did they go to hell? Of course, they didn't! I'd welcome their souls as my children, and I think God would, too!* That, in turn, made him think of his children, who were still in elementary school. They'd been raised with little knowledge about his true past, and suddenly he feared that they wouldn't benefit from his harsh experiences if he died. Then he thought, *Their mother will teach them, and besides—they all seem well adjusted to me. At least they have normal names—not like Riddick, Bub or Tweedits!*

Then Rick thought about recording his thoughts. *Could a story like mine help other people? Of course, no one wants to be bored with another person's psyche—but if I wrote the damned thing in a way that would attract attention, and people could relate to, it just might!* Then he considered the time and effort it would take. His latest test results had indicated that the interferon was not working. *Well, I could continue to be a guinea pig for other test labs, and that might buy me a little time. Shit! It couldn't be any worse than the hell that I've already been through, and that's for damned sure!* Then he laughed out loud as he remembered what a cellmate had once yelled at "Bub."

"Life's a bitch and then you die, so quit your damned bellyaching, goddammit!"

THE END.

ABOUT THE AUTHOR

Warwick J. Knox lives with his wife in California.

Please convey all regards to beltwaybub@warwickknox.com, or post to his blog at www.warwickknox.com, and, if humanly possible, have a nice day! ☺

www.ingramcontent.com/pod-product-compliance
Lightning Source LLC
Chambersburg PA
CBHW060936180626
46817CB00004B/1584